BYGORA VANDOS
Sinclair V-Log LB734/A

by Merita King

Published by Merita King

Eastleigh

Hampshire

United Kingdom

© Merita King 2013 all rights reserved

Cover art by J L Stratton. Copyright 2013

Bygora Vandos

ISBN 978-0-9570520-7-9

OTHER WORKS BY MERITA KING

The Lilean Chronicles: Book One ~ Redemption
The Lilean Chronicles: Book Two ~ The Sleeping
The Lilean Chronicles: Book Three ~ Changing Faces
The Lilean Chronicles: Book Four ~ Avalanche Effect

Floxham Island ~ Sinclair V-Log AZ267/M
Acts of Life

ABOUT THE AUTHOR

Merita King has loved the science fiction and fantasy genre in both books and movies since she was a young child. She has been greatly inspired by years of watching movies and reading books and has wanted to make a contribution to this genre for many years. Her stories all contain a strong spiritual thread as she believes that spirituality is universal and crosses all boundaries. She believes that the creative process is largely intuitive and can be very effectively blocked by too much pre-planning. "Plot lines, characters and events all come to me intuitively," she says, "and this makes the act of writing a constant pleasure." She is a psychic medium and lives alone in Hampshire, UK.

DEDICATION

For Dean and Sharon

CHAPTER ONE

This is V-log reference LB734/A, data log reference point 3380133/8392.

Okay umm, how is the camera doing? Just let me move this a little, that way. Uh? How is that? That is fine. Okay umm, now this case was one of those defining moments in my career, and in many ways, in my personal life too. It started out as just another job like all the rest, but even before I reached the location, things started to change. At first, some of these changes were exciting and meant I would be able to stretch myself a little, develop my skill base y'know? As time went on though, the changes that were taking place became less exciting and by the time it was all over, things had gone from change, to devastation and it took me a long time to recover. I am still not sure at what point during the job it became clear to me that not everything was all that it appeared to be; maybe it was a slow and gradual thing, I don't know, but there was a time when I was more than a little confused as to what was what. This often happens. The work I do cannot be choreographed, I have to think on my feet and sometimes I have to make it up as I go along. Ninety nine percent of the time, it all works out right in the end. That other one percent though, well those times are different. Very different. It was also one of those rare cases that affected me on a very personal level, and the emotional cost was so high that if I had known beforehand what was to happen, I would not have gone near the job. I seldom get personally touched by the cases I deal with; I'm able to retain some detachment and I think that's why I'm so good at what I do and why my boss gives me so much leeway. I am not made of stone though and on those rare occasions when I cannot avoid getting emotionally involved, I sometimes get knocked, and knocked hard. This was one such case and I still feel the effects of it today. I guess I always will and that is a good thing because there are aspects of the job I do not want to forget, despite the pain. Forgetting those things would seem like losing my humanity.

I had been through a bit of a dry spell work wise and had not been gainfully employed for three weeks or so when the job came in. I am one of those people who like to be doing something and I get bored easily with too much time on my hands. My contacts in the Law Enforcement Agency had told me to take a holiday, so as I hadn't had any real time off in a couple of years I accepted and went back home to Sigma Prime to catch up with some old friends and colleagues. I own an apartment in a nice high rise in a better part of Alimenika, the capital city of the easternmost continent and the location for the Law Enforcement Agency's Sigma headquarters. It is a nice part of town and as my job pays well, the location of my home was something I did not have to compromise on, especially as I am away from it for long periods. I called the cleaning woman I usually employ and let her know I'd be home for a couple of weeks, and as I closed my front door behind me, I could see she'd been in and done a great job on the place as always. Not only had she cleaned and aired the whole apartment, but she had filled my kitchen with food and even bought me a case of my favourite Kambino Beer. A note on the counter top informed me that she would take any laundry I wanted done, in the morning, and that there was home baked pie in the stasis unit I could reheat for dinner. I smiled as I thought of the dumpy middle-aged woman who looked after me as perfectly as any wife could and resolved to remind her how much she meant to me.

As has become my habit, I spent the first couple of days just doing nothing and enjoying sleeping in a comfortable bed again and eating proper food. I have all the facilities I need on board my own ship but they are basic, so whenever I get back home, I tend to spend a day or two just eating well and sleeping a lot. On the third day, I spent the morning at the hairdresser catching up with the cute redheaded woman from Earth who runs the place while she tidied up my hair and gave me a few shots of Tricholox to thicken it up a little. I am not the vainest person you will ever meet but I do like my hair to look good and I do like regular dermal treatments to keep my skin looking its best. After spending a couple of hours in a dermal optimiser, I smiled at my reflection. I'd lost a couple of years and a whole lot of stress off my face, my hair looked great and as I turned sideways in her full length mirror, I was pleased to notice that I seemed to have lost a few pounds too.

When the Head of Law Enforcement here on Sigma, Tinnias Vaylo, called me up and asked me if I'd call in and see him as he had a proposition to put to me which would bring me a substantial pay check if I chose to accept, I happily agreed. My job pays well and I enjoy a good standard of living but a bonus is always welcome. After a couple of days to myself with good food and plenty of sleep in a comfortable bed, a dermal and a haircut and a night with the cute redhead, I felt relaxed and wouldn't mind if my holiday ended rather sooner than I'd expected it to. I am so used to working all the time that when I do find myself with extended periods of time on my hands, it does not take me long to get restless and bored. Doing the job I do means I cannot maintain a circle of friends like ordinary folks do so I have become, by necessity, a bit of a loner. I sometimes only get home to Sigma a couple of times a year and I'd be constantly letting people down so I tend to keep a little detachment from people, which helps me do the work I do without distractions but it doesn't help my social life when I get time off. That is why I do not tend to take much holiday time.

I am a Freelance Law Enforcer, a cop of sorts but not in the ordinary sense. I am more of an inter-galactic cop; my patch is not a few streets or blocks, it is the whole galaxy and I share it with loads of others like myself. I am given a specific job to do by the Law Enforcement Agency as and when they need me. I am what is known in the trade as a chase, catch and deliver guy, which means I am given a specific target to acquire, restrain and hand over to the relevant Law Enforcement authorities. I used to be a regular Law Enforcer behind a desk in the very building I was now heading towards. I worked as a detective in Alemenika and seldom left Sigma. I can remember many times giving jobs just like the ones I do now, to other freelancers and never guessed back then that the roles would be reversed one day. Back then, I had good pay and regular time off but the petty rules and regulations sometimes got in the way, and too many times I found myself with no choice but to let some asshole walk because of some damn technicality. Eventually there came a time when I knew I could not take it anymore and it was either give up or go freelance. I liked my job; it was just the regulations and petty rules that irritated me, so I handed in my notice, took possession of an official tag that identified me as an officially recognised freelancer and went shopping for my own ship. In all the years I have been doing this job, I have never regretted going freelance, and apart from the ever present threat from the many unregistered freelancers, universally known as Mercs, I love my job. I often spend months at a time living on board my ship so I did not skimp when I was looking for one to purchase. It had to serve as not just my transportation and place of work, but my temporary home as well. I spent a good part of my life savings on her and she has all the facilities I need; fully functioning wash cubicle with shower, deluxe model nutri vend and auto snack and a double wide bunk in the small but functional bedroom. A substantial hold in her belly has space for up to seven prisoners to be safely restrained and plenty of storage space. A top of the range covert stealth modulator ensures I am invisible to ninety percent of the radar and scanning systems most of the worlds I visit use. She was in great condition and I was only her third owner. I did not hesitate. I christened her SC257 and grinned from ear to ear the first day I picked her up and admired her new paint job.

Tinnias Vaylo smiled and shook my hand as I entered his permanently untidy office on the third floor of the Law Enforcement Headquarters. I readily accepted his offer of a drink and sat opposite him. Although he is officially my boss, I like him, and we spent a few minutes catching up. I asked after his family and he invited me to dinner, which I was happy to accept as his wife is an amazing cook and his daughter is friendly and treats me like an older brother. It is the nearest thing to family I ever get to experience and I like the temporary closeness we share on these evenings. My parents both died years ago and I have no siblings and although I am used to my solitary status, it is nice to have that close feeling from time to time.

"Now Sam," he said as he tapped the screen on the digital console on his desk, "I have a job for you if you're interested. This is not like the usual jobs you do and will require you to blur the lines a little between your official resume as a straight chase, catch and deliver guy and a detective."

"Oh?" I replied in surprise. This was outside of my job description. My job is pretty straightforward; I am given a specific target to pursue, restrain and deliver to the authorities for trial or sentencing and my targets are usually escaped prisoners, criminals wanted for various misdeeds and all sorts of murderers and crazies. It's not my job to figure out who did what or why or how but just to catch person A, restrain them for a specific reason and deliver them to the relevant authorities at location B. Now here was Tinnias asking me to stretch my boundaries by being a detective. I was intrigued.

"I thought that would interest you."

"I'm not a detective Sir," I replied. "I'm a chase, catch and deliver guy as you know. Why the change now?"

"Well there are a couple of reasons. Firstly, there's talk of maybe giving all of our guys like yourself a bit more room to work out the why and how of the jobs you do. From the feedback you've all given us, we realise that many of you would like to be able to use more detective skills in your work. There have been many times, as you no doubt will agree, that your target has brought other aspects of his or her case to light that have a bearing on their eventual trial and often on the outcome of the whole case. Remember your experience with that Nembier guy?"

"Yeah, I remember," I nodded. Some time ago I'd been given the job of finding and catching this guy called Professor Nembier who was wanted for nine murders. As the whole thing worked itself out, I ended up having to be a detective in order that the real murderer be apprehended.

Everything worked out fine in the end but only because I stepped beyond the boundaries of my job.

"If I hadn't done my own detective work on that case, an innocent man would have been executed by now."

"Quite," Tinnias nodded. "Lots of our other freelancers have had similar cases where they've been forced to do their own detective work, which isn't strictly their job, but in all but a couple of the cases, innocents have avoided incarceration and the real perpetrators have been caught. It makes sense to give you all a little more scope to do your own research and make your own decisions in the field."

"Okay, that makes sense," I replied. "I'm sure that will help in some cases."

"Good, I'm glad you're okay with the idea. You're one of my most experienced men Sam and you've proved yourself time and again so I'm not going to send you on a detective's course."

"Thanks Boss."

"The other reason is that this job is going to take a while to complete. We know where to send you and we know something weird is going on there, but we do not know who is behind everything, why it is happening or how. You'll have to dig in and become part of the scene, take the time necessary to get to know everyone so you can eventually answer those questions for us. When you know what's going on and who our guy is, you have the authority to then arrest him and bring him in. All the decisions will be yours, but of course you'll take any flak should you bring in the wrong guy. I trust you Sam. I've known you since you joined the Agency and you've never made hasty decisions."

"It sounds interesting. What is the job exactly?"

"We've been in regular contact with our colleagues on Deligon 2 for the past year. It seems there have been a number of mysterious disappearances; seven in all during the past fourteen months. The Head of Law Enforcement over there, Adlion Garmast, tells me that all seven worked at a scientific station that was set up to do research into a new disease that's affecting the trees on Deligon. The last victim was discovered having apparently fallen while rock climbing while on leave from work. It wasn't until her family, who aren't native to Deligon, insisted on taking her body back to their home world for a full autopsy, that they found she'd died a week earlier than the Deligon report. Her body had been stored and some chemical added to her blood stream to slow down decomposition to make it look like she died many days later than she actually died. The cryo stasis process used to transport her body home affected this chemical compound and made it easy for her own doctors to find. If she hadn't been sent home in cryo, this chemical wouldn't have been found and everyone would've carried on believing she fell while climbing."

"So it's obviously a cover up," I nodded.

"Obviously," Tinnias replied. "Now we need to ask why cover up an accidental death?"

"And does that now bring suspicion on the other six deaths?" I continued.

"Right."

"So you want me to emigrate to Deligon and sign up for work?"

"See how good a detective you are Sam?"

"How long do I have?"

"As long as it takes. You take all the time you need. Keep in touch by the secure Unicom channel I'll give you and keep us updated. Anything you need, you just ask and I'll personally see to it you get it. Do you want the job? It's double pay by the way and all your expenses of course and anytime you want out, just call and we'll get a team in to extricate you if necessary. You want to think about it for a day or two?"

"I'll take it. I've never been to Deligon before and have no contacts there so it will be a good opportunity to add to my eyes and ears."

"That's great, thank you Sam. I'll get all your papers together and you'll be going with a large wedge of galactic credits to last you until you secure yourself a job within the scientific station. You won't be short of money, I assure you, and anytime you need more, just call."

"Thank you Sir."

"No problem at all. You'll have an alias for this job by the way; we can't have your real identity as a Law Enforcer coming out and putting you in danger before you decide it's necessary to reveal your true agenda. Any idea what you want to be called?"

"Joss Gilden," I replied without hesitation.

"Okay," Tinnias replied as he jotted it down. "You've used the Gilden alias before haven't you?"

"Yes Sir, is that a problem?"

"No I don't think so. Weren't you Demilo Gilden last time, and Tico Gilden one other time?"

"Yeah."

"That won't be a problem then, there's loads of Gildens here on Sigma. It's a fairly common name. Can I ask why you always use Gilden?"

"It's umm, well Sir it's the name of someone I used to know." I tried not to show him that this question made me extremely uncomfortable, but at the same time, I wanted him to realise that I didn't intend to expand on my answer. There was no way I wanted to remind him about her.

"Okay, no problem Sam." He pressed the button on his communication panel and called to his Assistant. "Can you come in here please Maddy?" The plump but pretty woman entered and smiled at me as she approached the desk. "Can you arrange for some papers for an alias undercover operation. Pilot's licence, intergalactic passport, DNA references and so on, the usual."

"Of course Sir," she replied. "What is the change of name?"

"From Samelan Sinclair to Joss Gilden."

"And the work history?"

"Ex-military, completed his statutory ten years then retired to start his own security business back home on Sigma Prime. Made some bad investments, lost his business and home and decided to start fresh somewhere else. Parents deceased, no siblings. That sound okay to you Sam?"

"Sounds fine to me Sir."

"And arrange for ten thousand galactic credits to be uploaded to Mr Joss Gilden's account would you?"

"Of course Sir," she nodded and left the room.

"Here's five hundred credits Sam," he said as he handed me a currency card. "Get yourself some new clothes, something a bit less umm,"

"A bit less what Sir?" I asked as I looked down at myself.

"Well, a bit less like an off duty law enforcer."

I laughed out loud but I had to admit that he was right. I'm no male model and my job hardly ever requires me to wear the latest fashions, so I tend to stick to what I know and all of it comfortable, sturdy and which enables me to do my work unhindered by trivialities. That does not mean I have no sense of style, far from it, but I seldom get the opportunity to look like I just stepped out of a clothes store.

"Don't be offended Sam," Tinnias grinned.

"I'm not Sir. You're right actually; my wardrobe could do with a bit of updating. When am I off?"

"Well, your papers should be ready in a day or two and I'll set up some accommodation for you on Deligon; that will take a day. How's your ship?"

"She's being refitted and serviced now. The guys said she'll be done by the end of the week."

"Okay then," Tinnias nodded. "Let's say five days from now then, provisionally."

"That's fine Sir."

"Thank you Sam. I know I won't regret putting my trust in you. You'll be an ambassador for this new change, if it should end up going ahead and your actions will be a benchmark for all our other freelancers. During this job you'll be setting the standard for them, so feel free to make it as high as you like."

"I will Sir and thank you for your trust. I appreciate it," I smiled as I stood and shook hands with him.

"Eight o clock okay?"

"Huh?"

"For dinner tonight."

"Oh, sure. That'll be fine. Can I use some of this money to buy Ambella a gift?"

"You could buy her a vidicom movie if you want; she'd love that new one by that favourite actor of hers. Umm that Elloway guy from Earth. You know the guy with the dark hair and blue eyes, the big fella with the muscles."

"Oh yeah you mean Jake Elloway," I replied.

"That's the one," he nodded. "She's madly in love with him and makes me and her mother sit through every one of his movies hundreds of times over. She's been nagging us to get her his latest movie."

"Okay," I nodded. "I'm a bit of a fan of his too. I may just buy myself a copy."

"You're shitting me Sam," Tinnias exclaimed.

"No shit Sir."

Tinnias laughed loudly and I could still hear him laughing as I left his office and headed for the lift.

I left my new clothes in a bag, along with a note asking my cleaning woman to launder and press them for me as soon as possible and examined the clothes I already owned. Tinnias was right, I do look like a law enforcer even when off duty and I resolved to buy myself more clothes suitable for off work times. I realised I did not own a single garment suitable for a smart occasion and not too many smart casual things either. I picked out the best shirt I had, an understated black number with a slight sheen to the light fabric and the one pair of good pants I owned. After rooting around in the back of the closet I came across a black jacket I bought on Terramora Prime a few years back and grinned. I forgot all about this garment and the cute blonde with the enormous breasts who sold it to me and then kept me company in my hotel room for the following three nights. I brushed it off and sprayed it with some Launder Fresh before putting it on and looking at my reflection.

I looked okay I decided. Smart enough but still casual and not at all like an off duty law enforcer, at least not one I'd ever seen. I picked up the vidicom movie I'd bought and had gift wrapped for Tinnias' daughter Ambella and left. As the hover cab swept through the darkening streets of Alimenika towards the Vaylo home I thought of the evening to come and realised I felt excited and happy to be spending time with people who were the closest thing to family to me. The only slight cloud on the horizon was Ambella herself. At fourteen she was still something of a kid but I was also aware of her burgeoning womanhood, and the way she always greeted me with a hug and a kiss on the cheek and the way she snuggled up to me as we all sat and talked and laughed, hinted at her growing awareness of her femininity. She's a pretty girl with a happy disposition and she shows her affections freely and that's the problem. I was beginning to get the distinct impression that she had a crush on me and I talked it over with Tinnias after our last meeting, nearly a year before.

"Don't worry Sam," Tinnias had assured me, "you're not around nearly enough to encourage her to fall for you. I trust you completely and she has plenty of young men her own age that she hangs out with."

"I don't want to hurt her feelings Sir," I replied. "I don't want to lead her on or anything. Give her false hope you know?"

"I know and thank you for telling me. Be your usual friendly self with her. Remember she's only thirteen and as fast as this crush has come, it will be gone and replaced with another."

"I guess you're right."

Tinnias greeted me with a handshake and looked me up and down before nodding with approval.

"That's more like it Sam," he nodded. "You scrub up very well."

"Thanks."

"Sam, how lovely to see you again. Come on in." Grellina Vaylo embraced me and gave me a kiss on the cheek. "You look handsome tonight," she smiled as she too looked me up and down.

"Thank you Mrs Vaylo, it's always a pleasure to be here."

"Oh stop it, call me Grellina, please. We're family Sam."

Thudding footsteps reached my ears and I looked up to see Ambella running down the stairs. She grinned and flung herself into my arms and hugged me, making me all too aware of her growing breasts and slimming waistline. She was no longer a child and I would have to be careful with her feelings. She hadn't yet realised how innocently provocative she could be and I could so easily be interested in her in a very non friendly way, but with her being so young and my Boss's daughter, there was no way I was going to allow her to give me an unscheduled hard on. In ten years' time maybe, but not tonight.

"Hi Sam. It's been ages."

"Hey there girl, wow look at you," I said as I held her at arm's length. "You're all grown up. You're a proper young woman now." She blushed and put her arm through mine and led me through to the sitting room where she plonked herself down beside me. I extricated my arm and took out the gift I'd bought for her. "I got you something, just in case I miss your next birthday."

Her eyes lit up and her full lips spread across her face in a smile that lit the room. "Oh Sam, thank you," she said as she took it and began to carefully unwrap it. When she saw the vidicom movie, she gasped.

"Oh wow," she exclaimed. "I've been wanting this for ages. Thank you so much. Oh Jake Elloway, he's so handsome." She leaned in and kissed my cheek.

"You're welcome hunny, I know you like the guy and a little bird told me you'd been asking for this new movie of his."

"You're the best Sam."

"That's another one her mother and I will get to know so intimately we'll both be able to play all the parts word perfect," Tinnias said and I laughed as Ambella made a face.

The dinner was delicious and the company friendly and I relaxed more during that evening than I could remember in ages. We talked and laughed for hours and it made me realise just how much I miss family life. I also realised that evening that the little Ambella whose cuddles I enjoyed so much was not little anymore and there could be no more innocent cuddles. I couldn't allow her to fall for me so for the first time, I didn't cuddle her back as she snuggled against my arm. I hoped she did not think I did not like her anymore and I made an effort to include her in conversation so she would know I still noticed her and valued her presence, but I had to begin the process of closing off the physical contact we had enjoyed during her childhood years as she ran headlong into womanhood. I thought back to all the times she'd sat on my lap and sang songs, fallen asleep in my arms with her thumb still in her mouth and forced me to play endless silly, wonderful games. The child was now a young woman and it felt almost like a death to me and I knew I would grieve for the innocent child with whom I had enjoyed so much comforting contact. In her place was a woman learning about emotions and having her first crush and my role in her life was now changed forever. As my Boss's daughter I couldn't afford to blur the lines between friendship and, something else. She didn't deserve that and I'm no cradle snatcher. As I said, in ten years' time maybe.

The evening was warm as we sat on their veranda and drank the rich green wine they save for special occasions. The Vaylo house looked down upon the city from the top of a hill where the most desirable residences are built. The city looked beautiful from up here and we could see for miles into the horizon, almost to the coastline. Ambella went to watch the new movie I'd bought her and left Tinnias, Grellina and I alone and Tinnias felt able to talk about the job he'd offered me. We discussed various scenarios and possible explanations for what might have taken place, played with a few ideas as to how I should approach my research and detective work to uncover the truth. He then told me I would be sharing an apartment with another guy who was also in the employ of the Law Enforcement Agency.

"He's a Damiklonian Sam, and he'll be helping you get to know your way around and will be a sort of assistant. He also works at the scientific station so use him in whatever way you feel he could be useful to you. He's prepared to do whatever you say. He knows you're the boss."

"A Damiklonian?" I said. "I've never met them before. What are they like?"

"They're nice people Sam. They look a bit different and they sound different too but they are honourable and trustworthy. I've worked with a couple of them in my time and wouldn't hesitate to trust them."

"That's good to know. What do you mean by different?"

"They have gills and can breathe underwater as well as in air and they have fangs."

"Fangs?" I replied in shock.

"Yeah," he nodded. "Really long ones too and their bite is venomous. Their fangs are retractable so you won't see them unless he wishes to use them or to show them to you. He also carries the only known antidote with him. It's galactic law that all Damiklonians carry the antidote when working away from their home world. He will make a point of showing it to you when you meet him so don't be fazed by it, he's just obeying the law."

"Okay thanks."

"His voice is a bit weird too," Tinnias continued. "Damiklonians talk differently to most other races and they have to be taught to speak in a way the rest of us will understand more easily when they leave Damiklon Prime to work."

"Right, thanks for the warning. I'll try not to offend him by being surprised."

"Don't worry, they're used to folks being surprised and so long as you're not openly rude or disrespectful, he'll be the best friend you could wish for."

"Thanks Boss," I nodded, little realising how pertinent those words were to become.

I took a hover cab back to the city, and Tinnias promised to call as soon as my papers were ready for me to collect. I stopped the cab at a local bar and after a few drinks, took home a delightful Sigma girl with long black hair and allowed her to take my mind off things. We spent the rest of the night and half the following morning having wonderfully wild and abandoned sex and after I saw her off in a hover cab, I showered and went for a walk. I ate lunch in a small cafe where an old friend was still the head chef and spent a happy hour and a half catching up with him. As I was leaving the cafe I felt someone bump into me and turned to see who it was, a ready apology for my lack of attention waiting upon my lips. The man turned and looked at me and the familiar dark spot fluttered within my heart. Our eyes locked for a moment, neither of us knowing what to say and both of us realising the weight of grief that would forever prevent any friendship between us.

"Hello Mr Gilden," I offered. "It's been a long time. How are you these days?"

"Sam. We're umm. Well, life goes on I guess. You look good, you haven't changed. It must be, what, over three years at least?"

"Yeah," I nodded. "I keep busy with work."

"Have you umm, been to visit?" he asked suddenly.

"No," I admitted guiltily. "I can't. I just can't."

"We do," he replied, "every week. We don't want to forget. We don't want her to think we don't love her."

"I'll never forget," I snapped back, "not ever. And she knows how I feel. Wherever she is, she'll know."

"Enjoy your life Sam," he replied as he turned and walked away. "How I wish she could too."

Damn that man. Why does he always manage to upset me whenever we meet? More importantly, why do I let him? I walked along the street, a rapidly growing knot of anger and guilt building in my gut. I strode along the city streets, teeth clenched, fists balled and the pain in my gut that ruined my mood. How the hell could he think I do not care? Surely he has not forgotten it was I that found her. Of all the people I had to bump into, it had to be Mr Gilden didn't it. The one person who can ruin a good mood just by being there and I have to run into him. Just my luck. At that moment, I was suddenly eager to get on with this new job and get away for a while to Deligon where I could concentrate on the job at hand and forget Sigma, forget Mr Gilden and his accusations, forget her. No, I couldn't ever forget her but at least being far away might ease the pain of the memories I tried so hard to put away but never quite managed to; the awful scene that met my eyes that I yearned to forget but couldn't. This was another big reason I did not intend to allow Ambella Vaylo to fall for me. I could not allow myself to get involved in an emotional commitment to someone as innocent as Ambella, with her whole life ahead of her. I could not put her at risk. I could not lose another love.

Merita King

CHAPTER TWO

I got the call from Tinnias that my paperwork was ready and promised I would call in the next day for a final briefing on the job before I was to set off. This meant I had one last free evening to do what I liked with and I decided to make the most of it, within reason. He warned me not to drink any alcohol as I would be making the journey to Deligon in cryo sleep and any alcohol in my system could put me at risk, so although my last night on Sigma was to be a dry one, it wasn't going to be totally devoid of fun.

I put on the same black shirt and semi smart pants I wore to dinner at the Vaylo home, checked out my hair in the mirror and left my apartment for the short walk to the home of my cleaning woman. She lived with her husband a half mile from my apartment block, in a small house with its own tiny garden at the rear. The weather was good and despite knowing I was leaving the next day, I was relaxed, my encounter with Mr Gilden now having faded into the background. No matter how long I spend away from Sigma, I love my home world and would not want to live anywhere else. I found the house and smiled as I knocked. A rather timid looking man opened the door.

"Yes?" he asked with a cautious smile.

"Oh hi," I replied. "You must be Raylen Cambly, Sondray's husband?"

"I am," he nodded.

"My name's Sinclair. She cleans for me."

"Ahh, yes," he replied and opened the door a little wider. "The law enforcement guy."

"That's me. Is she in?"

"Yes, she's in the kitchen. Come on in." He led the way through the small house to a kitchen that smelled wonderful. Sondray turned and smiled when she saw me.

"Hi Sam. What can I do for you? I thought you were leaving tomorrow."

"I am, but I just wanted to give you this," I said as I handed over a large box of her favourite indulgent delicacy. "To say thank you for looking after me so well."

"Oh my word," she exclaimed as she took the box. "Dried Lingmars. My favourite treat. Thank you so much." She gave me a peck on the cheek and offered me a drink.

"I'd love one, thank you but it'll have to be alcohol free I'm afraid. I've got cryo sleep tomorrow and I don't want to be ill."

"Where are you off to this time Mr Sinclair?" Raylen asked.

"Deligon 2," I replied. "It might turn out to be a long visit too, so I may not be back for a while. I'll call when I'm on my way home again."

"Are you allowed to tell us what you'll be doing?"

"I'm afraid not," I shook my head. "It's undercover this time. A little different from my usual chase, catch and deliver jobs. Sorry."

"Oh don't apologise," Raylen smiled. "We understand completely."

"And I'll air your apartment out every couple of weeks," Sondray said, "just as always. You just call me and let me know when you're due home and I'll get your supplies in as usual."

"Raylen," I said. "You're the luckiest man alive to have such a wonderful wife. I hope I find one as caring one day."

"Oh stop," Sondray blushed,

I left the Cambly home and strolled towards the centre of the city. Alimenika boasts a thriving nightlife, due in large part to Sigma's cosmopolitan inhabitants. Due to it being a big centre for trade and employment from many different worlds, Sigma was afforded the honour of being allowed to call itself a Prime world. Consequently, its major cities enjoy an eclectic nightlife. Music from many different worlds came to my ears as I wandered along past the bars and cafes and faces of every conceivable colour and design smiled or frowned as I passed by. I smiled and nodded to all of them in return. I headed for Tunipz; an area to the west of the city where a few of my friends live and hang out on evenings such as this. Tunipz is a rather run down area covering a few square miles of land and filled with shops, bars, cafés and whorehouses, all surrounding a beautiful area of parkland that nestles right in its centre. The inhabitants of Tunipz are what you might call, the lower classes and it is regarded by outsiders as a rough neighbourhood. Every city on every world has its own version of Tunipz and Sigma is no exception. During the daytime, water birds enjoy the small lake and folks stroll around on summer afternoons or enjoy free concerts by local musicians. By night though, the park becomes a no go area for anyone wanting to see their next birthday. It is not as bad today as it used to be, and I am part of the reason for that. I spent a few years working with the locals in the Tunipz area and over time, I encouraged them to clean the park up and keep it free of the worst of the crazies that could be found in there. I made sure the worst of them were put behind bars, especially those not native to Sigma and the locals came to trust me and responded in kind by forming their own security force who patrol the park at night and keep things to an acceptable level. It is still not safe to enter the park at night, especially for a woman but it is no longer a guaranteed death sentence to see someone go in there at dusk.

I smiled as I saw the light glittering off the tiny silver threads woven into the guy's suit. There was only one guy in Alimenika with balls big enough to wear that in public and not get laughed at.

"You're not still wearing that suit are ya buddy?" I said and grinned. He froze on the spot, his hand still on the door handle as he ushered Sigma Prime's younger generation into the deafening noise within.

"I don't even need to turn around," the deep velvet voice declared. "Sam fucking Sinclair." He turned and grinned as he opened his arms and came towards me. "Buddy. How ya doing?" The breath left my lungs as he hugged me to his massive chest and squeezed with biceps the size of my thighs.

"Leevine. You've lost weight man, are you ill?" I asked and he roared with laughter.

"And you're still as gorgeous hunny," he countered. "How long's it been? A year?"

"At least," I nodded. "How are things around here?"

"Oh pretty much the same as ever."

"Everything okay in the park these days?"

"Yeah," he nodded. "We've got four hourly patrols every night and three hourly at weekends now Sam. We ain't had a body in four months. The kids from the local school go there for their lunch breaks and a couple of the local old ladies started up a group to take care of the plants and keep it all pretty like."

"That's fantastic," I grinned. "I'm proud of you folks man, tell everyone I said it huh?"

"I will," he nodded. "You wanna know something hilarious?"

"Sure."

"Tunipz now has its own social committee that takes charge of anything that affects the whole area, like the park for instance, and they did this campaign thing to get a name for it."

"That's a wonderful idea," I replied. "You don't want to keep calling it Hellgate. Not now it's safer and folks are enjoying the place."

"Yeah that's what everyone thought when they had a community meeting about it. They told everyone to think of a suitable name and then they'd draw up a list and everyone would get to vote to decide the winner. Guess what name they decided on."

"I've no idea," I shrugged.

"Jahznirash," he replied. This Sigma word means beauty amidst decay and I smiled at the irony and insight of it.

"That's perfect," I nodded. "Just perfect."

"Do you remember The Team Sam?" he asked suddenly and I nodded again.

"Hey I'll never forget them. Why do you think I always come back here huh? I have to check in on the team when I can. I care about this place." During my days as a desk bound law enforcer, when I was working with the locals in this area and trying to befriend them and encourage them to clean the place up and make it safer for everyone, a group of the area's most influential guys got together the first Tunipz Security Group. A lot of these guys were crooks and many of them had done time but all had one thing in common; they cared about Tunipz. We came to call ourselves, The Tunipz Team and every time I get home to Sigma, I make a point of visiting the area to touch base with a few of them.

"Well you know what?" he continued. "The Team got together and ordered a fancy new children's play area in the park. For the very little kids you know? It cost a whole lot of cash Sam but everyone felt it was worth it now that the park is safer and they feel happier to take their kids there to play. Anyway, the guys took a vote and decided to name it Sam's Playground." I was stunned at this news and felt a lump in my throat.

"They did? Jeez that's wonderful. I'm honoured, really. Can I go see it?"

"Sure. I'll get my buddy here to cover for me and I'll bring my car around."

As the big guy's hover car cruised along through Tunipz, I rolled down the window and watched as the familiar streets flew passed. Here and there, a voice would call out and I would grin and wave. I felt like a celebrity on a meet and greet with his fans. The park was beautiful and even though it was dusk, I could smell the perfume from the Angral trees as we walked along the path from the main gate to the new kiddie's playground. A gaily painted fence, decorated with stylised animals and trees denoted the boundary of the little kids play area and I smiled as I saw that the locals had obviously raised a lot of money for this. Everything was top quality and brand new; no expense had been spared for their kid's pleasure and it choked me up to see Sam's Playground in huge painted letters above the gate. To know I'd had a hand in changing the nature of the area, and that I'd been able to help them rediscover a pride in their local community, so much that the Hellgate as the park used to be known, is now a beautiful place where they bring their kids to play, filled me with pride.

Leevine dropped me at what had become The Team's headquarters but which was actually just an empty store with a hand painted sign above the door that declared, 'Tunipz Security HQ' in large black letters. After another bone crunching hug, he drove off and I went in to find four guys deep in conversation over a map of Tunipz.

"Is this the local whorehouse?" I called and four pairs of eyes glared at me.

"Sam," the guy on the far left grinned. "How ya doin buddy?"

"Jinn, you don't look a day older," I countered.

"Come in and meet the guys," he said and waved me over.

I spent a couple of hours catching up with The Team and was pleased to see how they'd taken their community's wellbeing to heart. By the time I left I'd not laughed so much in months and had promised to return as soon as I was back on Sigma. I had my photo taken with the guys and asked them to give my thanks to the community for naming the kid's playground after me.

I headed back into the centre of Alimenika and my favourite bar for an alcohol free nightcap or three and maybe even some female company to while away the evening. The place was not quite half-full and I was pleased to see my favourite stool at the far corner of the bar was vacant. I sat down and ordered a Palmat juice and water and asked the bartender if there was any entertainment on tonight. Three hours later I stumbled out of the rear entrance and into the night to find a cab home. The Somborian dancers had been very entertaining and the three who took me into their dressing room at the end of their act, even more so. As I flopped into the cab my crotch ached and I was sure I'd never get a hard on ever again but boy it had been the best night I'd had in years. I dragged myself back to my apartment and took a shower. I winced as I soaped my groin; my balls ached, no doubt from over use but I couldn't help but grin. I'm not exactly a gigolo but I get my fair share and being a single guy with no ties certainly helps. I keep myself looking reasonable and have never had too much trouble finding female company but tonight I'd excelled myself. I fell into bed and was asleep within minutes.

Next morning I was keen to get back to work and was happy to notice when I showered that my balls no longer ached, the fact that I'd woken with my usual morning hard on assuring me that my health hadn't suffered as a result of last night's indulgence and my body relaxed as I showered. I dressed in some casual clothes and packed for my journey to Deligon.

Tinnias Vaylo smiled as he ushered me into his office and offered me a seat.

"I have all your papers here Sam," he said as he handed them over. "Galactic passport, work history and references from your ten year military career, birth certificate, DNA references and so on, it's all there. Here's your financial account details and your currency card. There's ten thousand credits in there and you can call for more whenever you need it. This is the secure Unicom number to use whenever you call here. It's been set up specifically for you and only a few guys here will be on hand to receive your calls so you should notice that you'll speak to the same six guys all the time. And of course I'll be on hand should you wish to speak to me personally."

"Thanks Boss. Is my ship ready?"

"Yeah, she's all done. We've stocked her up with supplies and given her a new paint job too, seeing as how Joss Gilden hasn't had her that long. We found a couple of those new AX27 model flight seats kicking around so we upgraded your pilot's and co-pilot's seats."

"Wow thanks," I smiled. "I was hoping to persuade you to let me have one of those cheap."

"No problem. Now here's some information on your contact and roommate, the Damiklonian guy. His name is Balian Renimir, thirty one years old, single and has been employed by the Inter Galactic Law Enforcement Agency for five years. He's been on site on Deligon for the past seven months and has been updating us regularly. He's known as Ren to his friends so you can call him that okay?"

"Sure. Is there a picture?"

"Oh yeah, here," he nodded as he handed me a photo of what appeared to be a rather finely boned but otherwise normal humanoid. His eyes were far too big, rather round and a strange blue grey colour but they seemed to look right into my soul. I could clearly see some horizontal marks on either side of his throat, just under the jaw line. Three horizontal lines on each side and I guessed those were the gills he uses to breathe underwater. He had his mouth closed so I could not see his teeth but I did notice his lips were full and wide, indicating that his mouth was capable of opening quite a bit wider than is normal for the rest of us.

"He looks like an okay kind of guy to me," I nodded. I like to think of myself as an excellent judge of character and I was confident I was not wrong this time. Doing the job I do means I get to meet and interact with all sorts of weird and crazy people from many different worlds and over the years, I have developed a skill for reading people. I have never yet met one person who can lie to me convincingly.

"He is," Tinnias replied as he put the photo away. "You can safely allow yourself to trust him completely Sam. As I told you the other day, Damiklonians are amongst the most trustworthy and honourable folks I've ever encountered. Make a friend of him and you'll have a true friend for life."

"Okay thanks," I said. "I'll remember that."

"Now," Tinnias continued. "Deligon is a long way away, so you'll be shipped out there in a military troop ship in cryo sleep. They'll wake you up and make sure you're okay before they drop you off three days out from the Deligon system. When you arrive, head for the northernmost continent and the small city called Bygora Vandos. Here are the exact co-ordinates. Arrive covertly by the way, we've given you a fake Deligon entry card so no need to go through the usual red tape and find they turn you away and scupper your mission. Here's a map of Bygora Vandos; the large building there is the scientific station and a few miles away to the left, with the red X, is the apartment complex you'll be living in. Tower 1784, floor 7, room 28. Ren will leave a spare key hidden under a loose tile at the right hand side of the door. Twelfth tile up, with a picture of a flower on it."

"Right, got it," I replied as I made a few notes.

"If you can sign for all this stuff, we'll get you a medical check with the Doc and you'll be ready to rendezvous with the troop ship which should be arriving in orbit anytime now."

"Hop up here for me would you Sam," the Doctor smiled as he entered my details into his digital medical scanner. I laid back and relaxed as he went through the usual routine and after assuring me that I was as fit as a man ten years younger, I shook hands with him and headed back to Tinnias' office.

"The Doc assures me that I'm still alive Boss," I reported as I handed him the medical data chip.

"Wonderful, now let's go downstairs to the ship shop." He led the way down to the basement level where all the Agency ships are repaired and upgraded. Everyone has called it the ship shop for as long as I have been working for the Agency and no doubt will continue to do so forever. I was stunned into silence for a few seconds when I caught site of my ship.

"Wow," I exclaimed as I approached her and admired her new paint job, "you look beautiful girl."

"Thanks buddy," the voice of Jola, the Chief Engineer cut into my thoughts and I turned to see him grinning at me.

"Fantastic job Jola," I smiled as I shook hands with him, "I mean it buddy. You're an artist man."

"Stop it Sam, before I blush. Come on; let me show you what we've done with her." He stood aside and I entered the side hatch. An hour later, I offered him my hand once again.

"Thank you Jola, I appreciate your skills and so does she," I said as I nodded towards my ship.

"My pleasure Sam," he replied. "When are you off?"

"As soon as I go back home, pick up my bags and get back here," I said.

"Okay," he nodded. "The troop ship is in orbit and they've told us they're ready for you so I'll get this girl here up to the roof landing pad to wait for your return."

"Okay, thanks," I said as I turned to go. "Give me an hour."

I settled myself into the wonderfully comfortable new model pilot's seat and grinned.

"You're looking sexy now Essy," I whispered as I started her up and got ready for take-off.

I call my ship Essy because of her registration SC257, which stands for Space Cop 257. It might seem a bit strange to think of her as a person but you ask any guy with his own ship and he will tell you, they have a real personality and appreciate a kind word here and there. Tinnias escorted me to the roof landing pad, shook my hand, wished me well, and made me promise to keep him updated regularly. My firearms locker had been restocked with ammo and I was delighted to discover a brand new model laser rifle amongst my array of weaponry. Tinnias had instructed me in using miniature surveillance equipment and gave me a tiny camera that looked like a shirt button, with an inbuilt microphone and told me to wear it at all times once the job got underway. The camera transmits everything to a receiver built into a standard vidicom camera that most folks possess these days and if there is nothing worth keeping, I can delete everything each night and just keep anything that will help our case against them. A stack of data chips, each one capable of holding six weeks' worth of continuous filming, were stored safely in the vidicom camera's carry bag, in a pouch under the lining.

"Okay Essie, let's get on with it shall we?" I whispered as I lifted her off the roof of the Law Enforcement Agency headquarters and headed up into the sky. My intercom beeped.

"SC257 this is Sigma Aerospace. We have you on our scanner. Your hosts are awaiting your arrival. Sending you co-ordinates now."

"Co-ordinates received, thank you Sigma."

"Safe journey Space Cop and come home soon. Sigma out."

Within a few minutes the huge hulking troop ship came into view. These things aren't built to be admired for their beauty and I was suddenly transported back twenty years to my years in the military when I'd done millions of space miles in ships just like this one in front of me now. I hailed them.

"This is SC257 wishing to rendezvous with you as arranged. I'm ready for docking co-ordinates."

"SC257 we are ready for you. Come around to docking bay twelve. Sending co-ordinates now."

"Received. Thank you."

I approached the docking bay and flipped into auto docking mode to let Essy do the work herself. The enormous maw of the docking bay approached and I looked up as the gap between us closed and smiled as I read 'Liberty' painted in forty foot high letters above the bay doors. It always makes me laugh the way Military ships are always given names meant to inspire. During my military career, I travelled in all sorts of vessels to all sorts of situations and this one reminded me of them all. They were all different shapes and sizes and served many different purposes but all had one thing in common, all were named in this inspirational way. Peacemaker, Brotherhood, Defiance, Allegiance, New Dawn and many others similarly named flitted through my memory as my ship docked automatically with Liberty.

"Mr Gilden," the tall muscular man smiled as he shook my hand. "Welcome to Liberty." Tinnias told me that from the moment I left Sigma, I was to be Joss Gilden and so as to get me used to answering to it, the crew of the Liberty were to call me by my agreed alias from the moment I came aboard.

"Thank you very much," I replied.

"If you'll follow me, I'll show you to cryogenics and hand you over to the Doctor."

"Lead the way."

The next four hours were spent in another medical check, this one far more thorough than the Agency one had been and by the time I was deemed fit for cryo sleep, I'd been poked, prodded and even had my cock inspected for infection by a man with very cold hands. Doctor Evelly signed me in as fit and handed me over to a young blonde man with bright blue eyes.

"Stannel here will take care of you from here Mr Gilden. He's our Head of Cryogenic Passenger Care and will help you prepare for cryo. I'll see you soon to see you safely off to sleep."

"Thanks Doc," I smiled a little nervously. I've done cryo sleep a few times but never for more than a day or two and it always makes me a little apprehensive. This time I was to be under for three months solid and the thought made me a little nervous.

"Follow me Mr Gilden," Stannel said and led the way out of the medical facility and along corridors, at the end of which I found my way blocked by a huge metal door.

"I'm going to show you the cryo facility," he told me as he punched a pass code into the entry pad. The door opened and I found myself looking into a huge room filled with what looked like thousands of clear, coffin sized pods, many of which contained a sleeping body. The pods were arranged in stacks of a hundred, each attached to a conveyor system that continuously circled up to the ceiling, over and back down again. As each pod reached the bottom of the ride, a technician checked its display and made notes into a scanner before it began its ascent once again. We walked along and Stannel explained the pods to me, showed me an occupied one and explained what the various beeps and blinking lights meant and one of the technicians showed me the digital record as he entered the details into his scanner. I felt better once I knew how the thing operated and saw how keenly they keep an eye on everyone.

"This is amazing," I said. "Scary but amazing."

"I know," he replied, "and our knowledge increases every day so that one day we can make cryo sleep just like going to bed at night. One day you won't need a pod. One day you can just go to bed in your room as normal and wake up weeks or months later in the same bed, refreshed and ready for the day, just like any other day. Ahh, here are the recovery rooms where you'll find yourself when we wake you up." He opened the door to one of the small rooms and I saw a large double bed. "Now if you can just fill out this form here so we know what your preferences are when you wake up." I blushed to the roots of my hair and he smiled. "Don't be embarrassed Mr

Gilden. We all work with cryo passengers every day and nothing shocks us anymore. We want your recovery to be quick and easy so you can get on and do the very important job you've been assigned." He held my gaze for a few seconds to push the point home.

"Sure, okay," I sighed and looked at the form. The reason for my embarrassment is the harmless but common side effect of long periods of cryo sleep. If you spend longer than a day or so in cryo sleep, you wake up with an all-consuming sexual urge that cannot be ignored. In the early days, they tried to get people to control it but after several rapes happened, they had to make allowance for it in their recovery procedure. Now, every cryo passenger fills out a form with his or her preferences in a sexual partner so when they wake up, they find a very willing and amazingly life like friend in bed with them. I filled out the form and handed it back.

"That's fine Mr Gilden," he smiled. "We'll have no problem accommodating your needs. Now, follow me and I'll show you where you can change your clothes. He led the way to a small room at the other end of the huge space and handed me a close fitting, white garment. "This is quite a snug fit," he explained, "but it needs to be so that the sensors get a good bond with your skin and give us accurate readouts. Have you emptied your bowels this morning?"

"Yeah."

"Good. Now take a pee before changing into the garment. The bathroom is just through there."

It was a bit of a squeeze getting into the garment and after much contorting and puffing, he led me into an adjoining room that contained nothing but an examination couch. The same doctor I saw earlier was there and smiled at me.

"Hello again Mr Gilden. I'm going to get you off to sleep now. Do you have any last minute questions or worries at all?"

"No I don't think so Doc," I replied.

"Great, now just stand still while I attach all these sensors to your garment." He clipped the sensors with practiced ease and then had me lie down on the couch. "I'm going to give you an injection now that will make you doze off. Don't fight it okay? Just let yourself drift off and let us attend to your needs. I will then attach a line into your bladder, through the perineum that will drain off urine and keep you clean and comfortable. After that, I will install a line into your stomach to feed nutrients to your body. Then we'll get you installed within your pod. Once you're safely down into cryo sleep, your pod will be attached to rack number twenty two and we'll talk again in three months."

"Okay Doc, and thanks," I replied as he prepared an injector.

I have vague memories of feeling sensations; hands on my cock, a prick of pain behind my balls and something touching the back of my throat, and then a peculiar taste in my mouth before my memory ends. You do not dream during cryo sleep because you are not strictly asleep. You're frozen at such a low temperature that the body's systems slow right down. It's more like suspended animation than sleep and it doesn't refresh you like sleep does and when you wake up, you feel like you pulled a couple of all-nighters on the trot. It's funny how cryo sleep makes you sleepy but everyone spends a good many hours sleeping off the effects when they're unfrozen. That is, after they've attended to their furiously driving sexual needs.

Well, I'm gonna get something to eat and hit the sack. I'll catch you all in the morning. Good night. This is V-log reference LB734/A, data log reference point 3380133/8393.

CHAPTER THREE

Okay umm, this is V-log reference LB734/A data log reference point 3380133/8394 continuing report.

The first thing I was aware of was voices, muffled and far away. I tried to concentrate but I could not understand the sounds. Then I must have fallen asleep because there's a bit of a blank spot in my memory until I awoke with a furious hard on that made sure I couldn't fall back to sleep no matter how much I tried. It is best that I do not go into details; some things are better not explained but I will say that the artificial companion I found alongside me in the bed was most accommodating with my demands. Frankly, I was surprised at the strength of my need and I did things to her I have never done to a real woman, nor ever will. To be truthful, I felt a little ashamed really but as I said, the cryo sleep has this effect and it has to be dealt with in a safe and healthy way. My memory is patchy, but I alternately slept and raped my companion for the better part of a day until I felt my body was spent of its need for both. When I awoke again, the sight of her next to me disgusted me so I dragged myself from the bed and into the bathroom to shower.

Once showered I felt relatively okay and went back into the bedroom to find Stannel unpacking my own clothes from a storage container.

"Good morning Mr Gilden, he smiled. "How do you feel?"

"Hi, umm okay I guess."

"Once you're dressed I'll take you for a check-up with Doctor Evelly and when he gives you the all clear, I'll show you to the mess and get you something to eat."

"Thanks."

Doctor Evelly shook my hand and indicated for me to strip to my underwear and sit on the examination table. He went through a similar routine to the one I had endured when I first arrived on board only this time he went through a psyche evaluation test as well. Four hours later he shook my hand again and called for Stannel.

"Mr Gilden is fit and well and needs some real food."

"Yes Doctor. Follow me Mr Gilden."

"Thanks Doc," I said.

"You have a couple of days before we drop you off so eat well and sleep as much as you like and if you need me for anything, you know where I am."

The mess was packed with soldiers and I was once again reminded of my own military career. I looked at the faces; most of them wide-eyed youngsters on their way to their first experience in a hostile situation, and it occurred to me that I must have had that same look when I was new in the military. From my own experience, I knew that within a year most of these young men would lose that wide-eyed excited look. At least the ones who were still alive. Most of them ignored my presence but a couple looked up and nodded at me and I nodded back. All in all I enjoyed my time in the military but I don't miss it and I'm not ashamed of how I exercised my duties back then. There was a lot of killing but it did not excite me and I was happy to leave when my time was done. My sense of humility has not deserted me despite all the hostilities I experienced and the killings and I hoped these young men would manage to keep theirs.

I ate a large meal and found that the food tasted wonderful, despite it being the usual military fare. Stannel told me later that long periods without solid food make your taste buds more sensitive so that when you do eat solid food again, your sense of taste is greatly enhanced. He showed me back to my room when I told him I felt sleepy again and said he would wake me in time for dinner. My artificial companion from earlier was back, this time sitting in a chair and dressed demurely.

"In case you find you need her again," Stannel explained. "Sometimes the effects resurface after the initial explosion of desire has been fulfilled so she's here for you in case. She's been cleaned and sterilised and repaired."

"Okay thanks," I blushed.

"No problem at all. See you at dinner."

I was asleep within minutes and don't remember dreaming but awoke sometime later on the floor, buried up to my balls in my now naked companion; her clothes ripped and strewn around the room. The knowledge that I had once again been driven to sexual violence was sickening and I carefully extricated myself and went to have a wash. Still racked with tiredness, I climbed back into bed and fell asleep; another seemingly dreamless void and awoke to find her back in the bed with me and obviously worn out from my assaults upon her person. If this were to continue for much longer, it would become a source of real worry for me. Groaning, I turned away and sat on the edge of the bed. It was a minute or so before I realised that I had a hard on but what pleased me was that I felt no compulsion to use her again nor even to relieve myself. With a sigh of relief, I yawned, stretched, and went to shower.

Stannel knocked the door when I came back through to the bedroom to dress. He smiled when I let him in. "Good morning Mr Gilden, how do you feel?"

"I feel fine thanks umm, morning? You said you'd wake me for dinner."

"That was last night. I came back to wake you and found you deep in the grip of delayed cryo sexual syndrome, so I fetched Doctor Evelly and dined alone."

"Oh shit," I groaned. Knowing what I'd done was bad enough but knowing this stranger had seen me acting like a crazed rapist was worse.

"Don't feel bad Mr Gilden," he said firmly. "This is completely natural, we explained before your journey. Everyone, and I mean everyone, who undergoes cryo sleep for longer than a day or two will experience this effect. It may go on for a day or two yet so don't get stressed about it. Your body knows what it needs and this is the safest place to let it work itself out okay?"

"Thanks," I nodded.

"No problem. Now come on, the Doc wants to check you out and then you can have breakfast."

My appointment with Doctor Evelly wasn't as long or as arduous as the last two had been but after talking with him for a half hour, he assured me that the fact I had the usual morning hard on but didn't feel the need to relieve it, showed I was now through all the side effects of cryo sexual syndrome. He also told me that Sigma folks have quite a high drive normally and tend to experience stronger effects. My experience did not surprise him at all. That was a huge relief; there's no way I wanted to turn into some crazed rapist for the rest of my life and although it made me a little nervous about going through it all again on the journey home, at least I knew what to expect and it wouldn't be a worry when it happened. In a way, it is cool to be able to let go of all of the basest desires we all keep under control, in a safe and controlled environment where no one has to get hurt and I can certainly say that for a while afterwards, I experienced an inner calm that was totally new to me.

I spent my last full day aboard the Liberty eating well and relaxing for the most part. During the afternoon, I even allowed myself to be talked into spending a couple of hours in the gym with a few of the soldiers who gave me some valuable tips on keeping fit and healthy. This so inspired me, that I promised myself some fitness equipment for my ship when this job was done. Times without number I have thought about getting some equipment and working out each day, but it is hard to get going with such a plan. Again, I promised myself I would do it this time. One last night in a comfortable bed and I awoke with dream memories finally apparent again, which further pleased me and helped me to accept that I was over the cryo sleep. Within an hour I was up, showered, dressed, packed, and was heading down to a final breakfast.

Doctor Evelly signed me off as fully recovered and I shook his hand. "Thanks for looking after me Doc, I appreciate it."

"You're very welcome Mr Gilden. Good luck with your job by the way. I look forward to meeting you again on your journey back to Sigma, whenever that should turn out to be."

Stannel escorted me back to my ship and wished me well. "I hope everything turns out the way you want it to Mr Gilden. See you again on the journey home."

"Thanks buddy," I replied as I shook his hand, "for everything."

As Liberty disappeared into the void behind me, leaving me alone in the vastness of the cosmos, I felt a moment of loneliness that I do not experience too often. I guess I am used to working alone; people just get in the way most of the time and I like the fact that I can work the way that suits me and make my own routine. Having spent three days amongst lots of people, I felt suddenly alone and it took me almost the rest of that first day to get back to my own self again. It was not true loneliness, just a shock to the system and being used to my own company; I was back to normal pretty quickly.

The journey to Deligon went without incident and I spent most of the time studying the files Tinnias gave me. The background information was scant at best; seven mysterious deaths, all connected to the scientific station, the sudden and unexplainable deaths of the trees and the obvious lack of information coming out of the scientific station all pointed towards something going on, but even I had to admit, it could all just be coincidence. I knew I would not be able to work anything out without getting inside the place first, so my obvious first task was to secure employment and take it from there. Despite the only known crime committed so far being covering up a death, I made a mental note to remind myself not to discard the thing about the trees. It may just turn out to be some genuine natural problem but my law enforcer's hunch told me it was relevant so I promised myself I'd investigate it. Next, I checked through the files of the seven deaths and one thing leapt out at me straight away. Every one of the victims not only worked at the scientific station but they worked in the same department – Research and Development. This was not coincidence and I flagged up the R and D department as first on my hit list. There were several other similarities between the seven victims besides working in the same department. They were all unmarried, between the ages of twenty and thirty five and none were native to Deligon and all of these factors told me there was a definite pattern worth following.

The next report was about the trees and although the science of it went right over my head, I got the general point and again, something interesting and relevant popped up. It seems the scientific station was set up when the trees in Bygora Vandos started dying off mysteriously. So far nothing sinister. It was not a huge plague or anything, just a few but all showed the same symptoms that pointed to poisoning of some sort. After the first eighteen months of operation, the scientific station suddenly expanded to twice its size and it was at this point that the tree deaths increased three fold and steadily increased in number until the current death rate, which is five times the original. I knew with every fibre of my being that this was relevant and again promised myself I would investigate this aspect as fully as I could.

I then turned my attention to the company that owns the scientific station and that is where it got even more interesting. The station itself is called Calmarin Research Station, which is run by the Calmarin Corporation. This Corporation is itself owned and run by Heibat Bio Research, which apparently researches diseases and develops cures. Heibat Bio Research also has a sister company called Heibat Power and Energy and one single man – Kaybel Abydell-Mirras, a native of Uraloma 2, owns both. Now, I would never describe myself as an expert in the ways of business but it seemed strange to me that one guy would be at the head of that long trail of companies, and it seemed to me as if there was an attempt to hide behind that trail. If he was trying to hide his connection with the events at Deligon, I wanted to know why.

My hand went instinctively to my Unicom and I got onto my contacts at Uraloma and asked them to investigate Kaybel and get back to me as soon as they had anything. Six hours later, just as I was standing at my nutri vend wondering what to have for dinner, I got the call. I learned that Kaybel Abydell-Mirras was eighty one years old and so ill he was now housebound and lives in his rambling mansion in the hills above Skellmanitch, a pretty coastal town on Uraloma's southernmost continent, a habitat of the very richest of Uraloma's elite. They also told me that although he is still officially the owner of the company, a committee now does the actual running of things. Apparently, there is a rumour that this committee is thinking of having the old guy deemed unfit to serve on the board so they can take over full control. My contact gave me the names of the twenty people on this committee and their backgrounds and one name almost made me drop my drink.

"Manno Lashling?" I exclaimed in surprise. "The military guy? Are you sure buddy?"

"I knew that would interest you Sam," he laughed. "Yep, the very same."

"Shit," was all I could think of to say. Manno Lashling, or Supreme Commander Lashling as he is officially known is overall head of the military in sector 48139, which means he runs all military operations in five whole planetary systems, one of which is the Sigma System, my home.

"Jeez I've met that guy," I said. "I hope this doesn't turn out bad or his career is over. Can you find out more about him? Anything that might indicate he has his hand in things that seem a little shadowy," I asked.

"Sure thing, no problem. Give me a day and I'll get back to you."

"Thanks man." I wondered whether to call Tinnias and tell him about this but decided to wait until my Uraloma contact got back to me. If he gave me anything more that could cast a cloud over the guy, then I'd report it. I ate my nutri vend dinner, which was almost inedible after the delicious food I'd enjoyed aboard the Liberty, and hit the sack.

Late afternoon the next day, my contact got back to me with worrying news. It seemed that Manno Lashling had a string of gambling debts stretching back twenty years and at one time lost his home rather than his kneecaps to pay one huge debt he had run up. He had been on the board of a few companies through the years and twice resigned his position in suspicious circumstances. Information about these resignations was scant but it looked like at least one of them was due to some trouble over misplaced funds that were never recovered. Most worrying of all however, was the mystery surrounding the Albalion massacre. Manno Lashling was responsible for taking the decision to send troops to Albalion 4 to help oust an invading force from Grollian 6, a very rich planet with a prime position in a major shipping lane. The Grollians live a military lifestyle and their whole ethos is that of the warrior. Left alone, they do not cause too many problems for their neighbours, although they are a little secretive. There were a few spats between the two neighbours for centuries but not until one of their high-ranking military leaders was assassinated did they make any real trouble for Albalion 4. They accused Albalion mercenaries of committing the crime and vowed to invade and wipe them out in revenge unless their leaders give themselves up for public execution.

Manno Lashling sent in troops to help the Albalions and all seemed to be going well until two thirds of Manno's troops were suddenly massacred in one day. In the conflict, the Albalion Emperor was captured and executed by the Grollians, who then returned to their own world, apparently satisfied that justice had been seen to be done. The strange part was that just a few months later, the Grollian leaders allowed Manno Lashling to set up a strategic military base on Grollian 4 and the two sides seemed to get along like a house on fire. There were many photographs of Lashling and the Grollian leaders having dinner together and generally looking like best friends and everyone who knew about it thought it was weird. My contact told me that the inside story was that the Grollian leaders offered Lashling a deal, the Albalion Emperor and enough of his own soldiers' lives to make it look good, in return for a financial reward and a permanent military presence on Grollian 4. What made it look even more damming was that in the year following the massacre, Lashling bought four properties as holiday homes for himself and his family as well as clearing his gambling debts. The underworld contract on him disappeared overnight and talk amongst those who move in such circles was that the debts were now settled with interest and he was no longer a target.

After thanking my contact, I sat back and sighed. This news might very well end Lashling's career but I had a duty as a Law Enforcer and I was not about to overlook his misdemeanours just because he is a big noise in the military. It seemed weird to me that a military man like Lashling would be on the board of a company like the Heibat companies. What would a die-hard soldier like him do with a scientific research company? Surely there was nothing there to interest him? No, it had to be money at the root of it. Money, power, or both. Lashling had just two interests in life, being a soldier and making money and the Heibat companies did not seem to offer him the first of those, so it must be the other two. I knew I had to find out so I called Tinnias on the secure Unicom number and relayed all of this to him and he was as shocked as I was. He told me he would have a discreet look into the Heibat companies and see what information he could glean and would tell me anything he found out when I next called in.

Finally, I turned my attention to the file on my contact on Deligon, Balian Renimir or Ren, as he prefers to be called. It was decided that our cover story was to be our shared military careers, so I refreshed my memory on the details of our supposedly shared experiences. I looked at his photograph and tried to get a handle on him. As I have said before, I like to think of myself as something of an expert at reading people and I knew right away that I was going to be able to trust this guy. His face spoke of honesty, integrity and high intelligence and I made a bet with myself that his IQ would make me seem like a Zinordic Swamp Rat by comparison. He was a fine boned man with slightly too large eyes of a strange blue grey colour, which seemed to bore right into my soul and see the real me. Those eyes were hypnotic; they held me. It was obvious that I would not be able to lie to him. Tinnias had already told me to make sure I was always on the level with him as he would take any deceit as a personal insult and I would lose his trust forever. I am not used to working with a partner and I was not comfortable knowing I had to share everything with someone else, but I needed Ren so I made the decision to put my own natural inclinations aside and trust him. He worked in the Personnel department at the Calmarin Research Station, which would be very useful whenever I might need to know about any of the workforce. He was necessary to getting the job done, so whatever my personal feelings were, I needed him.

I settled down to sleep my last night before arriving at Deligon. My journey had been a long one, I was anxious to get going on the job, and my restlessness prevented me from falling asleep for almost an hour. When I did fall asleep I dreamed of being stuck out in the middle of nowhere with the sounds of gunfire all around me. The first time I peeped out from behind the huge rock, I found to my horror that instead of soldiers coming to kill me, the army consisted of lifeless naked dolls with staring eyes all calling my name and telling me they wanted me. This sight filled me with dread and I awoke with a start and yelled out into the darkness of my ship, flailing my arms to protect me from the advancing foe. Once I realised where I was I groaned and went to my nutri vend to get a drink. I realised with a sigh that the effects of cryo sleep were going to take a while to get fully out of my system.

I eventually managed to get back to sleep and awoke feeling a little drained but ready for the job at hand. After a shower, I went to the cockpit and prepared for arrival at Deligon. Two hours later I took control and flipped on my newly enhanced Covert Stealth Modulator.

"Okay Essy my darling, time for me to take control hunny," I crooned as I entered the landing co-ordinates and headed down towards Bygora Vandos. Once the ship was safely locked down and stored within the community parking facility, I got out my map and headed for Tower 1874. The area was filled with residential tower blocks but pretty gardens and parks filled the spaces between and each had its own dedicated parking facility so I knew that the tower in front of me must be 1874. Shops and stores resided in the ground levels of each tower and stalls selling all manner of things lined the streets, their owners calling out to passers-by to try this or that. One caught my attention and I wandered over to look. A woman in a gaily-patterned skirt called out to me to slake my thirst on her wonderful array of juices, all freshly prepared that very morning. She had a pretty face and an engaging smile so I allowed her to tempt me to a bright pink liquid that tasted divine.

"That's wonderful," I replied. "What is it? I'm new around here."

"You have good taste Sir," she smiled. "It is the juice from the Moullin Berry. Some say it has the power to preserve a youthful complexion."

"Well in that case, I'll have another."

I entered tower 1874 and took the lift up to floor 7, noticing with relief that everything seemed clean and free from obvious vandalism so I guessed this was a decent enough place to live. The place was a maze of corridors and I walked along several before finding room 28 and looked for the tile with the flower on it. Sure enough, there it was and it flipped to one side easily and gave up the key hidden behind it. The door opened and I entered to find my new home was spacious and well kept. The rooms were large and airy, the big windows letting in plenty of light and the furniture seemed of high quality. A note stuck to the kitchen counter, informed me to make myself comfortable and to help myself to anything I might need. There were two bedrooms, one obviously occupied so I went next door and unpacked. My bedroom, like the other rooms, was large and comfortable and my window had a view over the neighbouring park. The bathroom was very high spec and I enjoyed a wonderful shower before changing my clothes and checking out what the kitchen could offer me for lunch.

I must have fallen asleep on the sofa because I awoke to someone shaking my shoulder gently.

"Joss? Joss, wake up buddy."

"Huh?" I groaned and sat up. "What the? Oh hi, you must be Ren. Sorry, I haven't been sleeping too well." I stood and shook his proffered hand.

"Take your time," he smiled. "Great to meet you Joss. Have you settled in okay?"

"Yeah, thanks. I took a shower, that unit is fantastic by the way. I must investigate getting one for my ship."

"It's something else isn't it?" he nodded. "Have you eaten?"

"I made a sandwich, hope you don't mind."

"Not at all, take anything you need. I've brought something for dinner. This is the local's favourite take out," he said as he unpacked a box he'd been carrying. The smell of meat came to my nostrils, followed by something that reminded me of something but I could not remember what.

"Smells nice," I said. "It reminds me of something but I can't for the life of me remember what it is."

Ren laughed loudly and I frowned. "That's what everyone says," he grinned. "It's this dish's secret and the reason everyone likes it. One of the vegetables in it, the Ground Ponkle, always tastes and smells like something you think you recognise."

"Really? How weird."

"This dish is called Slatchmak," he told me as he divided the contents of the various cartons between the two of us, "and it's very fattening so unless you work out every single day, keep it to a once in a while treat."

"Okay," I replied. "Thanks for the warning."

Over dinner, I studied Ren as much as I could without being obvious about it. Tinnias had told me that he would sound strange and he was right. Ren's voice was weird. It was as if he did not know how to keep his voice on one tone for too long and he kept raising and lowering the pitch of his voice a little. On top of that, he had an obvious accent, which only made things worse. I had to ask him to repeat things and I began to feel awkward about it but I just could not understand him half the time. When I had asked him for the hundredth time to repeat something, he laughed and I blushed.

"I'm sorry buddy," I said. "I've never met a Damiklonian before and it'll take me a while to understand your voice. Please don't be offended."

"I'm not offended, really," he replied. "It's just so funny seeing you struggling and not just asking me about it."

"Ahh, and I thought I was hiding it."

"You're no actor Joss, better stick to your day job huh?"

"Yeah, you're probably right," I nodded.

"Damiklonians don't talk like other races do. Our natural way of communicating would seem a little like singing to you and we have to learn to speak in a way other races can understand whenever we leave Damiklon to live or work. It's hard for us and we never completely lose our own natural way, much like someone learns a foreign language but always has a particular accent."

"Oh I see," I said, intrigued.

"Don't worry, you'll get used to it and having you around will help me perfect it, so feel free to pick me up on things when I make mistakes okay?"

"Okay sure."

"Oh, I almost forgot," he said and stood up and began to remove his shirt. "How stupid of me and you a law enforcer too, shit."

"What's up?" I asked.

"I am required by law to show you this," he said, revealing a short metallic tube attached to his upper arm. "Damiklonians have a venomous bite and this is the only known antidote and we're all required to carry it whenever we leave Damiklon. I have to report to the local security officer once a week to have it checked. You won't ever need to use it but I have to show you; as my roommate you may very well be asked whether you know how. Just pull it off like this, flip up the top like this and jab the tip into any exposed skin for ten seconds. It will automatically inject itself. Our venom is deadly but quite slow acting so you don't have to panic, there will be plenty of time to do what you have to do okay? Now you come and have a go."

I got up and approached him and grabbed the tube from its sleeve around his arm. The top flipped back after a bit of fumbling and I saw the tip of a standard auto injector just like one I carry as part of my restraining gear.

"Great job Joss," he smiled. "I guess you're no stranger to auto injectors huh?" he said as he put his shirt on.

"I have one just like it, for when I need to restrain prisoners. Sometimes they need a little persuasion to behave themselves. By the way Ren, would it be insulting of me to ask umm," I hesitated.

"You want to see em?" he grinned and I blushed again. "Don't be embarrassed buddy, it's not something you come across every day. Okay here they are," he said and opened his mouth much wider than I ever could and using muscles in his upper jaw, drew down a pair of the longest fangs I'd ever seen. They were easily two inches long and wickedly sharp.

"My god," I exclaimed, "they are awesome."

"Thank you," he laughed again when he'd packed them away and could talk again. "I've had them described in all sorts of ways but never awesome before."

"Have you ever umm, bitten anybody?" I asked.

"No," he replied as we resumed eating. "Unless it was to save the life of another who couldn't save themselves, or to save my own life when all other avenues have been exhausted, I would be jailed for a long time. A very long time ago Damiklonians were warriors and our ethic was one of fight and conquer or die trying. We left that way of life behind millennia ago but we remember that time as a way of illustrating how far we've evolved since then, since we left our ego behind."

The more I got to know Ren, the more I liked him and we spent the rest of the evening just talking and getting to know one another. We discussed the job and I told him everything I'd found out from my contact on Uraloma and showed him the files Tinnias had given me. By the time we went to bed we decided that the first thing was to get me a job.

"Come into work with me in the morning and I'll get you an interview. I know they're a couple of security guards short and with your fake background as ex-military and security, you stand a good chance of getting hired."

"Okay," I nodded. "I can't do anything unless I can get into the place so that's obviously my first task."

I went to bed and fell asleep pretty quickly, only to find my dreams of the same unsettling nature as they had been on the previous night and I again awoke with a yell, thrashing at the bed cover. Ren came rushing in and switched on the light, momentarily blinding me but waking me up fully.

"What the hell is the matter buddy?" he said, his face etched with concern.

"Sorry," I sighed as I wiped a hand through my hair. "It's these nightmares. Ever since the cryo sleep."

"Ahh, you had an intense reaction when they woke you up?" he asked and I nodded.

"Yeah, delayed cryo something they called it. Jeez man I was like a wild thing. I didn't recognise myself. It's scary looking back on it now."

"We all have many sides to our nature," he said as he sat down on the edge of the bed. "We are both aggressive predators and passive victims, all rolled into one. We control those aspects of our nature that we've learned through conditioning are not acceptable, but they are still a part of us and always will be. When our ability to reason with logic and learned conditioning are reduced, as they are for a while after cryo sleep, these aspects of ourselves will have free reign to express themselves. Accept it as a necessary part of your nature that you now have complete control over and you'll find the nightmares will stop soon. The more you fight it, the longer they will stay. These dreams are your sub conscious mind's way of showing you that you must embrace all sides of your nature."

"Yeah, that makes sense I guess," I nodded. "Sorry to wake you."

"No problem, now go back to sleep and dream well."

CHAPTER FOUR

Calmarin Research Station was a short hover bus ride from our apartment in Tower 1874 and took no more than thirty minutes to get from door to door. The other folks on the bus were friendly and most had smiles on their faces. Ren said hello to a couple of guys and introduced me as his friend from the military and told them I was here looking for work.

"These guys work at the Station too," Ren informed me. "Hitch here is security and Melk is in R and D."

"Hi there," I smiled, delighted to find Ren had a pal in the R and D department who may very well turn out to be a useful source of information later on.

"So what kind of work are you after Joss?" Hitch asked.

"Well my background is military and security. I'm not an office type."

"I know we're a couple of guys short in security at the Station so you shouldn't have a problem getting hired."

"That's great," I replied.

Three hours later I shook hands with Kobey, Security Chief at the Calmarin Research station. I'd filled out masses of forms, had my fake papers examined, had a firearms proficiency test and endured yet another but much shorter and far less thorough medical examination and now he was officially offering me the job of security guard.

"Welcome to Calmarin Joss," he said. "We run a pretty tight ship here as you'll discover. We may be just a research establishment but that doesn't mean we slack on security."

"Thank you," I replied. "I'm happy to be here Sir."

"Good, good," he nodded. "I'll take you down to the security HQ and introduce you to Pendle. He's your immediate supervisor. He'll show you around and get you a uniform and tell you all about the job. Follow me."

As we walked, I studied Kobey and knew right away that he was going to be useless to me as a source of any information. He knew nothing, and anything he might think he knew was just smoke and mirrors to make him feel important. I also realised that I might not be able to rely on him to help me out, especially if that help necessitated him telling a lie or turning a blind eye. His manner and speech showed me that he obviously had a strict code which he allowed to rule his every waking minute and he would sooner die than step away from that code. The first word that came to my mind as I looked at him was inflexible. His code and routine defined him so much that to step away from either would leave him unable to know what to do. This also meant that he would always tell the truth, should I choose to question him about anything but it would be what he perceives to be the truth, which may or may not actually be the truth. That depended upon people higher up the chain and knowing a little about Calmarin, I was not at all confident that they would tell him much. Kobey cannot read between the lines; he has neither insight nor intuition and would not know what to do with either if they slapped him on the ass. It would take a huge leap for him to change his ways and I realised that if something were to happen to make me have to rely on him in an emergency, I would need all of my people skills.

As we walked, I looked around the place to get my bearings. It was all corridors and offices in the main section but as we left the office building I noticed a door with a weird looking security locking mechanism keeping all but the favoured few firmly out. There was no sign on the door indicating what might be going on behind it so I asked Kobey.

"What's in that room Chief?"

"That's Research and Development," he replied without bothering to explain further.

"What kind of research do they do here?"

"They're trying to find out what's killing the trees around here and then stop it from killing more," he replied.

"Oh, okay," I said.

"You won't need to worry about what they do in there Joss," he said as he indicated for me to enter a building to my left. "They have their own security guys."

"Really?" I exclaimed in genuine surprise. "Wow."

"I guess they're dealing with potentially dangerous pathogens or something," he replied, "and they don't want to let any organisms out to create further havoc." He obviously didn't realise that he'd just told me he hadn't a clue what was really going on here, so I crossed him off my mental list of suspects.

"So you're Security Chief but just for the rest of us?" I asked and he nodded.

"Yeah. They run their security as a totally separate operation from us. You will notice their guys have different uniforms from ours. Now this here is Security HQ and this is where you'll operate from. See the main gate over there?" I looked and nodded. "When you arrive on shift each day you come straight here to report for duty, you take your breaks here and you end your shift here."

"Sure thing Boss," I nodded again. "Understood."

"This is Pendle," he said, indicating a tall, thin man who approached us, "and he's your immediate supervisor. He reports to me so your first line of communication is with him."

"Okay," I replied as I shook hands with Pendle.

"This is Joss Gilden," Kobey told him. "A new security guard for you. He's got an excellent military record and several years in security after that so you'll have no problem with him. Give him the tour and set him up."

"Yes Sir and thank you," Pendle called as Kobey left the building. "Hello Joss, nice to meet you. Everyone just calls me Pendle, we don't bother with titles unless he's around," he tipped his head, indicating the door by which Kobey had just left. "Are you okay with that?"

"Sure," I replied, happy to realise that Pendle and I were going to get along just fine.

"Let's get you a locker and then I'll give you the tour. This way."

The Calmarin Research Station covers forty seven acres of land, much of which is forest containing the diseased trees. The office block where I had my interview with Kobey, the Security HQ and a few isolated huts dotted about the place, were the only actual buildings on the whole site. All the rest is open land and forest. Pendle showed me around the whole perimeter on a company hover cart, giving me time to notice the perimeter fence, which would not look out of place on a high security prison. I instinctively felt I could trust my new supervisor, so I risked a question.

"Why such high security when they're just trying to stop trees dying? This place looks like a high max prison complex."

"I wondered when you'd notice that," he replied. "It's something we'd all like to know and I'll warn you now, you'll hear all sorts of rumours amongst the guys about what they reckon really goes on here, so just take everything you hear with a pinch of salt huh?"

"Okay, I'll remember that," I smiled.

"The truth is we don't know what's going on, or even if anything is going on but one thing's for sure – they," he nodded towards the office block, "don't welcome questions okay?"

"Right. Thanks for the warning. I guess I'm just the curious type," I shrugged.

"So are we all Joss," he replied. "Now let's get back to base and you can meet some of the guys."

I eventually got back to the apartment after taking the wrong hover bus and having to retrace my steps for a couple of miles but I discovered a store selling second hand surveillance equipment so it wasn't a waste of time. The place was packed with stuff, most of which I recognised, so I browsed the wares and noticed an ex law enforcement issue substance analyser for sale. It was an outdated model but I had used one like it when I was behind a desk before my freelance days. This was one piece of equipment I did not have; my job description was just to find a particular person, catch them and deliver them into the care of the relevant authorities so Tinnias had never issued me with one. The current job however, called for me to do actual detective work and this gizmo could come in handy so I approached the man I saw keeping his eye on me from the back of the store.

"Hi there," I smiled. "I notice you have an ex law enforcement G18 Substance Analyser for sale."

"What if I do?" he responded with suspicion.

"How much do you want for it?"

"Well now, that would depend on what you want it for and why," he said. This caught me off guard and for a moment, I struggled to find a suitable reply. He noticed my hesitation and grinned.

"Look at it this way buddy," he continued. "You're either a stuffed up collector, in which case such a modern instrument would be of little interest, especially as they're still in use, or you're law enforcement but don't want me to know that." He held my gaze and try as I might, I failed to stop myself from blushing. I sighed deeply and he gave a little snigger of triumph.

"Okay so you're a law enforcement guy but you don't want that to become public knowledge huh? That's fine, I'm not one for gossip," he said as he retrieved the analyser from the shelf and handed it to me.

"It's working perfectly," he said as I tapped the screen and made a few tests.

"How much?" I asked once I was satisfied it was working.

"Five hundred," he replied and I nearly fell on the floor.

"What?" I exclaimed.

"But if you just happened to be wanting to use it to find out what those crooks over at Calmarin are really up to, you could have it for seventy five."

I grinned. He was clever and I realised that I had found my second ally. This was too good an opportunity to miss so I decided to cultivate his interest and find out what he knew. I handed over my currency card and he deducted the seventy five. He introduced himself as Donal Efflan and offered me a drink, which I accepted happily and once we were settled in his back room, he related his story to me.

"I used to be a law enforcer myself," he said as he handed me a beer. "When the tree disease first came to public attention and the people from Calmarin came to take a look, we were pleased that something was going to be done to try and find out about it and maybe stop it. After a few months with no information about what they'd discovered, people started asking questions. It was only then that they said it looked like something was poisoning the trees and they wanted to find out what it was. They said they'd need to do proper investigations on the trees and even the land they grew in. As the land was poisoned with something and therefore not worth any money, they offered to purchase it for pocket change. They said it was either that or they couldn't do their job and they'd have to leave Deligon and not help us find a cure, so they were allowed to buy the land for such a low price as no one wanted to buy it and build there, not with some mysterious poison around."

This was interesting news and I immediately felt as though what was going on, had been going on since day one, and that whoever was in charge of whatever was going on was going to great lengths to cover it up. I also felt instinctively that money was at the root of it.

"Anyway, after a year or so a lot more of the trees outside of the Calmarin land started showing signs of the disease so again they offered to buy the land cheap so they could continue their work into finding the cause and hopefully clean it up and give the land back to Deligon. Seven families lost their homes that time but the big guys at Calmarin offered to compensate them by building them new homes and even gave them jobs at the Station when they'd lost their businesses too."

"So some of those who were originally affected now work for the company?" I asked.

"Yeah. Four guys who ran businesses from their original homes now work there."

"You wouldn't happen to know their names would ya?"

"Sure," he nodded and wrote them down. I noticed one of the names was the guy Hitch Ren had introduced me to that very morning. He worked with me in security so I would have easy access to him and I made a decision to befriend him.

"Thanks," I said as I pocketed the piece of paper.

"Do you have a job there yet?" he asked. "You're obviously going to work there, aren't ya?"

"I start in the morning," I replied.

"What's your job?"

"Security."

"Good. That'll give you plenty of access to stake the place out. The best time will be when you're doing perimeter duty out on the north western sector of the fence."

"Why?" I asked, incredulous that he knew so much and delighted that I had stumbled across him.

"Take the trouble to examine the ground in the north western sector, about fifty feet in from the fence. You may notice a slight dip in the ground or something else that'll look like an area of the ground is not quite the same as the rest. I can't be sure as I've never been in there but there's some kind of underground entrance there."

"An underground entrance?" My eyebrows were now level with my hairline.

"Yeah. Every week you'll be told that all perimeter duty that night is cancelled and that you're all to remain inside the security HQ. They'll tell you it's so that they can exercise and train the dogs."

"Dogs? I didn't see any dogs when I was there today," I replied.

"The other security guys, the R and D ones have them but you'll probably never see them unless you make a point of looking, which will probably put your job in jeopardy."

"So what's this underground entrance all about?" I asked.

"It all happens on the nights when they tell you they're exercising and training the dogs," he explained. "Several large shuttles land in the north western corner and disappear underground, through some kind of trapdoor or something. Each one goes down and an hour later comes back up and flies off. There are usually three or four of them. It takes the better part of the whole night."

"Umm, how do you know all this?" I asked. This all seemed plausible to me but I had to know that he wasn't just some wacked out crazy conspiracy theorist trying to get his rocks off.

"Because I spent my entire life savings buying an apartment three hundred yards from the perimeter fence and rather than spend my evenings getting laid, I scope out the place and make notes. I retired from the Law Enforcement Agency a few years ago but I guess old habits die hard and a law enforcer's hunch isn't to be denied, as you're obviously well aware."

"You live so close?" I exclaimed and he nodded. "Wow, well maybe Ren and I could come to dinner sometime?"

"Ren?" It was now his turn to look shocked. "You know him?"

"Yeah. We're sharing an apartment and working the case together. You know him?"

"Yeah. I'm one of his contacts. It was my concerns that actually got him interested in investigating the company in the first place. I'm also in touch with a few others who reckon there's more to the Calmarin site than meets the eye and if push comes to shove, I can arrange for a dozen or so guys who will be more than happy to put themselves out to help get this sorted."

"That's fantastic Donal," I replied. "Listen, I know you're Ren's contact and I don't want to step on his toes, but if he's okay with it, can I keep in touch with you?"

"Sure," he nodded. "On one condition though."

"What would that be?" I asked, wondering how much he was going to want.

"That you trust me with your real name." My surprise must have been obvious as he grinned. "Oh I don't want money Joss. I've got enough to satisfy my needs but I would like to be trusted with a man's real name when I'm helping him fight for my home world."

"Sam Sinclair," I smiled as I stood and extended my hand, "and I'm real pleased to meet you."

"Glad to know you Sam," he replied as he shook my hand.

I got back to the apartment and took a shower before writing up my notes. There was a lot of information that was coming to me on this job and I had only been there a day. Normally I never write anything down; I prefer to keep everything in my head so as not to leave a trail for anyone to find but this job was different. It was going to be a long job and I had to keep track of everything so I wrote my notes in the Sigma language and just hoped if it was ever found by the wrong person, that they would not be able to read Sigma. My belly grumbled and I realised that not only was I hungry, but that Ren would be home soon, so I checked out the kitchen and decided to make dinner. I'm no gourmet chef but I've been a single guy living alone for a long time and I've learned how to take care of myself and I figured I could feed the two of us without much difficulty.

Ren was amazed to hear I had bumped into Donal and confirmed everything he had told me as being the same information he had given him. He also assured me he had no problem with me keeping in touch with him and suggested we make a point of doing just that far more often from now on. I noticed Ren kept sprinkling copious amounts of some spice all over his food and wondered whether he was struggling with my efforts at feeding us both.

"I'm no gourmet Ren, is it awful?" I asked.

"What? No of course not. It's just that Damiklonians have different taste buds to you and we need pretty strong flavours to get any enjoyment out of our food. Have a try at this?" he said as he offered me a forkful of his newly spiced dinner.

"Yeuk," I hissed as I spat it out and wiped my tongue with my napkin. "That's disgusting."

"See?" he said as he roared with laughter. "That's my reaction to most of the stuff you'll eat."

"Hell, how can you eat that?" I exclaimed, still trying to wipe the taste off my tongue, and failing miserably.

"How the hell can you not?" he said, red faced from laughing.

After dinner, he called Donal and arranged for us to visit him for the next scheduled secret fly in at the Station, which was six days away. I decided to call Tinnias and update him with all the new information I'd been given and he was pleased. He told me his investigations into the Heibat companies showed that the power and energy side of things seemed to be the most vigorous of the two companies and that the bio research side didn't seem to be making any money at all and precious little actual research had come out of the company in years.

"It seems as if the bio research side is just a front," he said, "although we've nothing to prove it so far. There's been no obvious breakthroughs reported by them and when we tried to find out just what research they're involved in at the moment, all we could find was vague references to medical research, disease control and health optimisation."

"Health optimisation?" I repeated. "What the fuck is that?"

"I was hoping you'd tell me Sam," Tinnias laughed. "By comparison, the power and energy side is vigorously researching new forms of cheap and sustainable energy and have published a few papers with their findings on various things. Solar conduction power is one thing they spent time on. Apparently they're investigating whether they can tap solar energy by using Trigassium Waves."

"What are they?" I asked, realising too late that I'd no doubt regret asking pretty soon.

"Trigassium is a weird sort of energy wave given off by a rare mineral called Trigassicmolynuclear Iron. Apparently, this energy wave, when sent into a sun, collects the heat and retains it and when collected again in a receiver, it can offload its cargo of heat to be used in whatever way you want."

"Sounds great," I replied.

"Yeah and it would be, but for the fact that the mineral has only ever been found in three planets and is therefore too rare to be financially viable."

"So what else have they been involved in?" I asked, hoping it would turn out to be something I could at least pronounce.

"There were looking into many other forms of power. From solar power, wind power, water power and even collecting animal farts and using the gas as a power source." Before I could reply Ren roared with laughter and I couldn't help but join in.

"Sounds wholesome," I replied when I'd stopped laughing enough to speak.

"Indeed," Tinnias snickered. "There is something else that's interesting too. Some years ago, the energy and power side of the company was involved in a scandal. Apparently they went mining for some mineral but lied about what they were digging up. They said it was some kind of ore that was useful but not worth much, when in fact they were bringing up some fairly valuable minerals and precious metals. They had to pay a huge amount of money to compensate the locals but there's no way of knowing how much money they made before it was discovered."

"That is interesting," I agreed.

"And there is talk of other such scandals that didn't reach the public domain," Tinnias continued. "There's a significant number of ex-employees willing to tell all but of course they're just seen as wanting revenge for being fired and tend not to be believed."

"There's no smoke without fire," Ren cut in and I nodded.

"Quite," Tinnias agreed. "How are you guys getting along anyway?"

"Fine thanks Boss," I replied.

"Yeah, we're great," Ren called.

"That's good. Keep up the good work and keep me informed. How are you both for money or supplies?"

"I'm fine at the moment," I said and looked at Ren, who nodded. "Yeah we're both okay for now."

"Good, call if you need anything. Take care guys."

Ren and I spent the next couple of hours discussing what we had just learned. We both felt the news given us by Donal was significant and must be followed up, but how? The first thing was to see it for ourselves and that was six days away. Until then, all we could do was do our jobs and keep our eyes and ears open. Ren promised to check into the higher grade personnel and see if there was anything on their records of interest and I decided to check out the North Western sector of the fence as soon as my work rotation afforded me an opportunity. I was to spend the next week on the daytime shift, then the second week on twilight and a third week on nights, followed by a week off, after which the whole thing would start over with days.

With little for us to do to further our investigation immediately, Ren talked me into going out and sampling the nightlife of Bygora Vandos. I was not too keen but allowed myself to be persuaded so as not to be a party pooper and I ended up having a great time. He took me to a cosy bar around the corner from our apartment and introduced me to a couple of casual acquaintances he sometimes meets there. They were interesting guys and one of them had visited Sigma Prime a couple of times so we had something to talk about. After an hour, I noticed Ren disappearing out the back door of the bar and wondered where he was off to.

"Don't worry about Ren Joss, he's just saying hello to Darmella."

"Darmella?" I asked. "Who is that?"

"The cute redheaded barmaid who served us drinks earlier?"

"Oh, right," I grinned.

"She has this thing for off world guys," he grinned. "You might want to introduce yourself."

"Hell no. I wouldn't want to step on Ren's toes," I replied.

"Oh he don't mind sharing, believe me buddy."

"No, really?" I exclaimed. This shocked me. Ren seemed to be quite a straight laced sort of guy to me and to find out he was into threesomes almost knocked me out.

"How long have you known him Joss?" the other guy said with a grin.

"Well quite a while but this has never exactly umm," I struggled.

"Come up?" the first guy offered and we all burst out laughing.

CHAPTER FIVE

I spent the next three days learning how to be a Calmarin Security Guard and getting to know my work colleagues. It took me approximately half of the first day to become so bored that I wondered if I would be able to stick it out. As I had promised myself the day I first met Donal in his shop, I made sure to befriend the guy Hitch in the hope that he would confide in me about the time he lost his home to Calmarin. I did not want to hit him with questions right away, so I took my time and just befriended him for a while first. Ren said he would discreetly look into the personnel records of the top brass and tell me anything he found of interest and I looked forward to visiting Donal at his apartment to watch the mysterious shuttles arrive. I occupied myself during my boredom by going over various scenarios in my head about what these shuttles could be doing here. I could not wait to find out. Our duties were to patrol all the outside areas of the complex and to be on call if our assistance was needed in the office block. We had no other purpose than to ensure no one from outside got in without an invitation. I hoped that I would not be put into a situation where I would have to shoot any of the locals who tried to gain entry. That would put me in a very awkward situation and one I really did not fancy having to explain to anyone.

The other guys told me that Calmarin does attract a little attention from time to time and they sometimes find the media camped outside the fence for a few days and some of the guys said that these are the only times they get any excitement as the job gets a bit boring after a while. No shit! It was my third day on the job when my scheduled duty took me to the North Western sector of the fence with my co-worker and I scanned the ground for anything that looked out of place. I was not sure what I was actually looking for; Donal had been vague so I just swept my eyes back and forth over the ground as I walked and hoped that whatever it was would make itself obvious to me. Just as I was beginning to think Donal had imagined everything, a shout from behind brought me and my colleague to a stop.

"Hey Colm," Pendle shouted from the window of a hover cart. "Your wife wants you to call her. Your kid is sick again."

"Oh shit," Colm, exclaimed. "We thought she was getting better. Sorry Joss, I gotta leave you alone for a while. Will you be okay?"

"Sure thing," I nodded. "Go. I hope she gets better soon huh?"

"Thanks buddy. Just keep going the way you are and sweep the hundred meter strip from the fence inwards. When you reach the number seven marker post, you turn and make your way back to number eleven. That's our patch today. The next crew will relieve you for your lunch break and then you go and relieve crew ten so they can have their break. Pendle will tell you where their patch is."

"Okay," I nodded. "Gotcha." I watched him run to the waiting hover cart and leap in, worry etched across his face. I hoped his kid was not too sick but I was glad to have the opportunity to stake the place out without someone watching over my shoulder all the time. It was as I turned back to continue my patrol that I absent mindedly allowed my eyes to drop to the ground and noticed how the angle of sunlight highlighted so perfectly what I'd been looking for. I saw a perfectly circular depression, at least fifty feet in diameter and no more than an inch or so lower than the surrounding ground level. The rough grass looked the same and the tiny yellow flowers that grew amongst it were identical to the millions of others that surrounded me. If it had not been for the angle of sunlight, I would not have noticed it.

Luckily for me, this circular anomaly was well within my allotted hundred metre strip so I fished in my pocket and withdrew a tissue, which I dropped and trod into the ground to mark the position for when I returned on the way back, just in case the changing sunlight made it hard for me to locate the same position. As an added precaution, I glanced over at the Calmarin buildings in the distance, made a mental note of their position in relation to mine and resumed my patrol. An hour later, I was on the return journey and spotted my discarded tissue. After checking my position with the buildings in the distance, I retrieved the tissue and stuffed it into my pocket. Thankfully, the sunlight had not changed and I could still just make out the large circular depression in the ground so, as nonchalantly as I could, I altered my course slightly so I would walk right over it.

With my very first step down into the depression, I noticed immediately that it felt different under my feet. The ground I had been walking on was slightly soft underfoot; it yielded to my weight just a tiny bit with every step whereas I could tell that this new area had a far more solid foundation. I was not aware of any softness underfoot, and I felt a slight vibration as each foot touched the ground. Making sure to shift my gaze to my surroundings in order that anyone watching would see me doing my job, I allowed my feet and legs to analyse what they were feeling. By the time I'd made it across the circular area and resumed my normal course again, I realised what it was that was so odd. It was metal underneath the grass and flowers, of that I was sure. That tell-tale vibration with each step that gave away a suspended metallic surface assuring me that underneath that circle of ground was a space of some sort, an underground room and maybe Donal was not shitting me after all. Maybe this was indeed a trapdoor. Whatever it was, I knew I had to find out one way or another and I wondered whether I should risk asking one of my new workmates. Surely it would not harm just to mention I had almost broken my ankle falling into a section of grass that was an inch lower than the rest. Would it?

The unmistakeable sound of a twig breaking underfoot brought me to an automatic stop, my Calmarin issue laser pistol at the ready. All my training in both the military, and my twenty years in law enforcement took over, and I was ready. I snapped my head around and scanned the fence but saw nothing out of the ordinary. The fence that surrounded Calmarin was an imposing structure but luckily, for me, it was not a solid one. It was made of some pierced metallic substance that afforded me regular little windows through which I could see the forest beyond, albeit a somewhat restricted view. With practiced silence, I stood listening for a couple of minutes before resuming my patrol, my eyes and ears strained for the slightest thing out of the ordinary. Ten minutes later something hit me square in the temple and I yelped in shock, my hand going instinctively to my head. A spot of blood stained my fingers and a dull ache made itself apparent. Retrieving the tissue from my pocket, I wiped my temple, wincing with pain as I dabbed at it. I scanned the ground around me and noticed a small round rock by my right boot. Fishing in my pocket once more, I found my can of sterifilm spray and a fresh evidence bag and within twenty seconds, the rock was safely stowed in my pocket.

"If I catch sight of you, I'll shoot you, asshole" I called out. "I'll have that rock scanned for fingerprints within an hour and you'll be in a cell before nightfall." A stab of pain in my right knee had me dropping to the ground as another small rock made contact. As I looked towards the fence I heard the sound of someone clambering over undergrowth, twigs being snapped and a thud followed by a cry as someone tried to run away. Scrambling to my feet, I ran for the fence in the direction of those sounds and peered cautiously through the nearest hole. I saw nothing but trees until another thud came to my ears and I shifted my gaze to my left to see a young guy around seventeen or eighteen making a very bad job of escaping quietly. He was wearing a very distinctive patterned red neck scarf that I knew I'd recognise again. The second rock was packed as carefully as the first and I resumed my patrol and waited to be relieved for my lunch break.

"There ya go Joss. You'll survive," the medic smiled as he cleaned the small wound on my temple and sprayed it with Uniskin.

"Thanks buddy"

"No problem. Now just fill out the incident report and you can go back to your lunch. You'll probably have a bruise on your leg for a day or two so here's some painkillers if it gets uncomfortable."

"I appreciate your help," I replied and filled out the incident report with the approximate time and location of the incident, my injuries, whether I'd fired in defence or not and a description of my attacker. For some reason I chose not to reveal the bright scarf he'd worn around his neck; my law enforcer's instinct told me to keep that to myself as I'd rather meet the guy on my own than have Calmarin security find him first. I'd hate for some bored kid to lose his kneecaps just for throwing a stone at me. After having my gun checked and signed off as not having been used, Kobey signed the incident report and filed it away.

"Things like this do happen from time to time Joss," he said. "One of the hazards of the job I'm afraid."

"No problem, I've survived worse."

"Make sure to have the guards down on your helmet in future and I'll see if I can't hurry up the body armour order. You'll have your pads within twenty four hours, I promise. Even if I have to loan you my own. I won't have my men put at risk from stupid kids who should be at school or out working to help provide for their families."

"Thanks Chief."

"Take your proper time for your break by the way. I'll start your hour and a half now so you don't lose any time."

"That's great, thanks."

When Ren and I got back to our apartment he told me what he'd found out from the personnel records.

"I didn't have a huge opportunity today Joss," he said. "The end of quarter reports are due so we're all a bit pushed with those at the moment but I did manage to have a quick glance at the Station Commander's file."

"The head guy of the whole place?" I asked and he nodded.

"Yeah, and you know what his name is?" I shook my head. "Roben Abydell-Mirras."

"So he's related to the owner of the Heibat companies?"

"One of his sons."

"Wow, that's umm," I replied as I ran a hand through my hair and tried to see how this fitted in and what relevance it had. As I said before,

I'm not a businessman so this stuff is new to me but I am experienced at recognising clues and I knew this was potentially a big one.

"Yeah, it is," Ren nodded. "It shows that the Mirras family wants to keep their hand on the button."

"And I guess it suggests that there's a button here worth keeping their hand on huh?"

"Right. Anyway, Roben has only been in charge here since the expansion."

"The expansion?" I asked.

"When Calmarin suddenly doubled in size and people lost their homes?"

"Oh yeah. Sorry buddy, business isn't really my bag. I'm a cop."

"No problem," he smiled. "Before the expansion, the head guy was Symeal Gloak. Recognise that name?"

I frowned. The name was familiar; I knew I had heard it somewhere. "Yeah. I've heard that name recently. Who is he? Oh wait, wasn't he one of the seven victims?"

"Well done Joss. Yeah he was the first. Apparently burned to death in a hover buggy crash."

"Any idea where his body is?" I asked.

"No, sorry. That sort of information isn't contained in the Personnel files but Tinnias might know. Ask him to find out next time you call."

"Yeah, we'll call tonight, right after I write my notes and download this surveillance camera. There's something on it that's worth keeping."

"There is?"

"Yeah," I nodded. "I discovered what Donal was talking about. Y'know that trapdoor thing in the ground?"

"You mean he wasn't shitting us after all?"

"Apparently not," I said. "There is definitely a circular area approximately fifty feet in diameter out on the north western sector of the fence, about fifty metres in. It's about an inch lower than the surrounding soil and it feels different when you walk on it. If that's not metal under there I'll eat a Snagbott Fly and let you film me doing it."

"So we need to find out how to get down there and take a look," he said and I nodded.

"Yeah, and maybe you could see what you can find out about the other security guys, the R and D ones?"

"Sure," he nodded. "How's your head by the way? Did you see who did it?"

"It's fine thanks," I replied. "He looked about seventeen or eighteen at a guess and he was wearing a very distinctive red thing around his neck, like a small scarf."

"Red?" he asked. "Are you sure it was red? Bright red?"

"Yeah," I nodded. "It was very noticeable because of the colour. It stood out amongst the green of all the undergrowth and I remember thinking how silly he was to wear something so distinctive."

"That's great," Ren replied, "and it helps us to identify where to look for him."

"It does?" I asked.

"That red neck tie is a gang identification thing. Bygora Vandos contains three active gangs who get along pretty well most of the time, so long as they don't take their business into a neighbouring gang's territory. The guys with the red have the northern third of Bygora Vandos and their nearest boundary is about six miles or so north east of here."

"So this guy was obviously trespassing," I said and Ren nodded.

"Yeah. I wonder why."

"It does seem a little strange to risk a bust up with a neighbouring gang just to come and throw stones at a security guard, doesn't it?" I said.

"Very strange," Ren agreed. "You reckon it's worth following up? Maybe go have a beer tonight in the north of town?"

"I thought you'd never ask buddy," I smiled. "Now, I'll download the camera and write up my notes while you shower. Then we'll call Tinnias and after I've showered, we can maybe find somewhere to eat out? That sound okay to you?"

"You asking me on a dinner date honey?" he laughed.

Tinnias was very pleased with what I'd discovered and said he'd call in a couple of favours and get some covert surveillance to monitor the off-scanner comings and goings around Deligon. He also said he'd dig up what he could about Roben Abydell-Mirras and let us know if he found anything relevant, and he promised to find out where the body of Symeal Gloak was taken.

"I think perhaps an exhumation is called for," he said. "I'll get our top guys onto finding out exactly what killed him and I'll let you know as soon as I do."

"Thanks Boss," I said. "We're heading out tonight to try and find the guy who threw the rock at me today and see what that was about."

"Be careful guys," he said. "I don't want to wake up tomorrow to hear you've been murdered by irate gang members."

"Don't worry," Ren assured him. "I know my way around these folks. We'll be okay."

"Okay," Tinnias replied. "Sam? You do as Ren says okay? He's more experienced with Deligon folks than you are. Promise me."

"I promise Sir," I said, "and the name's Joss. Sir."

"Yeah, sorry. Okay guys keep in touch and be careful."

I switched off my Unicom and got up. "Right, I'm going to shower and then we can be off."

"Hey why don't we call Donal and ask him to tag along with us?" Ren suggested. "He's local and an old guy will help us look less like trouble makers."

"Okay," I nodded. "He might even have some useful information about the gang and its members. He's ex law enforcement so he might know their history at least."

"Right. Don't forget to wash behind your ears Joss."

"I won't Papa."

We took a hover cab to pick up Donal and then headed up to the northern end of Bygora Vandos. On the way, Donal told us that this end of town is the most up market.

"It's where the big companies have their headquarters," he said, "and it's the financial heart of the city. Wages are higher here and the folks who live and work here think of themselves as being guardians of the lower classes down south. They feel obligated to look after them but in doing so, they tend to look down on them a bit. Not in a condescending way but just because they have more money and opportunity."

"So why would a gang come out all this way to throw rocks at a security guard?" I asked.

"I have no idea," he shrugged, "but it must be relevant that he chose a Calmarin security guard don't you think?"

"I guess so," Ren said. "We know the people of Bygora Vandos don't like Calmarin being here, so it stands to reason that they'll pick on those who actively try to keep them out of the place."

"Maybe he wasn't trying to hurt you Joss," Donal replied. Ren and I looked at each other and frowned. "Maybe he wanted your attention," he continued. "Come on guys, how long have you been in law enforcement huh?"

"So that's why I noticed his red scarf so easily," I said and Donal nodded. "And probably why he thrashed around like a Promolian Snittel on heat. He wanted me to hear him, see him and maybe even recognise him enough to meet him again."

"So how do we go about meeting him?" Ren asked.

"Driver?" Donal leaned forward and called. "We want the Centora Bar please." The driver nodded and Donal sat back. "We go to their favourite bar, that's how," he grinned.

"I'm really glad I bumped into you buddy," I sniggered and Ren grinned. I realised then that this guy would make a very useful addition to my list of contacts, should I ever need to return to Deligon in the future. The problem was that he is Ren's contact and we Freelancers have a bit of a code about stepping on one another's toes. I decided to think about whether to ask Ren about it at some point before this job was over. It isn't unknown to share contacts with other freelancers and twice in the past, I've been asked by colleagues to share a contact of mine and I'm okay with that, if the contact is okay with it too and it works out okay.

"Okay guys, now let me do all the talking okay?" Donal said as our cab drew to a halt outside a smart looking bar with a brightly flashing sign in the window. "Just agree with everything I say and look like you're enjoying yourselves."

We entered and followed Donal to the crowded bar, where he ordered drinks for us and paid with local cash rather than the standard currency card. When we had our drinks, he led us to a table in a corner and we sat down.

"Real cash?" I said.

"Yeah," he nodded. "It's a quaint affectation amongst Deligon's up and coming youth. It's a way for them to feel as though they're preserving their culture and identity. Off worlders, as you two are known around here, will never be offered real Deligon cash in any transaction and if you asked for it, you'd probably get yourself a beating for your cheek."

"Really?" Ren asked.

"Yeah," Donal replied. "This Calmarin business has really soured the local's attitude towards non-natives and you'll find yourselves tolerated less happily here in the classier end of town than down where we live. Those down south are easier going, probably because they're less driven by the need to climb the social ladder."

We drank and talked for almost an hour before Donal nodded towards the door. I looked and found myself staring into the face of my mystery attacker from earlier that day.

"That's him," I hissed. "That's the guy from this morning."

"Are you sure Joss?" Donal asked.

"Yeah, absolutely," I nodded.

"Okay, here's what you do. Follow my instructions to the letter, don't deviate and we may just get some useful information out of this evening. That boy is Palko Garmast."

"Garmast?" Ren asked.

"The Law Enforcement Chief's son?" I asked.

"Yep," Donal nodded. Ren and I looked at each other in obvious shock. "Now listen Joss. You go up to the bar, just near enough to ensure he sees you but make it look like you haven't recognised him. You order us a fresh round of drinks and you come back here. Don't start a conversation with him."

"What if he talks to me?" I asked.

"Just pretend you don't know him. If he talks, say hello and leave it at that. Unfortunately we can't choreograph this so you'll have to use your initiative. Just don't make him feel cornered or he may run and the game will be off."

"Okay," I nodded. Picking up our empty glasses, I stood and headed towards the bar. The only free space was right next to the guy so I had no choice but to head over there. It would have looked odd if I had stood behind someone when there is a free space right there. The boy had his back to me as I clinked the glasses down on the counter and looked for the barman. Over the music, I distinctly heard Palko Garmast turn and look at me, the sound of my glasses on the counter catching his attention. I took a deep breath. Keeping my eyes firmly on the barman, I tried to look calm as I signalled for service. The big barman wandered over and I ordered our drinks. Keeping my eyes firmly on the barman was difficult for me and I had to force myself not to turn and question him or grab him by the scruff of the neck and give him a slap around for his assault on me.

"That'll be twenty five," the barman said and I handed over my currency card with a smile. When he handed it back, I gathered the glasses and turned to go back to Ren and Donal.

"Evening Sam," a voice behind me almost made me drop the glasses. I hesitated mid stride and didn't know how to react. Should I walk on and ignore him or turn and inform him he must have the wrong guy? I remembered what Donal told me so I ignored him and went back to our table, the look of shock on my face letting them know something had happened.

"What's up Joss?" Ren hissed as he sipped his drink.

"He knows my name," I hissed back. "He called me Sam."

Ren's eyebrows shot to the top of his head and Donal sighed.

"You know what this means," I continued. "It means his father's been gossiping and he may even be involved in this mess."

"Oh shit," Ren exclaimed as quietly as he could without letting the other drinkers around us know he was in total shock. "This is getting bigger than I imagined. What the fuck are we to do if Garmast is involved? He knows both our identities and if he blows our cover, our safety cannot be assured."

"Now let's not panic just yet," Donal whispered. "Keep your heads for fuck's sake okay? Don't lose it out here, so far from our home ground. Did you answer him?"

"No," I replied. "I didn't know what to say so I ignored him."

"Good. I wondered why you seemed to hesitate when you started back over here."

"Yeah I noticed that too," Ren nodded.

"The ball is in his court now," Donal continued. "Let's leave it to him to make the next move."

"Okay, yeah that's a good idea," I nodded.

"And that next move is gonna happen right about now," Ren said, "cos he's on his way over."

"Oh fuck," I hissed quietly and Donal kicked me under the table. "And then you know what?" he said loudly. "She tells me to leave. Just like that. Can you believe that guys?" We all dutifully burst out laughing. Suddenly I became aware of someone behind me, inside my personal space.

"I said, evening Sam," the voice said. "It's a little rude to just ignore me like that buddy." He plonked his glass down on the table and sat in the one vacant seat and looked into my eyes.

"I'm sorry," I replied with a fake smile that didn't touch my eyes. "My name's Joss. Joss Gilden," I replied as I extended a hand, which he shook with a grin.

"It's good to meet you again Sam," he continued, "and I hope I didn't hurt you too much this morning." My hand instinctively went to my temple and I mentally kicked myself for inadvertently letting him know I understood what he meant.

"Look, you've got the wrong guy buddy. But let me buy you a drink anyway huh?"

"Sam Sinclair," he said as if reading my own law enforcement file. "Freelance Law Enforcer, Tag Code Sinclair 27593-4/167AZP. Native of Sigma Prime. Forty two years old, unmarried. Ten years in the Sigma Military Corps. Shall I continue?"

"Okay okay," I sighed. "So why did you leave your territory and risk a clash with one of your neighbouring gangs, just to throw a rock at me?"

"Aren't you going to introduce me to your friends first?" he asked.

"This is Ren and this is Donal," I replied. "Now. The rock?"

"There was no risk from the other gangs by the way," he said. "Both of our neighbours knew of my expedition and both were okay with it."

"They were?" Donal asked. "That's unheard of."

"Indeed, but there's a first time for everything as they say."

"So why?" Ren asked.

"Because we all want to help you uncover whatever is going on at Calmarin Research Station. All of Bygora Vandos wants them out and we want to know what's going on. With all three gangs, I can happily assure you that you have four hundred and seventy six willing and eager young, fit and healthy Bygorans at your disposal. We'll do whatever you say Sam, err I mean Joss. We'll storm the place, keep watch on people, whatever, but we intend to be involved in getting this shit sorted. It's our world they're fucking with, our land and homes they've destroyed and our trees that are dying."

Ren, Donal and I looked at each other with obvious shock and Palko began to laugh. He extended his hand and looked into my eyes. I shook his hand and began to laugh with him.

Merita King

CHAPTER SIX

Palko Garmast showed us the best place in this end of the city to eat and we found ourselves in what looked from the outside like a rather run down square stone building. Looking at it from the outside, I was a little disappointed. I had expected the posh end of town to offer us something a little more, umm, swanky. Once inside though the difference could not have been more dramatic and I distinctly heard Ren whisper "wow." The walls were a dark shade of red and a lush carpet of the same colour lay beneath our feet. Thin black threads rippled through it and were echoed in the black wooden furniture. The room was long rather than wide; a single table on each side with a central walkway down the middle making it look like a converted mine tunnel but it was sumptuous. Music played in the background, just soft enough to lend ambience without being intrusive. Everything from the furniture to the crockery and glasses and even the small flower sprays on each table were of the highest possible quality and the overall effect was one of sophisticated but understated richness.

"Lovely place Palko," I said.

"This is the best restaurant in Bygora Vandos," he replied. "You'll love it." He waved at the smartly uniformed man who approached him with a smile.

"Mr Garmast, welcome once again," he said as he shook hands with Palko. "A table for four tonight?"

"Yes please," Palko nodded.

"Follow me gentlemen," the man said as he turned and led us to a table halfway down the room. After helping us into our seats and taking an order for drinks, he left to fetch the menu.

"This place only serves traditional Deligon food by the way," Palko said, "so just ask if you struggle to know what anything is."

"Thanks," I replied. "I reckon this is the swankiest restaurant I've ever eaten in."

"And the most expensive," Donal whispered with a grin.

"The traditional thing around here is for the known local to pay for the food and the guests to pay for the drinks," Palko explained. "Is everyone okay with that?"

"Sure," I nodded.

"Fine by me," Ren added.

"Absolutely," Donal agreed.

The waiter returned with menus and we spent twenty minutes learning what everything was. Some of it sounded disgusting and one or two dishes sounded positively indigestible so Ren and I went with a fish dish cooked in some kind of local wine and served with steamed local vegetables. Donal, being a native, knew what he was doing and chose an exotic sounding meat dish made of all the bits of some Deligon creature that I would not serve to my worst enemy. Eyeballs, lips, stomach lining and even the thing's testicles were seared at a very high temperature for just a couple of minutes before being steeped in a purple liquid made from the sap of some plant and served as a stew with vegetables. Palko ordered something that turned out to be a large vegetable stuffed with some kind of white gloopy substance with small lumps in. He told me it was a stew made from the Cagnall Worm, a bug about four inches long and bred for the table. Yuck.

Over the meal, Palko gave us the history of Calmarin, which was pretty much what we already knew but it was interesting hearing from the native's point of view. He was able to provide us with names of twenty-seven people directly affected by the presence of the Calmarin Research Station. We already knew about the seven families forced to sell their homes cheap, thanks to Donal, but the six others were new to us. He told us about this middle-aged guy who was an amateur scientist and had begun his own private research into the tree disease when it first appeared. He was one of the senior tutors at Bygora Vandos's largest college, so he knew his stuff but when he published an article about his findings in the city's largest newspaper, he was suddenly fired from his job and accused of sexually abusing the kids in his care. After being unable to find work again, he lost his home, his wife died of apparent food poisoning and he ended up losing his mind and being incarcerated in an asylum forty miles outside of Bygora Vandos.

"Might be worth paying him a visit," I remarked and the others nodded.

"I'll see if I can't dig up a copy of that article he wrote," Donal said. "My friends in law enforcement should be able to help me out. I'm owed a few favours."

"There have been three attempts to get inside the place," Palko admitted. "All three gangs co-ordinated an assault on the place but we never got anywhere near. The special security guys were there. It was like they were waiting for us."

"So you have a double agent within your ranks somewhere," Ren said and I nodded.

"Maybe you could find out all of the R and D security guys' names," I asked, "and then Palko here can tell us if any of them have links to any gang members he knows of. That way we might find out who can't keep his mouth shut."

"I'll do it tomorrow," he nodded. "First priority. Palko, if you give us your Unicom number, Joss and I will call you in the evening and give you the names. You tell us if you recognise any of them and we can proceed from there."

"Okay," Palko nodded as he jotted down his Unicom number and handed it to Ren.

"It might be better not to give the names over the Unicom," Donal remarked, "Unless it's a secure line. You never know who might be listening in, especially with a blabbermouth around."

"My line is secure," I replied, "So all calls between us must be on this number." I jotted down the number of my secure line and gave it to Palko. "Don't call Donal. If you need to talk to him, call me first and I'll call him and give him your message. The line is secure only when my Unicom is part of the call okay?"

"Okay," Palko nodded.

"My first priority must be to find out what's beneath that hole," I said. "But how the fuck do I achieve that?"

"What hole?" Palko asked. I told him about the trapdoor beneath the ground and was surprised that he didn't know about it. What he told me next shocked me to the core. "You want to get underground beneath Calmarin? Well why didn't you ask? I can get you down there easy enough."

"What?" Ren asked.

"Are you shitting us boy?" Donal demanded.

"Please tell me you're not tugging my wire Palko," I begged.

"Twenty or so years ago, the city bigwigs decided to upgrade the underground transport system. The system of tunnels was cleaned out, repaired and extended in some parts as the city had outgrown the old system. Other tunnels were blocked off and left to rot and I happen to know how to get into one of them right nearby where we met this morning Joss. That's how I got away without being caught."

"So you're telling me that you know of a tunnel that actually connects underground at Calmarin? Physically connects I mean?"

"Yeah," he nodded. "The boys and I go down there a lot, to see if we can get into the place but it's blocked off with stone and none of us has access to any equipment that could silently break through to the other side. We could blow it down but that would kind of give away our presence a little."

"Don't you worry about that," Donal said. "Like I said before, I'm owed a few favours and I can get an almost silent fluid drill loaned to me for an evening or two without too much of a problem. I also have some pretty sensitive listening equipment in the shop, so we can hear anything that might be going on."

"The first thing is to see it, so we know what we're dealing with," Ren said and we all nodded. "How soon can you show us?"

"What time are you off work tomorrow?"

"Four," Ren and I chorused.

"Okay," Palko replied. "I'll meet you all at four thirty in Donal's shop. I'll have to invite the leaders of the other two neighbouring gangs, just as a courtesy or it could jeopardise our current truce."

"Sure, not a problem," I nodded. "So long as one of them isn't the double agent."

"Shit," he replied. "Yeah that's a valid point. Okay umm, let's make it the day after. That way we'll know it's safe for me to confide our plan to them."

"Agreed," Ren nodded.

"Sure, that's fine," Donal said.

"Okay so we're agreed," I replied. "Sometime tomorrow evening I will call you with the names of the R and D security guys that Ren will get us. You tell us if you recognise any of them as having a connection to any of the gang members you know of, especially the other two leaders. If the other two leaders are not connected, give them both a copy of the list, they'll know their own members and you might find your leak. Then at four thirty the following day, we'll all meet up at Donal's store and you can show us the tunnel so Donal, Ren and I will know what sort of a job we have on our hands. Is everyone clear? Any questions? Good, now what do the Bygorans do for dessert?"

When we finally left the restaurant, I'd had the nicest meal I could remember in months and Ren and I decided we had to return from time to time. Palko agreed; it seemed the obvious place to meet with him should we ever need to and I looked forward to sampling a little more of the menu. Palko offered to show us one of the local clubs where the local young things gather for music and dance and Ren and I readily agreed. Donal said he was too old for clubs so we saw him to a cab and then let Palko show us the nightlife. The club was loud so we headed into the next room so we could at least talk without having to yell at each other. Glancing around, I noticed photographs of women lining the walls and each had a name beneath it.

"Who's in those pictures Palko?" I asked and heard Ren giggle.

"He's new around here remember," Ren said and Palko laughed.

"They are, umm, how did you put it? Dessert?"

"Oh I see," I hissed and Ren laughed.

"Come now, don't be shy," Palko said. "Which one catches your eye or would you like me to choose for you? Redhead or Dark? Blonde maybe?"

"He's not fussy," Ren replied for me.

"Hey," I cut in. "I'm very fussy thank you. Redheads or brunettes are my choice, depends on the eyes and breasts."

"Okay," Palko said as he scanned the pictures. "How about number fourteen? She's dark haired and has big eyes and a decent chest."

I looked at picture fourteen and I have to admit, she was cute. I was about to agree when I caught sight of picture thirteen and knew she was the one. Redheaded, with big purple Deligon eyes and huge breasts.

"Well?" Ren encouraged. "Come on buddy, I'm getting horny just looking at them. Pick anyone you want." Palko laughed loudly and I tutted at Ren.

"Thirteen is perfect," I said.

"Okay thirteen for you," Palko said. "I rather like number twenty and how about you Ren?"

"Seven for me please."

"You do realise Joss," Palko said with a grin, "that our umm, business will be conducted together."

"What?" I hissed.

"It's the Deligon way," Ren laughed. "Believe me buddy, if you refuse once you get in there, you'll cause a huge offence."

"Oh shit," I exclaimed. "I can't. I mean, I just couldn't. Not with you two there."

"Don't be such a wet blanket Joss," Palko grinned. "Once you get in there, you'll have the time of your life, believe me."

"Ren, help me out here buddy. You're on my side remember?"

"I am helping you," he laughed. "This is a way for you to ingratiate yourself around here. Word will get around the girls that you're an okay guy, and they will talk to other guys. We need the people to accept us."

"Oh shit," I sighed.

Palko made his way over to a desk in the corner of the room. When he returned he was grinning. "We're in luck tonight boys. All three are available."

We climbed the stairs and entered a comfortable sitting room with an attached bathroom. I noticed another door in the left hand wall.

"Okay Joss," Ren said as he began removing his clothes. "Into the bathroom and have a quick shower first."

"Showering time comes off our allotted time slot, so don't dawdle huh?" Palko added as he strode naked into the bathroom.

I took a deep breath, removed my clothes and followed them into the bathroom. When we were done and dried off, I followed Ren's example and wrapped the towel around my waist before following both men through the extra door in the sitting room. All three were gorgeous. Mine was dressed in lacy underwear that failed to fully contain her large breasts. She smiled and cooed at me from where she was sitting on the huge bed that dominated the room. Ren was over to his like a shot and had his dick in her mouth within seconds, while Palko took his from behind. Mine held out her right hand to me. I took a deep breath and walked over to her beckoning fingers.

In the hover cab on the way back to our apartment, Ren congratulated me on having ingratiated myself with the local way of doing things. He said it would make me more readily accepted by the Bygorans now that I had shown a willingness to conform to their culture and hadn't insulted them by regarding their customs as disgusting.

"These things mean a lot when you're trying to fit in Joss," he said and I had to agree, he had a valid point. "They have a very open attitude to sex here and sharing is a normal part of it. By this time tomorrow, word will have got around the whole of the Bygoran gang world that you're an okay guy. It'll help them trust us."

"Okay, gotcha," I replied. "I'll add to my notes when we get back and download this surveillance camera too so we have everything Palko told us on vidicom."

"You filmed our conversation?"

"Yeah of course. In case he turns out to be scamming us. If anything should happen to either of us, this bit of film might explain things."

"Don't let them catch you filming them Joss or you might just lose your kneecaps. Everything is done by word of honour here."

"Don't worry," I replied. "Word of honour is fine by me but a little hard evidence as backup never hurt anyone."

"Yeah, I know it makes sense. Just be careful okay?"

"I will. I've been doing this a long time. I know what I'm doing. You know, it would sure help if I could get a transfer to R and D security. How easy would that be to achieve do you think?"

"Well I guess it's not beyond the realms of possibility but I've never known it happen. All new R and D security guys are hired from outside the company and the majority are non-natives."

"Well I'm not a native Deligonian so I have one thing in my favour," I replied. "If only one of them would retire or get sick or something. I'm a little hesitant to just ask about it after only being there a few days."

"You don't want to show too much interest in what goes on quite so soon," Ren remarked and I nodded. "They're bound to get suspicious if you do. Take it slow, wait for an opportunity and then offer."

"Yeah. If I can become such a good employee that they trust me to do my job properly, they might begin to confide in me more. It'll take time to dig in deep enough, we just have to be patient."

"Our first job is to find the leak in the gang network," Ren said. "If we can find that and plug it, we have plenty of allies on our side if things get dirty."

"Yeah," I agreed."

The next day I decided a little more subterfuge would be in order, so I limped into work and made sure my colleagues saw me wince in pain from time to time.

"That rock to the knee hurting today Joss?" Pendle asked.

"Actually no," I replied. "It's my ankle. I forgot to mention it what with the kid throwing rocks at me and everything, but just before he showed up, I twisted my ankle out there. There's some kind of a dip in the ground out on the North Western sector and my ankle went over when I stepped into it. I'll be fine once I get going."

"Yeah. Dancel here broke his ankle when he first started the job and went over there for the first time."

"Hurt like damn hell for weeks," Dancel nodded.

"Why don't they do something about it?" I asked. "It's dangerous and it wouldn't cost as much to fill it in as it must've done in compensating injured workers."

"That's what I said at the time," Dancel replied. "I was off work for a month on full pay and yet how much would a few bags of soil cost huh?"

"Maybe Kobey could arrange something?" I suggested. "He seems like a guy who likes things to be done right."

"We've asked him a few times," Pendle said. "Nothing ever gets done. You're welcome to try again though if you want. He'll be bringing over your body armour today sometime, so I'll let him know you want to speak to him if you like."

"Okay, thanks," I nodded.

"Right guys, let's get to work huh?" Pendle called out and we all got up and headed towards the door.

Three hours later, I was dragging myself along by the Southern sector of the fence when the sound of a hover cart forced me out of my musings. I was already bored shitless with this job and the only way I was able to endure the hours of pacing up and down the fence was by reliving some of the more memorable experiences I have had during my years as a freelancer. In fact, it was during this job, after spending weeks with nothing but my memories to keep me from dying of boredom, that I first got the idea of maybe one day putting my stories out there for the public to share. I thought about writing a book but I do not have the patience or the skill for that, so as I have always been good at talking to people, I decided to make some video logs and tell some of the more exciting of my experiences.

Anyway, back to Deligon. I turned at the sound of a hover cart and saw Kobey draw up and get out, a big bundle in his arms.

"Morning Boss," I smiled.

"Morning Joss. I have your body armour here. There's a body shield, leg pads and arm guards. You shouldn't be bothered by kids with rocks anymore."

"Thanks," I said as I took the bundle and put the armour on. It was heavy and I didn't want to wear it but I couldn't think of a way to get out of it now that I'd made a fuss about a kid throwing rocks at me and besides, that rock had really hurt my knee. I had a four inch diameter bruise that ached painfully when I turned over in bed at night.

"You're welcome. Pendle said you wanted to ask me something."

"Oh yeah. I forgot to mention it yesterday with all the fuss with the kid throwing rocks at me, but there's a big area out by the North Western sector of the fence, about fifty metres in, and there's a dip in the ground. I fell and twisted my ankle yesterday. I told Pendle and the guys about it this morning and they mentioned that it's happened before. I thought maybe it should be filled in or something as it's a little dangerous don't you think? I know you're a stickler for health and safety so I thought I'd better mention it."

"Thanks for telling me Joss, I'll report it right away." He'd hesitated just a little too long before answering me and I knew right away he knew what I was talking about and was having an internal battle with himself as to whether to tell me what he knows or not. I remembered my initial meeting with him and how I'd summed him up so I took the biggest risk of my entire career and put all my faith in my people reading skills.

"What's going on down there Boss?"

"I don't know. Very few do. I'm not paid to know and neither are you."

"But what if it's something dangerous? What if it's something bad for the people of Bygora Vandos? Don't we have a duty to do something? Shouldn't we at least find out?"

"Don't Joss," he snapped. "Don't. This sort of talk is more dangerous and is far more likely to get you hurt." He saw me looking shocked and sighed. "No that's not a threat. I've worked here for a few years now and I've seen things that don't quite add up. I've known people who've asked questions and bitterly regretted it. Don't become one of them. I like you Joss. You remind me of my Brother's boy and I'd rather not see you get hurt."

"You know Boss," I said as I held his gaze. "If ever you see anything else that doesn't quite add up, you can always discuss it with me. Maybe the two of us together could figure out a way to understand it. Two smart guys with brains are better than one huh? Just for our own peace of mind, to help us both sleep at night."

He looked into my eyes for long seconds before giving the briefest of nods and I knew instantly that at some point in the not too distant future, he would be an ally. I watched him leave and decided that despite his lack of flexibility and his obsession with sticking with rules, I liked him. He was honourable and I like honourable men.

Ren was amazed when I told him about my conversation with Kobey.

"Joss you're amazing. How the hell could you take such a risk and come up smelling so sweet huh? Don't you ever fuck up?"

"Hell yeah," I laughed. "Quite often, but thankfully not today. Now, how did you do?"

"I got the names of all the R and D security guys and their supervisors and their Head of Security, here," he said as he handed me a list of seventeen names, none of which I recognised.

"That's great," I said and clapped him on the back. "Not only can we possibly find out who's the leak in the gang network, but if we give these names to Tinnias, he can dig around and see what else he can uncover about them."

"I also found out something else that might interest you," he said.

"Yeah?"

"In six weeks, their Head of Security, that guy at the top of the list, is retiring and returning to his home world on a fat pension. The third guy down the list is a Supervisor and he is earmarked for taking over his position. The seventh guy down is earmarked to take over his position as supervisor."

"So?"

"So they'll be a guy short."

"Oh my god," I replied and then grinned. "So I could get the job and get in there legitimately."

"As I said, it's never been done before since I've been here, which isn't that long but yeah, there's always a chance."

"Okay umm. I'll go and download this surveillance camera and make some notes. Then how about we call Palko and see what he says about the names, then call Tinnias and update him?"

"Sounds fine," Ren replied. "I'll go and shower now then."

Palko jotted down the names on Ren's list and recognised one of them. "Here's a name I recognise," he said. "This Badlok guy. I have two members with that same last name. It's not that common a name here either. I'll pass this list to the other two leaders and discuss it with them and get back to you within an hour or so."

"Okay, thanks buddy," I replied.

Tinnias was amazed to hear that the Head of Law Enforcement on Deligon had a son who is head of one of the three major gangs in Bygora Vandos. He assured us that Adlion Garmast was clean, which was a huge relief to Ren and I and he called up the guy's file right then and there and said there was nothing to indicate he'd ever had problems with his boy. He'd been a model student all the way through his education but had turned down a military career opportunity in favour of following his father into law enforcement, which he was due to start on his twentieth birthday. He also told us he'd found out where Symeal Gloak's body had been taken after his alleged death in a hover buggy crash.

"He was taken back home to Tallimak 7 where he was buried in an airtight pod in the family memorial. We're getting an exhumation order made up and we're already in talks with his relatives who are happy to help us as they've never believed he died in a buggy crash."

"That's good news Boss," I said.

"The airtight burial pod will ensure his remains will be pretty fresh," Ren said and I nodded.

"Exactly," Tinnias replied. "I've also found out about Roben Abydell-Mirras, Calmarin's head guy. There's not much to tell really. He's never been in trouble with the law, studied hard and did well during his education and went into the family's businesses. If anything he's a little ineffectual."

"All the better to control from afar," Ren said.

"That's exactly what I was thinking," I nodded.

"Good point," Tinnias said. "He's the youngest of Kaybel's sons. The other two both did pretty well for themselves. One runs Heibat Power and Energy and the other runs a banking firm that we've just discovered also traces back to the Abydell-Mirras family."

"Shit," I remarked. "Is there anything that family doesn't run?"

"It doesn't seem so," Tinnias said. "Keep in touch guys and be careful huh?"

Palko rang back and said both the other two gang leaders had gone over the list but could not recognise any connection between the names on the list and any of their members.

"So it looks like the leak could be in your group," I said.

"Yeah, the two Badlok boys. I talked it over with my two colleagues and we'll handle the problem, don't worry. We've put a couple of our most trusted members onto trailing them and I've already decided they'll never be party to any plans ever again."

"Don't get into trouble buddy," Ren said. "You have your whole life ahead of you, don't fuck it up before it's even begun okay?"

"I won't," Palko assured him. "Thanks. My two colleagues and I will meet you at Donal's shop tomorrow at four thirty. Wear something warm; it's a bit damp down in the tunnel."

Merita King

CHAPTER SEVEN

The following day was another boring one at work, with nothing interesting happening except that I managed to have a conversation with Hitch and broached the subject of him losing his home to Calmarin.

"How long have you worked here Hitch?" I asked as casually as I could.

"About four years now," he replied.

"Have you always been in security?"

"Hell no," he laughed. "I'm a carpenter. I make furniture."

"Really? So why are you boring your balls off working here? Why don't you work for yourself, making and selling stuff?"

"I used to do exactly that," he said. "I lost my home and business when this place expanded and they compensated me by building me a new home and offering me a job here."

"Jeez that must've sucked."

"Oh it did Joss," he nodded. "And it still does a little although I've got used to it. I still make furniture and sell it through a couple of the better stores here in Bygora Vandos and one in Shelbarr."

"You'd have thought they'd at least have offered to set you up with a new workshop so you could continue the job you had, rather than just offer you a job here."

"I asked them at the time but they said their offer only stood if I took the job. If I wouldn't accept the job they wouldn't build me a home so I'd be homeless and jobless and penniless. I had no choice."

"But that's against the law surely," I replied.

"I got advice about it but the law says that because the land was scientifically proven to be unsafe, we had to leave voluntarily or be forcibly removed and that the company was being generous by offering us anything at all."

"That would've seriously pissed me off."

"It seriously pissed me off too," he nodded, "and the other folks similarly affected but our hands were tied. You know what makes it worse?" he asked and I shook my head. "After being victimised like that and working for them for four years, nobody still knows anything about what goes on here. I sometimes feel like I'm helping the company to deceive Deligon, like I'm being disloyal to my own people and I hate that. I feel like a traitor."

"So you'd be interested if ever there was an opportunity to find out," I asked. "Maybe even possibly do something about it?"

He looked at me and frowned. I held his gaze as I watched him trying to figure out what I was getting at. "Just what are you telling me Joss?"

"Nothing," I shrugged while still holding his gaze. I wanted him to realise I was lying, without having to actually admit to him that I was lying. I wanted him to want to help and I felt confident that he would. "I'm just saying that since you feel forced into a corner by them, if something ever happened that gave you an opportunity to fight back and get the truth out, you'd be wanting to be a part of it."

Long seconds of silence hung between us as we held each other's gaze before he shrugged and nodded. "Yeah. Yeah I guess I would."

Ren and I arrived at Donal's shop and headed through to the back, where he had hot drinks and a snack waiting for us.

"We don't know how long this is going to take," he said. "We may be eating late tonight and I happen to get very grouchy when I'm hungry."

"This is delicious buddy," I said as I took another bite of my sandwich. "What is it?"

"Well it's umm," he hesitated.

"On second thoughts, don't tell me," I grinned. "Probably best I don't know huh?"

"You're catching on Joss," Ren laughed.

"I've put together a few bits of equipment here," Donal said as he indicated a holdall. "There's an almost new Sobberlander and three sets of headphones so we can hear if anything's going on behind the wall Palko told us about."

"You have a Sobberlander?" I exclaimed in surprise and he nodded. "Jeez we can hear a heartbeat a mile away with one of those."

"I've also been in contact with a colleague who says he can let me have his fluid drill for a weekend in a couple of months' time. He's using it on a job out on Deligon 4's second moon at the moment and it won't be back for a couple of months, but he's promised me it's mine as soon as it gets back."

"That's great," Ren said and I nodded. "That way, if you have managed to get a transfer to R and D security by then, you might know more of what's going on yourself Joss."

"You're getting a transfer to R and D?" Donal asked.

"There's a retirement coming up," Ren explained, "and a couple of the other guys are earmarked for promotion to close the gaps, which will leave an opening for a security guard. Joss would like the job, although neither of us know how he'll go about obtaining it yet."

"Well let's all hope you find a way," Donal replied. "There's flashlights for everyone in the bag too by the way, it's bound to be dark down there and I'd rather not break my ankles by stepping into a hole in an abandoned underground tunnel if it can be avoided."

"I hear ya buddy," I nodded. "By the way, did you manage to get a hold of that article that guy wrote about the trees?"

"Yeah," he said as he reached into his jacket and retrieved his media viewer. He tapped the screen a few times and then read us the article and Ren and I listened, our mouths opening wider in shock with each passing second. Ganfrey Tamlik was a science tutor at one of Bygora's largest colleges and in his spare time he decided to do his own research into the new disease that had befallen the city's trees. With his own extensive laboratory in the basement of his home and the indulgence of his adoring wife, he took samples and analysed them and wrote up his findings.

He came to the conclusion very quickly that whatever it was that was afflicting the trees, it wasn't a living pathogen. There was no parasite and no systemic fungus or virus could be found. Once he realised he wasn't looking for a living organism, he turned his attention to poisons and after weeks of methodical tests, he discovered that the results he was getting seemed to indicate the presence of a heavy metal that was toxic to the trees. From soil samples he found that not only the leaves, fruit and bark of the trees contained traces of this heavy metal, but the roots did too, indicating that whatever it was, it was in the ground and leeching up into the tree's root system, where they were drawing it up with the moisture they took in from the ground's natural water table. He concluded this initial part of his report with the suggestion that the trees were being poisoned by some naturally occurring heavy metal that had somehow begun to leech up into the surface where it was taken up by the trees through their root systems.

If he'd just left it at that, he might not have lost his home, his wife and his mind but, being a diligent scientist, he had to know what was going on, so he continued his research and drew upon some contacts he had in the scientific community in order to identify this heavy metal whose identity had so far eluded him. He'd been able to rule out every heavy metal he knew of, without identifying this mysterious substance, so he called in a favour and got a colleague from a science research company to help him out. The guy got back to him and thought at first that he was tugging his chain and accused him of trying to catch him out in some stupid game and demanded an apology. After assuring the guy he was asking a legitimate question, Professor Tamlik told him about the trees and his own research that indicated a heavy metal was the cause. He told him that despite his best efforts, he had so far failed to identify the heavy metal and asked him to put his greater knowledge and far more sophisticated equipment to work on it and tell him what the stuff was. Donal then read from an old news report.

"He laughed at me and asked me if I was sitting down," Professor Tamlik told us. Donal read. 'The Professor, a highly respected tutor of sciences at one of Bygora Vandos's largest colleges then told our reporters what his colleague told him of their findings. "At first he didn't believe me when I told him this substance, whatever it was, was poisoning our trees," the Professor told us. "It took me several minutes to convince him that I wasn't kidding him. He told me that he and his colleagues had done the tests three times just to make sure it wasn't a mistake, as it was so rare that none of them had ever actually seen the stuff or its effects upon living tissue before. He told me that some people in the scientific community now think of it as nothing more than legend," the Professor continued. He then told our reporters something so extraordinary that if true, would really put Bygora Vandos, and indeed the whole of Deligon, firmly back onto the galactic map. "He told me it looked as if I'd found Zanbadellium."

For those of our readers who may not know the legend of Zanbedellium, it is said to be a rare heavy metal that has a frightening and deadly effect upon any living flesh, rendering it into a state like that of death but without actually dying. A few anecdotal tales can be found of people supposedly under the influence of Zanbedellium and most tell of their deathly grey skin, staring eyes and slow, lumbering gait. Some of these tales say that sufferers of Zanbedellium poisoning lose their minds and become like empty vessels, devoid of any power over their own thoughts, without their own will to think, feel or act. Like walking corpses, these tales say, those unfortunate souls are as lifeless as androids, living but without a soul. A truly horrendous affliction indeed. Of course, our reporters cannot in any way presume Professor Tamlik's report to be either fact or fiction, suffice it to say that if true, the consequences for Bygora Vandos and indeed the whole of Deligon, could be serious. We will keep you updated as to any further findings Professor Tamlik should share with us.

"Holy Shit," I exclaimed. "A substance that turns you into a walking corpse?" Please tell me it can't be true."

"I'm afraid it's true, Donal said. "At least so the legend goes. This stuff Zanbedellium is said to turn anything living into something resembling a dead version of itself, without actually dying. People become like walking corpses without a mind of their own. They die quickly if they are in continuous contact with the stuff. The heavy metal somehow renders them almost catatonic and death occurs quickly with continued contact."

"Let's hope this Professor whatsisname was mistaken," Ren hissed as he ran a hand through his hair.

"I did a little digging," Donal said, "and I haven't been able to find any verifiable accounts of Zanbedellium having been found, anywhere. The last report of it was over three hundred years ago and that story was told via some mouldering writings left behind after some planet's inhabitants were wiped out by some disease or other. There was no proof though."

"If that shit is what's going on here we're gonna all have to be mighty careful guys," I said and looked at each one in turn with a grave stare. "No heroics huh? None, ya hear me?"

"But what if?" Ren began.

"No heroics Ren," I repeated. "Not for me anyway okay? Okay?"

"Okay buddy," he replied quietly. "And none for me either okay?"

Now it was my turn to hesitate. "Okay," I whispered and tried to smile. "Donal, you're not officially involved in this so you keep right out of it once we've identified the danger. That's an order by the way, from a Law Enforcer."

"Okay," he nodded. "I'll do as you say Sam, but I want to be involved as much as possible. This is my world here."

"Sure buddy, you'll be involved, don't worry."

The sound of the front door opening and closing, followed by several pairs of feet walking across the tiled floor caught our attention and I looked to see Palko and two young guys strolling towards the back office. We shook hands and he introduced us to his colleagues.

"This is Doniss Kelman from the local group and this is Marlo Hoklop from the eastern group. Guys, this here is Sam Sinclair from Law Enforcement. He's Joss Gilden while he's here working the case. This is Ren and you already know Donal."

"They do?" I asked and Palko smiled.

"There's not much we don't know Joss," he said. "We keep an eye on all the law enforcers in Bygora and retirement doesn't make any difference to us. For what it's worth though, we long ago identified Donal as a good guy."

"Thanks buddy," Donal nodded with obvious pride.

"We've got the two Badlok boys under surveillance by the way," Palko continued. "They won't be giving us any more problems, I promise you that. Now, how are things with you? Do you have any news?"

"Yeah I'm afraid we do," I nodded. "You'd better take a seat guys. You ain't gonna believe what we've got to tell you."

"Problems?"

"If what we've heard is true then yeah," I nodded. "A potentially lethal one."

"Okay, shoot," he said as they sat down.

By the time we'd finished telling them about Professor Tamlik's article and the legend of Zanbedellium, all three boys were white, their eyes wide and mouths open.

"If all this is true then you boys are gonna have to keep out of the place," I said. "You've all got the rest of your lives ahead of you and Palko, you're the son of the Head of Law Enforcement here on Deligon. I can't allow you anywhere near that sort of danger. You have to be okay with this, all of you."

"You can't shut us out now Joss," Marlo said and all three nodded in agreement.

"I'm not trying to shut you out," I explained, "but I am trying to save your lives. You can be involved in everything where there is no danger to your lives, but I have to be able to trust that you'll do as I say, even when that means keeping out of danger and even when I know you'll not want to. Do we have a deal?"

"Sure, we'll do as you say," Palko nodded after exchanging glances with his friends.

"Thank you guys. There's another thing you have to be aware off also. Ren and I are working this case with two objectives in mind. First to find out what the fuck is going on and second, to gather any evidence we can that will help us bring those who may be breaking the law to justice. This means that there will be some stuff we can't share with you, for legal reasons. We have to do everything right so that those crooks don't get away on some stupid technicality. Are you okay with that?"

"Yeah that's fine," Palko nodded. "I understand all of that, what with my dad and everything."

"And with you going into law enforcement yourself soon, you have to be seen to have a totally stain free record buddy," Ren added. Palko nodded.

"Okay guys," I said in an effort to lighten the mood. "Who wants a drink before we go? We've got some sandwiches here too if anyone wants to grab a bite. Just in case it's late before we all get a chance to have a meal."

We all piled into Donal's hover car and set off, Palko acting as navigator. The drive took us around an hour and we found ourselves three miles to the rear of the Calmarin Research Station and an area I'd not yet visited. This was on the very boundary of Bygora Vandos and bordered the several thousands of acres of countryside between it and Shelbarr, its nearest neighbour and slightly larger city to the north. Dusk was beginning to fall as we parked up and set off to walk the three miles through the forest to the tunnel entrance and Donal made sure everyone had a flashlight.

"No one touch the trees guys," I said. "We don't know how easy it may be to be poisoned by that stuff okay?" Everyone nodded.

"Best not to touch any of the plant life here, just to be safe," Ren offered.

"I'm wondering if it's got into the food chain," Palko remarked. "Supposing everything we've been eating for years has been dosed with the stuff. We could all be dying slowly of Zanbedellium poisoning."

"My guess is that if that's the case, then it must've been going on for a long time," Donal said. "Possibly even hundreds of years, in which case we might've built up some sort of resistance to it that we've passed down the generations."

"It could even be that none of you could survive without it," I said as I remembered my experience on the planet Amphallium 6. "I once had reason to visit a planet where some stuff had been found in the soil and everyone was worried about it. They fed it to lab animals and they all died horribly and everyone was full of doom and gloom about it. It turned out the planet had been giving off tiny amounts of it for thousands of years and the indigenous life had become used to it and couldn't survive without it. When they first started exploring space they couldn't understand why everyone got sick once they were away from their planet and it wasn't until they discovered the link to this stuff that they realised it had become essential to their survival."

"I don't think that's the case here Joss," Donal said. "Deligonians travel away from the planet all the time without ill effects."

"Okay, well unless there's been an increase in the number of unexplained deaths by poisoning and no one's reported seeing walking corpses strolling around, there may not be too much reason to worry yet."

"That's a valid point," Palko nodded. "Come on, we take this path."

We walked for an hour before Palko stopped us and pointed into the bushes. I could just make out the almost overgrown path and noticed the remains of buildings amongst the trees. What were once pleasant homes and thriving businesses were now just foundations surrounded by piles of rubble and overgrown with vegetation, amongst which hardy flowers were still bravely fighting with the undergrowth for the few precious hours of sunlight. Palko noticed me looking at the derelict buildings.

"This used to be the village of Timperly," he said. "When Bygora Vandos expanded to its boundaries, the villagers either left the area or moved into the city and what wasn't swallowed up by the city was left abandoned. Children come here to play sometimes."

"There's something sad about abandoned buildings," I said as a shiver went through me. "They creep me out."

"Why is that?" Ren asked. "To me they speak of generations of love, laughter and families. To me they're happy places. Why do they bother you?"

"I uh," I hesitated as the memory flitted through to the front of my mind. I didn't want to remember that. I didn't want to remember how she died, where she died and how I found her. "Someone died in an abandoned building," I said quietly. "I found her and couldn't save her. I always remember that whenever I see a derelict building."

"I'm sorry buddy. You wanna talk about it sometime, I'm here for you."

"Thanks," I replied and strode onwards with purpose.

"Here we are guys," Palko announced a few minutes later. The flight of steps leading into the ground was well overgrown and in the dark of the forest, was a danger to anyone who might happen to come by and fall down them. We picked our way down gingerly, trying to avoid contact with the undergrowth as much as possible and entered total darkness. The air became colder as we continued on and the ground beneath our feet felt harder, dryer, the further we went. I swung my flashlight around and saw the tiled floor and walls dotted with damp and fungus. We heard creatures scurrying away from our flashlights and I hoped nothing dangerous had set up home here.

"Look at this," Ren said as he approached the left wall, his flashlight held up in front. A poster hung limp in its frame and we could just make out the vague outline of a beach scene. A young girl smiled, her hands running sensuously through her hair as she gazed up at the sun in the now grey and mouldering sky.

"Tasmik Sun Cream," Donnis said and Donal nodded. "I have that same poster in my collection."

"You'll have to excuse Donnis," Palko grinned. "He collects ancient advertising posters. Poor dear can't hope to ever get laid." Guffaws filled the tunnel and Donnis tutted.

"Some of them are worth a lot of money," he replied, "and money will impress the ladies long after your dicks have gone limp." I laughed out loud and decided I liked the way this guy thinks.

The tunnel swerved away to our left and we found ourselves at a junction. We took the right and continued on, past more fading posters and saw evidence that the city's dropouts had sometimes made a temporary home here. Graffiti adorned the walls, crude images of giant penises, enormous breasts and open lips alongside words I wasn't able to read. Discarded clothes lay rotting on the ground, a shoe, a blanket, a tin cup. Around another bend we suddenly found ourselves on the platform, the ancient transport system long since overdue.

"We have to hop down onto the transport rail now guys," Palko said. "Watch your footing." For what seemed like a mile we wound our way along the dank tunnel, our flashlights lighting the way so we didn't break our ankles tripping over the transport rail. Palko flashed his light at a sign on the wall that was long since faded and only offered us a capital D followed by what could be either an e or an o. "Okay guys, through the next opening on the right." I could have missed the small door had not Palko pointed it out with his flashlight and we were all pleased to be able to get off the transport rail. My legs ached from having to walk with my legs slightly too far apart and I guessed the others were feeling the same from the way they stamped their feet and massaged their knees.

Through the door was a small room which looked like it had once been a store of some kind. A few rotting crates were still stacked against one wall and an oily smell pervaded the air despite this section of the transport system having lain dormant for twenty years. Palko flashed his light to a poster on the wall, covered in some hard, clear substance that had kept it in pristine condition and made it easy to read even after all these years. It was clearly a map of the transport system tunnels and Palko pointed to a red line painted onto the surface.

"This is the journey we've just done," he explained, "and this X is this room. You see this whole section beyond?" We nodded. "That is beyond this wall here," he said as he pointed to the far wall of the room. "As you can see from this overlay we made," he indicated to Marlo who produced a transparent map of Bygora Vandos which they taped over the transport map, "beyond this wall is Calmarin land and fifty yards that way," he tapped on the map, "is that hole in the ground you talked about."

"You've really done your homework guys," I said. "I'm really impressed."

"We're not bored kids Joss," Doniss said. "We're Deligonians who want our world back and we're willing to fight to get it. Whatever is going on here just doesn't feel right and we want to know or we want it gone."

"Right," Donal said. "Let's see if we can hear anything through that wall shall we?" He placed his holdall on the ground and began to unpack the Sobberlander. He handed Ren and I a pair of headphones each, before donning a pair of his own and approached the wall. He gently pressed the nozzle of the machine's microphone to the wall and adjusted the sensitivity. For agonising seconds we heard nothing but then a low hum came to our ears and we looked at each other.

"What can you hear?" Palko asked.

"Just a hum," I replied. "Here, take one of the earpieces." I handed him half of my headphones and we listened. Ren shared with Doniss and Donal shared with Marlo.

"I wonder what's making that noise," Ren said and I shrugged.

"Could be anything but it's definitely something mechanical don't you think?"

"It's an engine of some sort," Doniss replied. "A large one too with a self-contained fuel and air cooling system."

"How the fuck would you know that from a hum?" Ren asked.

"My dad works for the biggest industrial engineering firm on Deligon," he replied. "I've grown up around engines and when I come of age I'm going into the firm. He's taught me a hell of a lot while I've been growing up."

"I can tell you guys," Palko remarked, "that if he says it's this, that or whatever else, then it is. There's nothing he doesn't know about engines."

"Okay then what would that sort of engine be used for?" I asked, having decided to take advantage of this guy's knowledge and skill.

"Can you also hear that high pitched whine just above the level of the hum?" he asked and we strained our ears. "That tells me that this engine is being used to power a pump of some sort, although it would be a pretty huge pump, judging by the size of the engine powering it."

"What would something like that be pumping?" Ren asked.

"Could be all sorts of things," Doniss replied. "Water, air or gas though most probably. I don't think this is being used to pump anything with solid particles. The noise is too uniform for that, which tells me whatever is being pumped doesn't have much physical mass to cause pressure on the pump, like say lumps of rock would do. My guess, seeing as how this is Calmarin and we know a little about the place, is that it's pumping air or gas. If it was water, we'd see evidence of outflow somewhere and in all my wanderings around here I've never seen water I can't identify."

Suddenly a noise joined the hum and whine and made us all jump. It sounded like the excited barking snarl of a pack of predatory creatures around a fresh kill. Then a second new noise joined the snarling and we looked at each other and frowned as we listened.

hiss, thunk, foo

hiss, thunk, foo

"What the fuck is that?" I said and Ren shrugged. I looked around at all the guys and everyone shook their heads.

hiss, thunk, foo

hiss, thunk, foo

That reminded me of something and I strained my memory for it but it stubbornly refused to come forward. I was just about to swear when it suddenly leapt to the front of my mind and I knew where I'd heard that noise before.

"Doniss?" I called and he looked over at me. "You were right buddy, that machine is pumping air or gas."

"How do you know?"

"Because I've just remembered where I've heard that hiss, thunk, foo before."

"And where was that?" Ren asked.

"In the military," I replied. "My unit was sent to Garnal 7 to help quell an uprising and they used poison gas on us. We had to wear breather units and they made that sound, hiss, thunk, foo all the time you breathed with them on."

"He's right," Donal called back to us. "I've used similar breather units before too. I had to help arrest some guys who were trying to manufacture an illegal drug. Something had gone wrong in their little home factory and we had to wear breathers when we went in to arrest them."

"And that snarling noise must be one of their mysterious dogs," Ren said and I nodded.

"So we know there's a guard in whatever room is immediately beyond that wall," I said. "Shit."

"It may just be a corridor Joss," Palko said. "Let's keep listening and see when he returns, then we'll know how much time we have in between passes. If it's an occupied room, there will be sounds of people in there all the time don't you think?"

"Good idea," Marlo nodded.

We listened as once again the hum, with its quiet but ever present whine once again ruled supreme until, fifteen minutes later, we heard the guard return and listened once again as he strolled along on the other side of the wall not ten feet from our ears.

hiss, thunk, foo
hiss, thunk, foo
hiss, thunk, foo

Well, I am going to take a break for a couple of hours, get some reports written up, and have some food. I will catch up with you later. This is V log reference LB734/A data log reference point 3380133/8395.

CHAPTER EIGHT

Hey there, I am back. This is V log reference LB734/A data log reference point 3380133/8396 continuing report.

We all now realised that noise was the sound of a breather unit working. The hiss as the wearer breathed in, the soft thunk as the valve reversed, followed by the exhalation, unencumbered by filtration. We continued listening for a couple of hours and noted that the guard passed by every fifteen minutes with his snarling creature, the mysterious dog.

"What exactly is a dog?" Ren asked. "Does anyone know?"

"I haven't the faintest idea," Palko replied as Doniss and Marlo shook their heads and shrugged.

"From what we've been told," he continued, "we've guessed it's some fearsome creature they use to enhance security but we've never seen them and no one's ever described them."

"They're from Earth," I said. "They are kept as domesticated pets mostly but they're intelligent and are often trained for use with security guards and the military use them too."

"How do you know that?" Doniss asked. "I've heard of Earth and I met a girl once from there but I don't know much about them."

"I have a couple of contacts there and I've been there a few times on jobs. I was once chased by a pack of them when trying to apprehend my target."

"What are they like?" Ren asked.

"Well umm. They're four legged carnivores, covered in fur. Beyond that they're all sizes, all colours and many different body shapes. Some are tiny and others are huge. Earth people give them names and treat them like children sometimes. They keep them in the house like family members."

"Jeez, they let animals live like family members?" Marlo exclaimed in disbelief and I nodded.

"Yeah, and the dogs get very attached to their owners. It's almost as if they have the capacity for emotional bonding and many owners swear blind their dogs actually love them."

"But that's crazy," Ren said. "No animal can feel the same type of emotion in the same way that a humanoid can."

"Well I don't know," I replied. "One of my contacts had a big dog who was very friendly, even to me when I visited. If my contact said my name, the dog would look at me like he understood that the word meant me and not another person. He liked to play games and I spent hours throwing sticks for him that he would run after and bring back to me to throw again. I was there for a couple of weeks once and I admit I became quite attached to the thing and kind of missed him when I left."

"That's weird," Marlo said and everyone nodded.

"Yeah and it's probably safest to assume that these dogs, if that's what they are, are not the friendly ones. Let's assume they're trained to be vicious huh? That way I get to keep my balls."

"Good idea Joss," Donal snickered. "I think that it's," he began but then a new noise came to us from the other side of the wall and everyone fell silent as we listened. What sounded like many shuffling feet approached from the right and got louder as it approached our position. Heavy boot steps followed behind with the ever present breather unit.

hiss, thunk, foo

hiss, thunk, foo

hiss, thunk, foo

"Keep walking," a voice commanded and the shuffling continued. Suddenly, right in front of our position, we heard a thud followed by the angry snarling of the creature. "Stop walking," the same voice yelled and the shuffling stopped. Running boot steps and the click, click of claws on tile approached. "Crusher, quiet," the voice commanded and the snarling stopped. "You two, fourteen and sixteen, help him up." A few moments of nothing but the breather unit ensued until we heard what sounded like fabric tearing and the same commanding voice. "Walk." The shuffling began again and continued until it was beyond the range of our Sobberlander and we were once again left with the lone guard.

hiss, thunk, foo

hiss, thunk, foo

No one spoke for a couple of minutes. We were all trying to make sense of what we'd heard beyond that wall and with what we'd all learned that very afternoon about the mysterious legendary substance called Zanbedellium and its effects upon the living, we each shared the same horrific mental imagery that none of us was able to put into words right away.

"I umm," Marlo began, trying to break the spell we were all under. "I umm, think that umm," he gave up and sighed.

"Yeah," I nodded. "Me too."

"Oh shit," Ren whispered. "What a situation. I never dreamed this job would turn out like this. How do we deal with this shit huh?"

"We may be just discovering that this job is beyond our limited capabilities to deal with," Donal said quietly. "Maybe you should inform your superiors Joss and ask them."

"I can't give him anything that isn't hard evidence or we don't have a leg to stand on," I countered. "Sure, I'll tell him everything we've found out today and what we've heard tonight but that doesn't actually prove anything at all. I'm still obligated to continue with my investigation until we have actual evidence that makes it clear we should all withdraw."

"Of course," Ren nodded. "You and I will carry on with our plans just like we said we would. I'll find out what information I can and help in any way that I'm able to, while you continue doing the job of security guard and seeing what you can find out that way. We carry on and see what develops as we go."

"Yeah," I nodded. "But you three boys and you too Donal, you mustn't become involved in anything that puts any of you in danger. If it does turn out to be that Zanbedellium stuff, then once we know, you step right back and work in the background okay? That's an order by the way, not a suggestion."

"Sure Joss," Palko replied and the other three nodded reluctantly.

"We still need to see what's on the other side of this wall though," Marlo said. "That will be some hard evidence won't it?"

"Yeah," Doniss and Palko replied in unison.

"We have two months until I can get the use of the fluid drill for a weekend," Donal said, "so that will give all of us time to work in the background and find out anything we can. We have the shuttles arriving the day after tomorrow so that might give us something to go on."

"And if I can secure a transfer to R and D security when the other guard retires in six weeks, I'll have access to what's on the other side of that wall."

"In the meantime," Palko said, "we can have our boys tail all the station's top brass and we'll write reports of their movements, who they speak to, even what time they take a shit in the morning, everything."

"Good," I nodded. "We all have something positive to do and it will all help to bring this out of the shadows, so don't you boys think you're not involved okay? If your surveillance brings up anything like secret meetings or anything suspicious at all, you might just be witnessing the most important evidence of this whole case. Don't underestimate the importance of the job you're all going to be doing. You're all valuable to this."

We packed up and headed back through the tunnel system and the subject of conversation was, of course, the Zanbedellium and its alleged effects upon the living. None of us welcomed the idea of becoming living dead men and for the first time in a long while, my job gave me a twinge of fear. People think my job is glamorous, which it is not at all but I am happy to cultivate that image if it helps my social life, if you know what I mean. People also see my job as dangerous, which it is, but my training helps me to deal with the dangers, and experience has helped me to deal with the fear in a positive way so that I seldom feel actual fear anymore. We walked back through the forest as the dusk settled around us. The derelict buildings brought unwanted memories back to my mind and I felt a fear I had not felt in a long time. It was the sort of fear you get when you realise you might just be out of your depth; the sort of fear you get when you think that maybe, just maybe, you might not survive this experience.

I've faced death many times during my career, both in the military and in law enforcement and since going freelance I've been shot at, beaten and almost eaten alive by all manner of hellish creatures but during all those experiences, I had this inner knowing that if I did die, I would die the same man I had always been. This time however, as the night birds left their nests and called into the Deligon evening, I realised that what I feared was not death, it was something worse. The thought of being a soulless husk without will, doomed to shuffle my way through the coming weeks unable to think or act from my own mind was more horrible than anything I had faced before. For an agonising couple of minutes I almost ran away but then Ren appeared at my shoulder and walked beside me. He did not say anything, he just walked with me, so close I could feel his shoulder against mine and as we walked, I felt my strength and resolve returning. I guess it was at that moment when our friendship became something deeper, something only two single guys far from home can understand. Although neither of us could describe it, the bond silently worked its way around our souls, so gently but so naturally that it did not feel strange or inappropriate at all. His presence by my side strengthened me, and it was then that I realised he had taken a position I thought no one would ever be able to take. In that moment, he became my best friend.

Donal parked up in the community parking facility behind his apartment tower and we headed off to get a hover cab. He offered to buy dinner so we found a small restaurant not far from the apartment tower Ren and I were living in and wandered in. The place was lively and this lightened our spirits as we ate our meal and talked over our plans for the next few weeks.

"Tomorrow, I'll get names and addresses of all the top brass and the R and D personnel too," Ren said. "Then you guys can organise your members to trail them for a while."

"We've got enough members between the three groups so that we can guarantee day and night cover," Palko said.

"Be careful though guys," I told them. "Be discreet okay? If they see you, you're safety might be an issue and I don't want that to happen."

"Don't worry Joss," Doniss replied. "We'll be fine."

"Are we all meeting the day after tomorrow at Donal's apartment to watch for the shuttles?" I asked and everyone nodded. No one wanted to miss it and I hoped Donal didn't mind me inviting the three boys on the spur of the moment. It seemed a little rude not to include them and I was still acutely aware that although they were still just boys, they were part of a very strong and effective gang culture that effectively helped to run Bygora Vandos. I didn't want to jeopardise the success of this mission by offending them. We needed them on our side.

We left the restaurant and said our goodbyes, after arranging to meet at Donal's apartment at nine in two days' time. I gave everyone my secure Unicom number so they could call me if they felt they needed to without worry of anyone listening in. As we walked, I looked up at the stars and sighed deeply. At that moment, I felt old, burdened by worry, and needed something to take my mind off things for a while.

"Hey buddy. I could sure use some female company right now. Are you game?"

"I'm always game Joss," Ren grinned. "Come on then. What is it to be this time? Redhead or brunette? How about a blonde this time?"

"I'm not really into blondes, sorry. Let's find a couple of cute brunettes with big asses huh?"

"Suits me fine. And you're paying this time okay?"

"Okay, deal," I grinned and followed him across the street.

Nothing noteworthy happened during my shift the next day but I did catch Hitch looking at me funny a couple of times. I supposed he was remembering our conversation the day before and was probably still wondering what I was on about. Although I was eager to get him on side, I decided not to mention it again just yet. It would be best to let him think about it for a while and besides, there was nothing he could do just yet so why risk putting him off. When things started happening, I would make the move on him and I felt sure that after a few moments of hesitation, he would be willing to join me in a fight if necessary. Ren and I caught the hover bus back to our apartment and he cooked dinner while I wrote up my notes and took a shower. Tinnias was stunned when we told him about Professor Tamlik's research, the Zanbedellium he said he had found and his subsequent arrest for alleged child molestation and incarceration in the asylum.

"Fuck it Sam, if all that is true then you have to be careful guys," he said, the shock evident in his voice. "I'd never forgive myself if the two of you ended up like that and there's no guarantee I'd be able to get you both out safely. If it looks like things are getting too big to handle on your own, you call me and we rethink this okay? That's a direct order."

"Yes Sir," I assured him. "We won't be silly, don't worry."

"Call me tomorrow and let me know about the shuttles. Film it. I want to see it myself."

"I will."

"How are you both for money?"

"I'm fine," I replied and looked at Ren who nodded. "We're both okay Sir."

"Okay, now what are your plans for this evening?"

"We don't really have any yet," Ren said. "Why?"

"Then I order you to spend the evening doing nothing connected with the job. Stay in and watch movies, go out and find a whore, whatever, but take a mental rest from it okay? Just for tonight."

"We will," Ren said and grinned at me. I tried not to laugh.

"Think of it as a team building exercise," Tinnias said. "You've worked alone for too long Sam and it'll do you good to have a buddy around for a while."

"Yes Sir," I replied. "We'll call tomorrow. Actually it'll be more likely the early hours of the next morning. Donal told us the shuttles take most of the night to arrive, do whatever it is that they do and leave again."

"Okay then, call me when you can. If I'm not here personally, one of the team will be here and play me your conversation when I get here. Take care guys and enjoy your evening off."

"What are the vidicom channels like here Ren?" I asked.

"Pretty shit actually but there is a movie channel that has some good stuff. Try channel 567." We spent a couple of hours laughing our heads off at a dreadful old movie, after which Ren said he was going to work out.

"I didn't know you worked out buddy," I said.

"I work out every day," he replied. "I normally do it before going to bed but as there's nothing going on I might as well get on with it now."

"You have some weights and stuff?" I asked. "I keep meaning to start a routine and I promised myself when this job is over I'm going to get some equipment for my ship so I have my own on board gym."

"I don't work out with weights Joss," he grinned.

"Oh," I replied. "Then what do you do?"

"Come and watch."

I followed him into his bedroom where he indicated for me to sit on the bed. After making myself comfortable, I watched as he stood, ramrod straight and breathing deeply. After a couple of minutes, he opened his eyes and began to move his body; kicking, twisting, punching, leaping and lunging. It was as if he was fighting some invisible opponent and I was transfixed. His movements were rhythmical and followed a definite pattern I was able to follow, after the first couple of minutes, and soon I was anticipating his next move. After five minutes, he changed the routine and once again, I struggled to follow until I recognised the pattern. This was obviously some kind of martial art and I realised he would be a formidable opponent. He went through four different routines before, with a loud cry and a jab to the front with his right hand, he stood straight once again, eyes closed and breathing hard. His body was strong and muscular but still that fineness was evident, from his bone structure to his muscle mass and I was envious of his physique. I am no slob but I do not work out regularly. Yeah, I know I should, and I want to but it is just the getting started that had always eluded me, until that night. After watching Ren do his martial art, I knew I wanted to learn. I was amazed and impressed.

"That was incredible Ren," I said when he opened his eyes. "Amazing buddy."

"Thank you," he puffed.

"What is that? Some sort of martial art or something?"

"Yes. It's the Damiklonian martial art. It's purely ceremonial nowadays. We use it as a way of not only keeping fit and healthy but also to remember and honour our old warrior ethos and keep our old fighting skills alive."

"So you actually used to fight like that? In the old days?"

"Yeah. With these," he said has he pulled a large case from under the bed. Inside were at least a dozen or so knives of every conceivable shape and design."

"Wow," I exclaimed as I knelt down to get a better look. "These are awesome."

"Be careful," he said as I reached for one. "Our martial art may now be purely ceremonial but these are always kept ready for use and they are deadly sharp."

I reached in and took hold of what looked like a metallic glove with four razor sharp talons extending for three inches beyond the ends of the knuckles. I slipped my hand in and grasped my fingers around a horizontal leather bound bar, effectively making a fist with four lethal talons sticking out the end. It was slightly too big for me but I was stunned and amazed.

"This is just," I began, "just. Wow." Ren laughed.

"Want a demonstration?"

"Hell yeah," I said.

"Okay choose one for me."

I handed him the talonned glove I still wore. "This one. It has to be this one."

"Okay, sit down and watch."

He put on the glove, a perfect fit and I noticed for the first time how his hands were just slightly too large. A moment later, I noticed his fingers were slightly webbed and I remembered he could breathe underwater and realised he obviously uses his hands as paddles. No wonder his arms were so muscular. He reached around to the back of the glove and touched something near the wrist and a single bladed knife fell away from the main body of the glove itself. I had not been aware of it there; it was so well disguised. The blade was long and thin and he held it with the blade sticking up, rather than down as one might expect. What followed was the most awesome display of fighting skill I had ever seen and ended with him disembowelling his opponent with the glove, before stabbing him through the heart with the single blade. When he finished he was breathing hard. Rivers of sweat ran down his body and I knew I was not half as fit as he was, but I was hooked from that moment.

"That was amazing. The most incredible thing I've ever seen. You have to teach me, you have to. I wanna do that."

He laughed out loud. "Thank you for the compliment Joss. I'll help you to work out if you like and you can learn the moves as you go. How does that sound?"

"Fantastic."

"Okay. Take off your shirt and stand beside me. We'll start with some stretches to get your muscles warmed up. Do you work out much?"

"Not really," I admitted. "But I'm going to now, I promise."

"Okay," he grinned. "We need to get you going slowly or you'll do yourself a mischief. Now, follow what I do."

An hour later I was exhausted and sweating but felt great. That hour taught me how much I'd neglected my body and I vowed there and then to remedy that and Ren promised to help me. It would give us something to occupy our minds during the coming weeks as we waited for things at the Research Station to develop.

Another uneventful day at work dragged by and it seemed like weeks before Ren and I headed back to our apartment. I ached from the previous night's workout; my body shocked beyond belief that I suddenly had the ridiculous idea of demanding it do some real work for its living. The pain told me that the workout had done some good, and I was happy to have something physical to take my mind off things. We worked out for another hour, after which I cooked while Ren showered. It seemed sensible for us to take it in turns to cook and I was okay with that. I was careful to put his jar of spice on the table so he would be able to appreciate his food and after my exertions, I really enjoyed the meal. Once I had showered and dressed, I packed my vidicom camera and we headed out to Donal's apartment. We decided to walk the four miles; it was a lovely evening and it was good exercise for my aching legs. We passed many shops and stores on the way and stopped to look in the windows of some of them. One sold pretty jewellery and I thought of Ambella Vaylo, Tinnias' daughter. I knew I should get her a present, as I always did on my travels so I asked Ren if he would mind if we went inside.

"Hey buddy, do you mind if we go inside? I should buy a present for someone."

"Sure, no problem."

We entered the small store and I found myself surrounded by jewellery of every conceivable design and colour. I wondered what to get her; I did not want it to seem too personal; I had to be careful not to give her the wrong signals.

"What are you looking for Joss?" Ren asked as I browsed.

"I don't know really," I replied. "I've never bought a woman jewellery before."

"So it's for a woman huh?" he grinned.

"It's not like that. She's just a friend's daughter that's all."

"That's what they all say," he laughed.

"Oh stop. You're a bad guy you know that?" I replied but couldn't help grinning.

"You didn't tell me you had a girl."

"That's because I haven't," I replied as I glared at him, which only made him grin even more.

"So, you're just buying sparklers for some friend's daughter huh?"

"Well, yeah."

"And there's nothing between the two of you?"

"Nothing. We're friends. She's Tinnias' daughter actually."

"Your boss's daughter? Wow Joss you do like to live dangerously."

"For fuck's sake Ren, there's nothing between us. I've known her since she was a baby, sat on my lap with her thumb in her mouth. She's like a little sister to me."

"So how old is she now?"

"Fourteen."

"And that doesn't make you uncomfortable?"

I hesitated before answering him and that silence told him everything he needed to know.

"Well, yeah things have changed a little over the past couple of years I guess. I have noticed she seems to be changing towards me and it has been on my mind. When I think back, it only seems like yesterday she was sitting on my lap and learning to read and I used to tuck her up in bed and read her a story. Now, when she snuggles against me on the sofa when I go around there for a meal, it's like I can feel her motive has changed."

"And how do you feel about that?" Ren asked.

"Well there's no way I'd," I began. "No way. She's fourteen and my boss's daughter. But, I'm pretty sure she thinks she wants me to. I'm trying to gently put some barriers between us but it's become a habit that I always buy her a gift when I go off world and to not do it would seem a little heartless."

"So you want to buy her a gift but one that says friend, not lover," he replied.

"Yeah, that's what I'm trying to do."

"Then jewellery isn't your answer my friend," a female voice cut in and Ren and I looked up to see a middle aged woman with a bright smile looking at us. I blushed. "I couldn't help overhearing your conversation," she continued. "Would you like some help to choose something?"

"Oh yes please," I nodded with relief.

"Okay," she replied. "Stay away from anything that is in any way connected with her body. Clothes, jewellery, shoes, make up, that sort of thing. By buying her those types of gifts you are giving her a message that you've noticed her body, that you want to have a hand in enhancing it, and the unspoken message is that you want her to use the gift to enhance her body for you."

"She's talking complete sense buddy," Ren said. "Listen to her."

"You need to give her something unconnected to her person. Something that just lets her know you thought of her but not in a personal way."

"I understand that," I nodded.

"When you think of her, what is the first thing that comes to your mind?" she asked.

"Her happy nature," I replied without hesitation. "Everyone who knows her comments about it. She has this innate ability to make you feel happy."

"That's good," the woman smiled. "So you want something to reflect her happy nature, her sunny disposition, the way she brightens the atmosphere when she's around, yes?"

"Yes, that's perfect," I said.

"Then how about one of these?" she said as she turned and led me to a display of big crystals. Each one was several inches in diameter, with many sides and had been cut into a point at the top. "These are called Sun Spots here on Deligon," the woman continued. "Take one to the window and hold it up to the last of the daylight." I did as I was told and took a medium sized crystal and walked to the window and held it up to the remaining daylight. As soon as the light caught it, the whole shop was filled with golden twinkling sunlight.

"Wow, that's beautiful," Ren said with a grin. "I'd like one myself."

"It'll be perfect for Ambella," I said as I held it up again. "Just perfect."

We left the shop having bought two of the crystals and given the helpful woman a large tip for her kindness and continued on our way to Donal's apartment.

"Does Tinnias know?" Ren asked.

"Yeah," I nodded. "I talked to him about it a year ago, when I first noticed she seemed to have a crush on me."

"How did he react?"

"He was okay. We talked about it and he said he trusted me, which was a relief and kind of puts an obligation on me not to do anything to ruin his trust. He said she hangs out with kids her own age and that she'll soon get herself a boyfriend."

"That's good. You seem to have a good relationship with Tinnias."

"Yeah. They're like family to me. My parents died a few years ago and I have no siblings or relatives left, so it's nice to get that family feeling once in a while y'know?"

"You never married?"

"No," I replied without explanation, before realising that Ren was my friend and deserved a little more honesty. "I nearly did, once, a long time ago but it didn't work out."

"What happened?" he asked.

"She umm," I hesitated. "She died."

"I'm sorry buddy," he replied. "Really. You wanna talk about her?"

"Not right now. Not yet okay?"

"Okay. You should though. How long ago was it?"

"Twenty years."

"That long?" Ren looked startled and I nodded. "Do you talk to Tinnias about it? About her or what happened?"

"No," I replied. "I've never discussed it with anyone before."

"Shit. Buddy you really need to get that out of yourself. That shit will poison you as effectively as that Zanbedellium will."

"I've got used to just leaving it behind I guess," I replied. "My job necessitates me being alone most of the time and I'm used to that. It's normal for me."

"It's become normal," Ren said. "And leaving it inside isn't leaving it behind."

"I suppose you're right," I nodded.

"What was her name?" he asked quietly.

"Merellia Gilden," I replied as my eyes began to sting.

"Gilden? So that's why you chose Gilden as an alias huh?"

"Yeah," I nodded, embarrassed but not knowing why. "I always use a Gilden alias when I need one."

"And you still think you've left it behind?" He held my gaze for a few seconds to push the point home and I realised he was far wiser than I would ever be able to give him credit for.

"Was she the one you meant the other night, in the forest? You said you didn't like abandoned buildings and that you'd found a woman dead inside one once. Was it her?"

"Yeah," I hissed as I tried to control my emotions. "Yeah it was her."

"How did she die?"

Long moments of silence passed before I had the strength or courage to answer. I'd told Ren I didn't want to discuss it but he'd successfully got the story out of me within a few minutes with a few simple questions and here was I, on the point of bursting into tears in the middle of a crowded street on Deligon 2. And I thought I'd left all that shit behind me.

"How did she die Joss?"

"She was shot seven times by a murderer I was making a case against. I'd been in law enforcement for less than two years and it was my first big case. I'd had to rattle a few cages to get the information we needed to secure his arrest and he took offence and got a colleague of his to pay me back by shooting Merellia. The guy kidnapped her, took her to an abandoned warehouse, stripped her naked, raped her and shot her seven times. It was one week after I'd asked her to marry me and she'd said yes."

"Shit," Ren exclaimed. "Shit and fuck. I'm sorry that happened buddy. I can't imagine how that must've made you feel. One thing I do know though, is that trying to forget it is not dealing with it in a healthy way, a way that honours her memory."

"You're probably right," I nodded.

"I know you're gonna hate me for this Joss, but I won't stand by and watch you torture yourself about something awful that happened in the past. I'm gonna make you tell me about her, about what happened and how you feel about it and you can yell at me all you want, but you're gonna get that shit out okay? You hearing me buddy?"

I looked at him and saw the most determined look I'd seen on his face since I'd known him. His eyes were fixed into a steely gaze of determination and his jaw was locked so hard the muscles in his neck stood out. So far he'd been a really easy going guy but now he was a solid wall of defiance and the contrast was so complete it made me laugh.

"Okay buddy," I said as I laughed.

Merita King

CHAPTER NINE

Our detour into the store to buy Ambella Vaylo a gift meant that Ren and I were a few minutes late arriving at Donal's apartment. He showed us in and offered us a drink while we sat down and said hello to Palko, Donnis and Marlo who had all arrived ten minutes early.

"We were getting worried about you guys," Palko said.

"Sorry," I replied. "It was my fault. I saw a store and remembered someone I needed to buy a gift for and we got delayed."

"I've made some sandwiches and got some snacks together," Donal said as he entered the room with a tray of drinks. "It'll probably be a long night."

"You should've told us all to bring something," Doniss said and we all nodded.

"Oh jeez no," he laughed. "I'm more than capable of providing a few snacks."

"Well next time we all bring something," Ren suggested and everyone agreed.

"Okay then," Donal nodded.

Ren handed the three boys a copy of the list of names he'd managed to get from the personnel records. "Here's the list of all R and D personnel, including their security guards. Their names, addresses and even Unicom numbers, they're all there. You'll see most of them live fairly local to the Research Station itself."

"That's okay," Marlo said. "My group won't be able to trail all of them so we'll pull all three groups together and forget the territory boundaries for a while. If that's okay with you two?" he asked and looked at Palko and Donnis.

"Sure thing," Palko nodded. "My group are more than happy to join forces with the two of you to get this done."

"Same here," Doniss added.

The three spent the next hour studying the list and dividing it up between the three groups and I was happy to see the three gangs working together. It reminded me of the Tunipz Team and I thought of all the good that had come out of the work they had done once they managed to find something worth believing in and working for. I hoped these three boys could build something as good from the situation that had forced them into a truce and I decided to do my best to encourage them as much as I could. Donal told us that the shuttles normally start arriving around one in the morning, so we switched on the vidicom and watched a terrible movie, whilst taking it in turns to keep watching the Research Station through his powerful scope. When the movie finished, I set up my own vidicom camera to film the proceedings as Tinnias had asked me to, although I still hadn't told anyone but Ren about the miniature surveillance camera I now wore at all times. I realised I probably should tell them but something just kept niggling me about it and I held back from telling them. Doniss was doing a shift at the scope when things started happening.

"Here we go guys," he said suddenly. "Something's happening over there." I leapt out of my chair and nudged Ren who had dozed off and was snoring quietly. I went to my vidicom and watched as a group of what I now recognised as the R and D security guards appeared from a door at the rear of the R and D department, and made their way to several waiting hover carts.

"So those are the mysterious dogs," Ren said as he sat and peered through his own scope. "Jeez I'd hate to be on the wrong side of one of them."

"Those aren't dogs," I said. "The dogs I saw on Earth were nothing like these things. No way." The dog my Earth buddy had was a fairly big, solidly built animal with brown and black colouration, a shortish snout and no tail. He did tell me what breed it was although I have long since forgotten. I do remember its head was around my mid-thigh level as it walked beside me. The creatures I now looked at were a head or so taller; their heads were almost hip height, their bodies very stocky in appearance, solidly built with muscular legs. Their heads were overly large and their jaws were wide rather than long, the bottom jutted out slightly further than the top, giving them an undershot appearance. They had huge fangs both top and bottom which overlapped their lips and what looked like a pair of short pointed horns sticking out just above their eye sockets. Being night time, I could not make out what colour they were, but they were uniformly dark all over and their bodies looked like they had a slight sheen, as if they did not have fur but something slightly shiny.

"Hell fire," Donal said. "Look at those things. You two have to be careful if you do get to go down there. You wouldn't last five seconds if those things got to you."

"Don't worry," I said. "I have a sedative pistol as part of my armoury.

"Yeah but your sedative is meant for humanoids with soft skin," Ren said. "Can you get your hands on some stronger sedative and maybe some stouter darts?"

"That's a valid point Joss," Palko said and I had to agree, he had a point.

"Yes he can," Donal said. "I have just what you need in the store. Stop by in a couple of days."

"Thanks buddy."

"I have enough to equip you both with plenty."

"Thanks," Ren said.

"Couldn't you just bite them Ren?" Marlo asked.

"That depends on their skin," he replied. "If they have skin, even fairly thick skin with fur I could, but from what I'm seeing I don't think they have fur. It looks different to me, thicker somehow and in that case no, I couldn't."

"I know what you mean," I nodded. "It's got a sort of sheen to it, whatever it is."

"Like scales," Palko said.

"Yeah," Ren nodded. "Just like that. Good thinking buddy."

We all watched through scopes as the four hover carts made their way towards us, to the North Western sector of the fence where I knew the circular dip in the ground was. They divided themselves into two groups and stood in two lines, twenty feet apart and each lit a flare. After placing it on the ground in front of them, they stood, apparently waiting for something. I could see at once they'd made a landing strip.

"It's a landing strip," I said. "They've lit the place for something to land."

"It's always the same routine," Donal remarked. "In a few minutes the shuttles will arrive and descend one by one."

Sure enough, five minutes later we saw the first of four shuttles arrive and each had the same logo painted onto its side, a huge capital letter H with what looked like a lightning bolt running through it.

"Heibat power and energy," I said quietly.

"That's just what I was thinking," Ren replied.

"What?" Palko asked.

"Calmarin is owned by a pair of companies called Heibat," I said. "One of them is called Heibat Power and Energy. The letter H and a lightning bolt? It has to be Heibat Power and Energy."

"What would a power company want here at a Research Station that's apparently trying to find out what's killing trees?" Marlo said.

"What indeed?" Palko replied.

The first shuttle edged forward onto the circular area and began to descend into the ground. It was obvious to me that the metallic surface I'd felt underneath the grass was some kind of elevator, taking anything on it down into whatever underground rooms they had down there. Fifty minutes later, it reappeared and took off into the night sky and the second shuttle edged itself onto the platform and began to descend. This happened with all four of the shuttles and after the last had taken off, the security guards put out the flares and made their way back to the waiting hover carts, which then returned them to the same rear door of the R and D department they'd come out of, over four hours earlier. Thirty minutes later, we saw the normal security guards resuming their patrols. I packed away my vidicom and sat down with a sigh.

"So this happens every week?" I asked Donal who nodded. "And it's always the same?"

"Yep, the same routine every time."

"Absolutely the same?" I asked. "I mean, exactly? There's never been anything even a tiny bit different?"

"No," he shook his head. "Apart from the shuttles of course."

"What do you mean?" Ren asked.

"Well, once every couple of months, the shuttles that turn up are different from these ones. They still have that same logo and everything else is the same, but they're bigger."

"Bigger?"

"Yeah."

"Oh," I remarked as I ran a hand through my hair and let this information sink in. This had to be significant but as yet, I did not know how or why. "So when is the next lot of bigger shuttles due?"

"Umm, about a month. Let me check my notes," he replied as he got up and left the room. We heard a door opening and closing and then he appeared with a digital console. He tapped the screen a few times and then nodded. "Yep, five weeks from tonight. According to my records, the bigger shuttles turn up every nine weeks."

"That's weird," Ren said. "Weird but umm, relevant I guess."

"It has to be relevant," I replied. "I wonder what the bigger shuttles do? I wonder what the small ones do. This not knowing is damn irritating."

"Now you know how we've felt for years Joss," Doniss said and I nodded.

We talked over what we had witnessed for nearly an hour before saying our goodbyes and arranging to meet for dinner the following day. Palko, Marlo and Doniss would begin trailing the list of R and D personnel Ren had supplied and might have some information for us that would prove interesting. There was not much else we could do until Donal could get hold of the fluid drill that would enable us to get through the wall in the underground tunnel, which he said was in a couple of months. I hoped to be able to get a transfer to R and D security in six weeks, when one of their top brass retired and unless something out of the ordinary happened, the next few weeks were probably going to bore me rigid.

Ren had the next day off and I was due to start my first twilight shift, so we had most of the day to ourselves and we caught a hover cab back to our own apartment and went to bed. I awoke around midday and found Ren making lunch.

"Sorry, did I wake you crashing around in the kitchen?" he asked.

"No," I yawned. "But that smell might've done. What is it?"

"You want some?"

"Yeah," I nodded. "Smells delicious."

An hour later, we worked out and I found myself really enjoying getting fit and learning the movements Ren was teaching me. I ached still but I knew that meant my body was reacting in the right way and I was happy to put up with it. Ren suggested we go for a gentle run around the park next door to loosen up the legs so I readily agreed. After a shower and a couple of hours relaxing, I felt fitter than I could remember in years. When it was time for me to head out to start my shift at the Research Station I wandered into the kitchen to look for something to take with me to eat.

"I've packed you something Joss," Ren called from the other room. "In the stasis unit."

"Aww thanks hunny," I grinned and heard him laugh. "Now you behave yourself while I'm gone ya hear? No talking to any strange men."

My shift went the same as all the others; I wandered along my patch and was glad to have a companion to talk to. The hours dragged by without incident, the only highlight being our scheduled break time. I got along well enough with my co-workers and found them all to be as curious as I was about what really went on at the station, and especially the mysterious R and D department. My shift finished at two and I caught a hover cab back to the apartment and tried not to wake Ren as I took a shower. I crept into the kitchen to find a note reminding me it was my turn to cook dinner the next day and to have it ready for five, as Donal and the three boys were coming over and I would be leaving at seven thirty to get to work for eight. Yawning, I got myself a drink and headed to bed.

I awoke mid-morning and called Tinnias to update him. He was intrigued when I showed him the vidicom footage I had taken of the shuttle landings and told him about the larger shuttles that turn up every nine weeks. Then he told me that the covert surveillance around Deligon had seen the four shuttles arrive at the planet and leave again five hours later and confirmed that all have been using some sort of covert mode to keep themselves invisible to the Deligon Air Security Force.

"This proves they're up to no good Sam," he said and I nodded. "Whatever it is they're doing, they don't want the Deligon Air Security Force to know about it. Those shuttles docked with a large research ship that also carried the Heibat Power and Energy logo and headed out of the Deligon system. We have a ship trailing them at a discreet distance so we'll know where they're going soon enough."

"Great," I nodded, glad that Tinnias was actively helping us out.

"So what's next on your agenda?"

"Well not much for the next few weeks," I replied. "The boys are trailing the R and D personnel, just to see if anything comes up of interest. We just have to wait until Donal can get his hands on that fluid drill so we can get through that wall and see what's going on. That'll be our next excitement, unless something else comes up of course. I'm still hoping to get a transfer to R and D security in six weeks, when one of their guys retires, and if that comes off, I'll have open access to what's down there. Next week I might miss the early stages of the shuttle landings. I'm on twilight shift and don't get off till two and it'll take me a few minutes or so to get to Donal's apartment. The following week though, I'm on nights so I'm planning something that might give us all a better look at what they're doing."

"Be careful Sam," Tinnias said. "Those animals look like nothing I'd want to get tangled up with."

"I will," I assured him. "And Donal is going to equip me with some heavier sedative darts just in case."

"Good. Keep them with you at all times when you're likely to run into those things. Oh by the way, I almost forgot. Ambella has gone and got herself her first boyfriend."

"She has?" I grinned. "That's fantastic. Is he okay?"

"He's a pimply kid Sam," he laughed. "He's got a nervous stutter, no sense of style and says he wants to be in the military when he gets older.

He's also a fan of that Elloway guy that Ambella loves so much, so I guess that makes up for his pimples."

"That's awesome," I laughed and Tinnias laughed with me.

"I thought you'd be relieved to know."

"I am," I nodded. "Very relieved."

"Call me when you have anything more," he ordered, "but call me anyway in three days okay? Even if you've nothing to report, just so I know you're both still alive and kicking. Now you're starting to find out stuff, I want regular scheduled check ins every three days without fail."

"Sure thing Boss," I replied. "Will do."

Palko and the boys arrived promptly at five and assured Ren and I that they had organised round the clock surveillance on all the R and D personnel from Ren's list. They told us it was too soon to have any news for us but promised they would call me on my secure line whenever they had anything of interest. Donal called and told us that his colleague with the fluid drill had called and told him their job had finished early and that he would be able to have the drill in four weeks instead of two months.

"That's awesome news buddy," I said. "Fantastic."

"Any news from the boys?" he asked.

"Not yet, it's too early. They've set up surveillance but it's only been a couple of days so far.

"Okay. Call by the store in a couple of days. I'll have some stronger tranquiliser darts for you and Ren. Does he have a tranquiliser pistol by the way?"

"Yeah he has a decent armoury. It's just the darts we need."

"Okay, give me a couple of days to get them here and they're yours."

"Thanks buddy, we really appreciate your help."

"No problem at all. See you in a couple of days."

The days dragged by, one very much like another. I was bored to fuck with the job of security guard but anxious to find the underlying cause of what was going on. Ren and I had a couple of hours together after he got home and before I went to work, so I ate early and we spent an hour working out, after which he sat down to dinner while I showered and got ready for work. It also gave us an opportunity to compare notes on anything that might have happened during the past day, which was precious little and as the days passed, we both became impatient. When the time came for the shuttles to land again, I knew I had to rush back to Donal's apartment in order not to miss too much. Ren had agreed to bring my vidicom camera with him and set it up for me so I could just come in and get on with it without any fiddling.

"Have I missed anything?" I asked.

"The security guards are just lighting their flares now," Ren said. "You haven't missed much."

Everything went off exactly as it had done the week before and when it was all over, I told them about my plan for the following week.

"I start on the night shift tomorrow guys," I said. "Which means that I'll be on site when the shuttles land."

"Yeah but you won't see anything," Ren said. "They always make the security guys stay in the HQ until after five. They say they're exercising their dogs."

"I know," I nodded, "but I have a plan that will hopefully get us a much better view of what's going on down in that hole."

"You're not going to be doing anything daft I hope," Ren said.

"Hey buddy, you're sounding like my mother," I laughed and he grinned. "If Donal can set me up with a Consoria P30 surveillance camera or something like it, I'm going to plant it right smack bang in that dip in the ground so that when the shuttles go down, it'll go down with it and film everything. It'll send what it's seeing to a receiver in my vidicom camera so we can record it."

"I doubt I can get my hands on a P30," Donal said, "but I should be able to manage a P25, or even a P26 or P27 if we're real lucky."

"That'll be fine," I nodded. "Can you get it by the day before the next shuttle landings?"

"Yeah. It shouldn't take more than a day or two. I'll call a favour in."

"How are you going to plant the camera?" Palko said. "Won't they see a camera lying on the ground?"

"They won't see a Consoria," I said. "It's no bigger than a shirt button and has a weighted spike underneath so if you drop it on the ground, it always lands spike downwards. Then I just tread on it to make it disappear into the grass and no one will see it unless they're looking for it. Its camera looks upward and is really wide angle so we'll see the ceiling and everything down to around waist height."

"That'll be fantastic, Doniss said.

"Any news on your surveillance of the R and D personnel yet?" I asked.

"Well," Marlo said. "The head of department is having an affair with the wife of the Manager of one of Bygora Vandos' biggest banks."

"Really?" I grinned. "Do you have any pictures of them together? Y'know, in case we need to persuade someone to help us out at some point?"

"Hey Joss, what do you take us for, amateurs? Of course we have pictures, here." He brought out a small digital console and tapped the screen a few times. My own unit began to beep and I picked it up. "I've sent the pictures to your unit." The photographs clearly showed a man and woman meeting, kissing, going into what looked like a hotel room and then there were several images showing them having the most incredible sex.

"That's awesome buddy, well done," I grinned. "These could come in mighty handy if things get sticky later on."

"There's a couple of other of the personnel who are having affairs too," Marlo continued. "One of the security guards is fucking his own brother's girlfriend, and one of the technicians is having it away with the wife of your security supervisor, Pendle."

"Pendle's wife?" I exclaimed in shock. "Oh man. He's a real nice guy. Are there pictures?" A few more taps on his digital console and my own beeped again. "Thanks buddy. Anything else of interest?"

"No," he said after hesitating a moment too long and I knew he was lying. I looked him in the eyes and found him wide eyed, holding my gaze. He had his digital console in his left hand and I saw him tap a finger to its display. I looked back into his eyes and back down to his hand. The finger tapped again and I knew he had something to show me that he wanted to share privately. I gave him a slow blink and he smiled, the briefest of smiles to let me know he understood.

"I'm on nights for the next week so I'll be around all day from lunchtime onwards," I said to everyone. "Ring me anytime you have anything for me," I added as I gazed into his eyes once again.

Ren and I caught a hover cab back to our apartment.

"Marlo has something to tell us that he didn't feel able to share with everyone," I said once the cab was safely underway.

"I caught the look he gave you," he said. "I guessed something was happening between you two. Any idea what it could be?"

"Well it's obviously something that he's found out through the surveillance."

"And the fact that he didn't want to share it would suggest it's something that might put our little family in jeopardy," Ren added and I nodded.

"Yeah, shit." Just when things were going along smoothly, something happens to fuck things up. This quite often happens; my job is not the sort of occupation that can be choreographed and things often happen unexpectedly that have the potential to fuck things up. I tend to find though, that these sometimes lead to breakthroughs in the end. They always seem like huge obstacles when they occur but later on when I look back, I realise they actually helped me out. It is not always the case, and sometimes these things really do fuck things up but around half the time, they are actually helpful in the end. I just hoped this was one such occasion.

I took a shower when we got in, while Ren fixed us a drink and we settled down to watch a movie on the local vidicom movie channel. I'd just sat down in my underwear with my drink when my Unicom beeped. I answered and found Marlo on the other end.

"Hi Marlo," I said as I switched it to loudspeaker so Ren could hear. "What was it you didn't want to tell me earlier?"

"Thanks for understanding Joss," he replied.

"Hey buddy, I've been doing this job a long time and I'm something of an expert at reading people. Now there's just Ren and I here so you can talk freely. And don't ask me to keep this from Ren okay? I won't keep anything from him, are you okay with that?"

"Oh sure," he replied. "Hi Ren."

"Hey buddy."

"It's just that something came up during our surveillance yesterday that shocked me. I thought you ought to know about it as it might put your safety in danger."

"Oh shit," I said and looked at Ren who sat, wide eyed and looked back at me.

"A couple of my lads were tailing Professor Jakelham, the Chief Technician in R and D. They followed him home yesterday, where he had dinner with his family and then left in his hover car. He went into a community parking facility on the outskirts of the city and parked up. He then gets out of his hover car, walks over to another parked vehicle and gets inside. That vehicle belongs to Adlion Garmast, the Law Enforcement Chief and Palko's father."

"Holy shit," I exclaimed.

"Oh fuck no," Ren gasped.

"Exactly," Marlo replied. "Now you know why I didn't want to say anything in front of Palko."

"We understand completely," Ren said. "Thank you buddy, you'll make a great detective one day with that instinct."

"Thanks. Now I've instructed my lads to fit the vehicle with a surveillance device. It's only audio I'm afraid but if they meet up again, we will be able to hear what they say. Until then we must be careful what we say around Palko. I've also got a couple of guys onto trailing him."

"That's great," I replied. "Good work. He may very well not know what his dad is up to but we have to be sure. My boss assured me that Adlion Garmast is clean but he could be wrong I suppose. It's been done before. The Law Enforcement Chief on Minostrall Prime was found to be a double agent ten years or so ago. He'd been doing it for years without anyone finding out and it was only accident that it came out at all."

"I'll be back in touch as soon as I get anything else. If nothing happens then I'll see you both at Donal's for the next shuttle landing."

"Thanks Marlo," I said. "Good work buddy."

Ren and I lost interest in the movie and spent the next hour talking about the possibility that the Chief of law enforcement for the whole of Deligon 2 was corrupt. We both went to bed realising that we no longer felt as safe as we had done. From this moment on, we would have to filter what information we gave to Palko, in case he was being used by his father to spy on us. This job was now a whole lot dirtier and both Ren and I got the first little tickle that we might just be in slightly more danger than we had thought.

CHAPTER TEN

The next morning was the start of my week on the night shift. It was also Ren's day off so after going shopping for supplies, we worked out for an hour and went for a run before having a light lunch. I decided to call Tinnias and give him the news about Adlion Garmast.

"He's not going to be happy about this at all," Ren said.

"You can say that again," I replied as I dialled. He was right too, Tinnias went nuts.

"What?" he bellowed. "Are you absolutely sure about this Sam?"

"Unfortunately Sir, we are. I trust Marlo and I just can't believe that he'd fit up Palko to screw this up. Everyone here wants Calmarin gone and I trust him."

"Shit. This really fucks things up. Okay umm, let me think on my feet here a second. Maybe we should get you both out of there as soon as possible. He knows you're both there, he knows why you're both there and if he's in bed with them, you're both in danger."

"Sir?" Ren said. "Let's take a breath here for a minute huh? Now, okay Garmast met with Jakelham but there's no way to know why he met him or what for. They might be buddies or they might be setting up a secret birthday party for another friend, it could be anything."

"He's right Sir," I said before Tinnias could ignore Ren and insist on extracting us from Deligon and fucking up the mission. "Let's not jump to conclusions here. There could be any number of reasons for them meeting. The boys have bugged Adlion's vehicle so if they meet again, we'll hear what they say. I think we should hold on until something else happens."

"And something else Sir," Ren added. "The fact that Jakelham went to meet Garmast, went to Garmast's car, might just hint that it's Jakelham talking, not Garmast."

"Unless Garmast called him and asked him to meet up so he could inform him about you two," Tinnias replied.

"Look," I cut in. "We could argue this back and forth all day but the truth is, we don't know why they met, and we won't unless we hold on and continue trying to find out. Please Sir, let us hold fire a little longer huh?"

"Ren?" Tinnias asked. "What's your position buddy?"

"I agree with Sam. I think we should stay until we know more."

"Okay, then it's your decision. You're the ones in the field so you call the shots. I must have your promise though, that you'll call for help the moment anything proves you're cover has been blown okay?"

"You have it Sir," Ren said.

"Sure thing Boss," I added.

"Okay. Now I can also tell you that we've exhumed Symeal Gloak's body and our top guys are examining him as we speak. We're also going to get exhumation orders on the other six victims and re-examine them. I'll let you know what they find as soon as I know."

"Thanks."

"Another piece of news that might just be useful to you guys is that I showed the pictures of those dogs to some of our researchers and they scanned the galactic web for hours trying to find out what they are. Apparently, they're called Hymilonts and they're native to a planet called Asmeria 3. They're covered in scales; that's why they look shiny and you need a powerful weapon to bring them down. Those scales are very hard, like armour plated kind of hard."

"Damn," I said. "That means a dart won't be any good either."

"Now hold up Sam," Tinnias said. "There are a few areas of their bodies that don't have the scales, so if you need to use a dart, you're gonna have to know where to aim. Their heads don't have the scales but their skulls are thick so that won't do but you could dart them through the eyeballs and the sedative will go right to the brain real quickly from there. Also, the inner surface of the ears is just skin, as is inside the mouth, a strip along the belly, and the area around the genitals."

"So if we've missed their eyes and ears and it's chased us down and is sitting on top of us, go for its balls," Ren said and I sniggered.

"You never know," Tinnias laughed, "that information could save your life."

"We'll remember Boss," I replied.

"Take care guys and keep in touch regularly okay?"

The next few days passed without incident. I kept the apartment clean and cooked dinner and Ren joked about me being the perfect homemaker, but the truth was I was bored and even housework was something to do to occupy my mind. We worked out, went for a run each evening, and watched awful movies on Bygora Vandos' only vidicom movie channel. After three days I had cabin fever so we went out and had a few beers and a couple of women. We called into Donal's store, he kitted us out with heavy-duty darts and strong sedative, and we told him what Tinnias told us about the Hymilonts. We kept in regular touch with Marlo in the hope that he would have some news for us from his surveillance of the R and D personnel but so far, all was quiet.

"I'm bored Ren," I said on the fourth day. "I don't know how I'm going to stick this for too much longer. I have all next week off too, what the fuck will I do with my time?"

"Listen buddy," he said with a snigger. "I've noticed you getting more restless by the day so I booked a couple of days off to coincide with my normal day off. That gives me three days off, so why don't you fly us out to Halimantera for a weekend in the country? We can go hunting."

"Hunting?" I said. "You mean we have to catch our own dinner?"

"Hell no," he laughed. "Not that kind of hunting. Out in Halimantera they have a Warrior Games station."

"Warrior Games? What the fuck are they?"

"Joss, where have you been all your life?" he laughed. "It's the most fun you'll have in years, trust me. It's just what you need to de-stress. Now, I'll write a list of all the supplies we'll need and you go shopping tomorrow. We'll camp out in your ship. We can leave right after the next shuttle landing, which is your last day on night shift and have three days away from here okay?"

"Well okay," I nodded.

"Trust me, you'll love it. A change of scene will do us both good. Being on my own here I haven't bothered with too much social life so it's just what we need."

The next day I visited Donal in his store and asked about the Consoria camera. He handed me a small package with a triumphant smile.

"You got one?" I said.

"Take a look," he grinned.

I opened the package to find a brand new Consoria P30 surveillance camera still in its wrapper. "Wow, you got a P30? And it looks brand new. You're amazing buddy, I hope your ass isn't too sore."

"Like I told you Joss," he laughed, "there are more folks around here than you know who want to know what's going on up there beyond that fence. Some of them can't say so publicly but they're more than willing to help if they can do so without risking their balls or their families."

"This is awesome," I grinned. "This is gonna give us a real good view of what's going on underground up there. Thank you, I mean it."

"You're welcome. Now, have a drink with me."

Ren was delighted when I showed him the P30 and promised to vidicom the whole event.

"This will transmit to a receiver in my vidicom camera," I told him, "so you gotta use mine, not yours okay?" He nodded as I showed him the enhancement I'd had done to my camera and how to operate it.

"Don't worry Joss, we'll get the whole thing and the moment you get back, you'll see it."

The following night, I made my way along my allotted patch, which was once again the North Western sector of the fence, from marker posts seven to eleven and dropped the Consoria into the grass right at the edge of the depression in the ground. After carefully treading it down below the level of the grass, I pretended to need to re-tie my bootlaces and took the opportunity to make sure the device was well hidden by the grass. My partner did not notice anything out of the ordinary and we continued on our way. When I got back to the apartment the next morning I switched on my vidicom camera and tested it out. I was delighted to get a fabulous view of blue sky and fluffy clouds and I even saw one of the security guards strolling past scratching his balls and spitting into the grass.

Ren and I worked out for an hour and then went for a run before eating dinner. While he showered I called Tinnias and gave him the good news about the Consoria. He was pleased and made me promise to send him a copy.

"That's fantastic Sam," he said. "I want a copy of that, even if there doesn't appear to be much to see, let me have it anyway."

"I will Boss."

"I have some news for you too," he said. "We have the report on Symeal Gloak's body and we think we know what killed him."

"Please tell me it wasn't a hover buggy crash," I said.

"It wasn't a hover buggy crash Sam," he replied and I sighed with relief. "It is very weird though. It seems as though he's been dead a lot longer than his official date of death."

"That's the same as that other victim," I replied. "The girl who apparently fell while climbing."

"Yeah. There was some stuff in his blood and his brain tissue too."

"Stuff?" I asked. "What kind of stuff?"

"It seems to be a derivative of Zanbedellium."

"A derivative? So Professor Tamlik was right."

"It would seem so," Tinnias replied. "It's not the raw stuff though. It's been put through some process that refines it somehow and minute particles of it, small enough to get through individual cell membranes, were in his brain. In fact his brain was riddled with it."

"So what the fuck are they doing with it?" I said, knowing Tinnias didn't have the answer.

"We haven't the faintest idea," he replied, "but I can tell you that all those stories you've heard about the effects of the stuff are not exaggerated. Our guys said that anyone with that level of refined Zanbedellium in their system would probably be exhibiting really strange behaviour."

"Like what kind of strange?"

"Well it's hard to tell unless we had a live victim, but our guys told me that every part of the brain was affected. Just about every brain function we know about would be affected and all of the senses would be giving off false signals so the victim would see, hear, feel and even probably believe stuff that wasn't true. The stuff also affects the brain's ability to control the body's movements, so their walking would be weird."

"Hence the shuffling we heard," I said.

"Yeah. Apparently the victim's sleep would be disrupted and our guys think that maybe they wouldn't be sleeping at all and after prolonged absence of dream sleep, they'd be hallucinating anyway, so this stuff would just make that worse. Eventually the brain just stops functioning altogether."

"Holy fuck," I hissed. "How long does all this take?"

"Well we know that the female victim, the one they said fell whilst climbing, began working at Calmarin five months before they said she died. There's no way of knowing when her exposure began though. It could've been right from day one or a few days before she died. We can't know that at the moment."

"My god, what are those assholes doing up there?"

"We think they're either mining it and refining it on site, or they're shipping out the raw stuff and refining it elsewhere. Those shuttles are either shipping out the raw product or the refined stuff."

"But what the fuck do they want to do with it?" I said. "Turn the whole galaxy into shuffling half dead shells?"

"I certainly hope not," Tinnias replied. "But we have to accept that it's a possibility. If that is their intention, then I fear for countless lives, my own included."

"Can't you get hold of some and find out more about it?" I asked.

"Oh we're trying that too Sam," he said. "But it's so rare we're having a hard time tracking down any known samples. We have a couple of leads though. I'll keep you updated."

"Okay, thanks Boss."

"You and Ren take care of yourselves you hear?"

"We will."

The next day was shuttle day and while Ren was at work, I called Marlo and asked if there was any updates on the surveillance. There wasn't, but he was also able to assure me that Palko had not done anything suspicious, which was a huge relief, as I couldn't think of a way to exclude him from the proceedings without him realising something was up. He promised all surveillance would continue for as long as necessary and would get in touch if anything came up. We arranged for the three boys to arrive at our apartment at nine so we could all travel to Donal's together and I would leave for work at a quarter to one from Donal's apartment.

Ren and I worked out and went for a run before showering and then having dinner. As we ran through the parkland that nestled between our tower block and the neighbouring ones, I thought back over my years as a freelancer and how often I had faced death. I have lost count of how many times I could have died but this job was the first time I was so acutely aware of how many more things there are that are far worse than death. I looked at Ren and realised that for the first time in my life, I had a best friend who not only got along with me but also understood my job first hand. Not only was he a fun guy to be around but I could talk to him about my job, discuss tactics with him without having to hold back and without him being baggage. I remembered how he walked beside me as we left the tunnels just days ago, how he seemed to know I needed support at that moment and how sincerely he wished to give it. Then I realised that if anything happened to him on this job, I would be sad to lose him and I knew without doubt that he would be sad to lose me too.

I stopped running. "Ren, buddy?"

"Yeah Joss, what's up?"

"If this job doesn't pan out the way we want, y'know? If something goes wrong. I can't become one of those things, I just can't. Promise me you'll, umm," I hesitated.

"I promise," he replied immediately. "And please do the same for me huh?"

"I promise," I nodded. "I umm."

"What?" he asked.

"I just umm. This job is dangerous, perhaps the most dangerous of my career so far and there's a real possibility that one or both of us might not come through this. I just don't umm."

"What's up Joss?"

"Well I just. I don't want to lose another friend without saying thanks, for being a friend. This job doesn't really allow time for real friends."

"I know," he nodded, the beginnings of a smile on his lips.

"I never really had a best buddy before and I can't lose another person without making sure you know I appreciate you. That's what I wanted to say, just in case, well you know."

"Thank you," he whispered. "Can I tell you a secret Joss?"

"Sure."

"When I got the call that they were sending me a partner for this job, I raised hell about it."

"You did?"

"Yeah," he sniggered. "I was really annoyed that they were making me babysit another freelancer who'd either just get in the way or bulldoze his way through my carefully laid plans and if he didn't fuck everything up he'd do very little and take all the glory."

"Tinnias never told me that," I grinned.

"Well, for what it's worth Joss," he said. "I'm real glad you're here with me on this."

"Thanks."

"Now come on, let's get back and eat."

The five of us arrived at Donal's apartment shortly before ten. He made drinks while I set up my vidicom camera and reminded Ren how to make sure the additional enhancement recorded everything the Consoria would be transmitting. Once we were sitting down I updated everyone on the details Tinnias had given me. When I finished, the room was silent as everyone tried to digest what they had heard.

"Shit," Donal replied and ran a hand through his thinning hair. "Holy fucking shit." This was the first time I'd heard him curse and I knew he was scared. "I suddenly feel very old and frail," he whispered.

"I'm suddenly scared that I won't have a chance to get old and frail," Palko said, his voice shaking ever so slightly.

"I know buddy," Ren said. "We're all scared and it's okay. Being scared means we care about our lives and that's a good thing. Never wish to be unafraid, not ever. That would mean you'd lost your love for life."

"Well this scares me more than I've ever been scared in my whole life," Doniss said. "But it also makes me more determined that I'm gonna fight with everything I have to stop them doing whatever they're doing.

This is too serious not to fight for and I would rather die fighting it than end up one of those things."

"Here here," I replied. "We're all in this together okay? No one is fighting alone, remember that, all of you."

"Thank you guys," Marlo said and everyone looked at him. "Ren and Joss, you're not from Deligon but you're here helping us fight this awful shit and you might not get out of it with your lives or your minds intact. I appreciate that and I want you to know it." He blushed as we all looked at him.

"Thank you buddy," I replied.

"Thanks Marlo," Ren smiled and nodded.

"Now I have to get to work guys," I said as I stood and reached for my jacket. "I'll be back shortly after eight in the morning so I'll try not to wake you up."

"Here's a spare key Joss," Donal said. "Let yourself in and find a spare place to crash. Help yourself to anything you need okay?"

"Thanks. See you all in the morning guys."

I found the security headquarters building packed with guys all laughing and talking and fooling around. Music was playing and in the centre of the room a large table was laden with food and fruit juice.

"Someone's birthday?" I asked.

"Hey Joss," Hitch smiled. "It's dog night tonight so we get to party."

"Dog night?" I enquired, trying to seem ignorant.

"The R and D security guys are out tonight exercising their dogs so we have to spend the night cooped up in here and entertain ourselves."

"Oh," I tried to look bemused, "okay. Dogs? They have dogs here?"

"Yeah," Pendle said. "You know what they are? You've seen em?"

"Yeah," I nodded. "I went to Earth once to visit a military buddy of mine and he had one. Real nice creature it was too, I was kind of tempted to buy one for myself and take it home to Sigma."

"Well these ones ain't nice," Dancel replied. "They ain't nice at all. That's why we have to stay inside here while they're out getting exercise. If one of them got you, you'd be history."

"My Earth buddy told me some folks train them and use them for security and the Earth military and security forces use them a lot for guard duty and crowd control."

"They certainly look the part," he nodded.

"I wonder why only the R and D guys have them," I said. "You'd think that we'd have them. After all it's us that patrols the fence and deals with trespassers. Those guys never see the light of day so what do they want dogs for? What do they need to guard?"

"Twenty seven," the entire room yelled and everyone laughed. I frowned and Pendle came and clapped a hand on my shoulder.

"Congratulations Joss. You're the twenty seventh person to ask that question. Here," he grinned as he handed me a marker pen, "see that board up there above the roster? The one with all those crosses on it? Go make your mark buddy."

Everyone applauded as I made a cross on the board. I bowed low and grinned.

The night passed slowly but it was fun with the guys and the conversation was all about the mysterious R and D security guys and what really went on behind that locked door. The theories were many and varied and ranged from secret weapons manufacturing to a new and highly secret Transmortal Army installation.

"Transmortal Army?" I laughed out loud. "Come on, that's the craziest thing I've ever heard. They're extinct now, that Lilean guy sorted that problem out."

"Maybe not so crazy," Stimlik replied. "They could've found a live one and brought him here to do experiments on him. Find out how they did their shit so they can do it too huh?"

"Hey guys," Hopple cut in, "it could be a massive inter galactic whorehouse they're setting up down there."

"Now that would explain the dogs," Pendle said and everyone roared with laughter.

And so it continued, hour after hour through the night and although I had a laugh, I would much rather have been with Ren and the guys up in Donal's apartment watching the feed from the Consoria P30. I wondered what they were seeing and looked forward to seeing it too when I got off shift. Looking around at my colleagues, I decided they were all nice people. Once again, I hoped I was going to be able to bring this situation to a satisfactory conclusion for everyone and I hoped that none of them would lose their livelihoods, or their lives, in the process. Everyone seemed to share my curiosity about Calmarin and I wondered how many of them I might be able to rely on when things started to get difficult, as I knew they were going to, in the not too distant future. One thing was certain; they would all fight for their families and their survival, so I would have to make sure that they knew the only way to do that would be to fight alongside me. I sighed as I realised the enormity of the task ahead. Not only was I to uncover what was really going on at the station, but I knew it would be in everyone's interest to get as many people on my side as possible. Although I have never suffered from problems with self-esteem, I have never regarded myself as a leader of men. Ninety-nine percent of the time, I work alone, but here I was, knowing I had to inspire solidarity and a willingness to take risks, in men who just wanted to earn enough money to keep their families and take a holiday now and then. There were many lives depending upon my decisions and actions and for a moment, I wished I were far away from Deligon 2.

"You still awake Joss?"

The voice made me jump. I turned to see Hitch looking at me. "Oh hi buddy. Sorry, I was miles away."

"Y'know all this silly talk about what's going on here has got me thinking."

"It has? What about?"

"About you."

"Me?" This caught me unawares. "Why me?"

"Because I remembered another umm, silly conversation we had a while back. I remembered when you umm, joked with me about whether I'd be willing to put myself out if something happened here. Remember that joke Joss?" His gaze held my eyes as he spoke and I understood perfectly.

"Yeah, I remember."

"Well I've been thinking about it. About that silly conversation and your joke and I reckon that with everything that's happened to me and my family over the past few years, I'd be more than happy to take a more active role in finding out what's going on here."

"You would?" I replied, both shocked and delighted at the same time.

"Yeah, I would. But of course we both know it was just two guys joking around. Don't we?"

"Of course," I nodded, still holding his gaze. "Just a joke."

I crept into Donal's apartment as quietly as I could and found Ren asleep on the sofa, Doniss and Palko snoring in chairs. Marlo was nowhere to be seen. On tiptoe, I went to the bathroom to take a pee and have a wash before heading to the kitchen to make a hot drink. A cushion and blanket were stacked neatly on the floor, so I commandeered them and sat down with my drink. I heard a noise to my left and looked up to find Ren stirring. He opened his eyes and yawned, stretched and looked around.

"Sorry buddy," I whispered. "I tried to be quiet."

"Hey Joss," he yawned again. "That's okay, I need to pee anyway." He got up and went to the bathroom. I was dying to ask about the night's filming but I was aware that they'd all probably not got to sleep before five, so I held back as much as I could.

"How did the night go?" I asked when he returned.

"I can't wait for you to see the film Joss," he replied as he sat down and looked at me. He ran a hand through his hair and sighed. "That camera is awesome. We saw what was happening very clearly."

"That's fantastic," I replied. "I can't wait to see it."

"Sleep Joss," he said and yawned. "You're gonna need a fresh mind when you see it, and remember we're off to Halimantera today."

"Okay," I nodded and realised I was really tired.

"Joss? Hey Joss, wake up buddy. It's half past one. Time for some lunch."

"Huh?" I groaned as I forced my eyelids open to find Marlo shaking my shoulder. "Oh hey buddy, you're back."

"Back?" he frowned. "I never left."

"Oh," I replied as I sat up and yawned. "I couldn't see you around here when I got in this morning."

"We drew lots for Donal's spare bedroom and I won," he grinned. "Ren's gone shopping for something for lunch so you've time to shower. He brought a change of clothes for you, here in the bag."

"Thanks." I stood and stretched. My back was stiff from sleeping on the floor but I felt reasonably rested despite it. I heard murmuring from the kitchen and wandered through to find Donal, Palko and Doniss whispering to each other.

"Hey Joss," Donal smiled. "Hope you slept okay on the floor. We didn't want to wake you so we came in here to talk. Go take a shower and then you can see what we saw last night."

"Okay," I yawned again. "Was the Consoria worth the effort?"

"You have no idea Joss," Doniss said. "Just wait till you see the film. It's gonna blow your socks off."

"That's good news," I replied and headed to the bathroom. The water was hot and revived my aching back. I was looking forward to working out with Ren later and getting the last knots out of my muscles. I did not linger too long in the shower, despite it being wonderfully soothing; I wanted to see that film.

We skimmed the film through the bits we had seen from Donal's apartment windows and concentrated on the times the shuttles went down underground, thereby reducing the time spent watching. Two hours later, I ran both hands through my hair, and sighed. What we had witnessed not only confirmed that something very secret was going on at Calmarin Research Station, but it also confirmed our worst fears and each one of us sat in silence as we contemplated the ramifications of what we had just seen. For several minutes, I wondered if I was the man to deal with this and I knew Ren was thinking the same. Then I realised that Donal and the boys were looking to us to sort it out for them and despite the fact they wanted to help fight for their world, it was us they trusted to ultimately save Deligon from this terrible nightmare.

CHAPTER ELEVEN

For a moment, all we could see was the star filled night sky and the dark forest that loomed in the background. A faint golden glow of the security guards' flares played on the dark grass and I knew they were lined up behind the camera, marking out a landing strip. After a minute or so, I noticed movement against the dark sky, accompanied by a faint hum and a black shape grew and as it got nearer, it became obvious that it was a shuttlecraft coming into land. All four flew across the film and disappeared out of the range of the Consoria hidden in the grass. Ren moved the film forward a few minutes. One of the shuttles came into view and landed right in front of the camera and the hum of its engine stopped. Then a loud metallic knock followed by the sound of a gear mechanism clicking into place and the camera began to vibrate slightly. The vibrating continued for a couple of minutes accompanied by the metallic grinding noise that told me the elevator was descending. An intermittent squeak told me something needed oiling and the patch of star filled sky gradually got smaller until it was too small to see.

Bright light suddenly exploded as the elevator reached its destination and we saw the white walls of what looked like some sort of cargo bay, a domed roof and the dark circle of the elevator shaft above. I heard the familiar sound of a shuttle hatch lowering and was annoyed that I had positioned the Consoria so it only saw the nose of the shuttle. I wished I could see the hatch area and resolved to move the camera to a new position the next time my shift pattern took me to the North Western sector. A man leapt out of the shuttle and walked out of sight, a digital console in his hands. A few seconds later, he reappeared with two others and stood by the shuttle as if waiting for something. Faint murmurings told us they were talking, but the surrounding noises, hums, metallic knocks and the general noise one hears in a cargo bay, prevented us from hearing their conversation. We heard the sound of an engine; probably a hover cart or buggy, and the three men looked round and smiled. The rear portion of a large hover cart came into view and we clearly saw the loading platform filled with several large drums, all painted with the Heibat Power and Energy logo. They were fitted with what I recognised as security jackets so I knew right away that whatever those drums contained, it was highly toxic.

"Security jackets," I murmured.

"Huh?" Palko asked.

"Those drums have security jackets," I explained as I continued watching the men load them into the shuttle. "That means the contents is either highly toxic or flammable or both. It also means that if there's a spill on board, they can jettison them and they'll automatically explode after twenty seconds of zero gravity without causing problems by landing on a planet and killing everything."

"Oh, okay."

I counted a dozen drums in all before the hover cart disappeared; replaced three minutes later by another and the whole process began again. All the drums looked identical to me and as the process repeated the third time, I took the opportunity to concentrate on what else I could see in the shot. In the far background, hover carts manoeuvred crates and empty drums into what was obviously a storage area. A couple of security guys with their fearsome Hymilont companions wandered across the shot, then a door opened, and we got the shock of our lives. A security guard and his Hymilont stepped out and stood to the side, the creature snarling and dripping drool to the floor. Then a line of people emerged and began shuffling forwards. Their heads bowed slightly, they slowly shuffled along in single file, looking as if each step was painful. Their one-piece garments were a dull grey and their faces equally so. Most of them showed signs of losing their hair but not in the way people normally do. Their hair loss was patchy and uneven, some were obviously women, and they were equally balding. Suddenly the guard shouted at them to stop and they obeyed without question. From the right, a man in a white lab coat appeared with a box, which he placed on the floor and slit open with a knife. He lifted out several trays of auto injectors and as the line of people stepped forward one by one, he gave each one an injection, after which they turned tail and shuffled back through the same door from which they had appeared.

"I wonder what they're injecting them with?" Donal said.

"Hmm," I responded. "I intend to find out as soon as I'm able."

Once again, I heard the familiar sound of a shuttle hatch closing and then the elevator started its climb back to the surface, before the whole procedure started over with the second shuttle. The second shuttle went down and was loaded with the same drums as the first one had been, but this time there was nothing of special interest in the background. As the third shuttle was loaded, luck smiled upon me as I saw someone stand right next to the camera. Whoever the man was wore a white lab coat and black pants; we could only see the very edge of his right shoulder, arm and leg down to mid-thigh level so I would never be able to recognise him again.

The door from which the shuffling, grey clad people had emerged opened once again and another line of equally grey people shuffled out. This lot looked worse than the previous group; all were completely bald and many had obvious patches and sores on their heads. Their eyes were ringed with black and their skin, a lifeless grey. They hunched forward much more than the previous ones had done and their shuffling was slower, more laboured. As with the previous ones, they each received an injection, but these auto injectors were different.

"That's a different injection these ones are getting," I said.

"How the fuck do you know that?" Doniss said.

"The auto injectors are different," Ren answered for me and I nodded.

"Are they? I didn't notice that."

"Yeah," Ren replied. "These ones have a pointy top, whereas the last ones had a flat top."

"I wonder why they'd give them a different injection," Donal said.

"Probably because they need something different because of the state of them." I glanced at Donal and saw him frowning at me. "Look at them; they look three quarters dead. The others weren't so bad so they're probably giving them something stronger or different to try to keep them alive longer, to get the most work out of them that they can I guess."

Donal nodded slowly. "Shit. Those poor people. We have to help them guys, we have to. What they must be suffering down there I'd hate to even guess. We can't let this kind of treatment continue for fuck's sake."

"We will buddy," I replied with as much conviction as I could, "we will." I was about to say something else when a clear voice made me shut up and listen. The guy by the camera obviously had a buddy with him.

"How long will these last?"

"No more than three or four days before their usefulness is gone."

"Is there room in storage?"

"Yeah, the freezer is only half full. We'll last another three weeks without a problem."

"Good. How's production going?"

"I reckon we're running at optimum now."

"What's your estimate of how long the seam will produce?"

"From what we can see, I'd guess a couple of years at our current production rate."

"Workforce turnover is a problem though. What are your guys doing about that?"

"We're building more housing for the workforce so we can double our intake and work them one day on, one day off. That will double their working life and halve our clean up problem."

"So you haven't come up with anything to block the stuff yet?"

"Not yet but we have been able to design a special suit that slows down penetration by almost half."

"What about slowly desensitising them by gradual immersion?"

"You mean like a sort of vaccine? Allow the body to build its own immunity?"

"Yeah."

"The only way that would work would be with a solution equivalent to one drop per twenty gallons of water, given no more than monthly and we estimate it would take five years for the average humanoid immune system to build up enough of a defence to make total daily immersion safe. It's just not a viable prospect, seeing as how we expect to be gone from here in a couple of years."

"Okay, then the best way is to double the workforce and maybe triple it as soon as you're able to. Disposal is becoming a chore."

"Yeah, we're hopeful we can double the workforce within the next six months and then we could probably triple it within another six, so long as recruitment can keep pace."

"It will, don't worry about that. There are innumerable planets out there and all have drop outs, low life's and bums just waiting for an opportunity to make their fortune and get away from the home worlds that outcasted them."

"Good."

The rest of this conversation was lost as the elevator started to rise again and I looked around at my companions, eyes wide and sighed with shock.

"Yeah," Ren nodded. "I thought that would interest you."

"Shit," I responded and ran both hands through my hair while we waited for the final shuttle to descend. The fourth shuttle descended and offered us nothing more. The two guys had obviously finished their conversation or taken it elsewhere and we saw no more shuffling grey people.

"This is big Joss," Donal said as I packed away the camera. "This is some serious shit that's going down over there. You gotta be careful guys. If you start digging around and they find you or your reason for being here, you're both as good as dead."

"Or worse," Marlo said. "Much worse."

"Well at least we know a little more about what's happening down there," I replied. "They're obviously mining Zanbedellium and taking it off world somewhere. We know they're using untraceable folks from other worlds, probably to do the actual digging, and we also know the way it affects them."

"We know they don't live long," Doniss said, "and that when they die, they take em away from Deligon for disposal."

"And we know they give them injections," Palko added, "which are probably an effort to make them live longer or stave off the worst of the effects a bit longer or something."

"I wonder what they meant when they said immersion," I thought aloud.

"What?" Ren asked.

"Those two guys. They kept saying about immersion. Any idea what that could mean?"

"None, sorry."

"Listen Joss, Ren," Donal said suddenly. "Isn't this film enough to get the place shut down? You've got the evidence right here. There's no need to put yourselves at further risk by going in there."

"And you now know what killed those seven victims," Marlo said. "That proves it's Zanbedellium they're bringing up and with this film, you can sort it all out without any more risk."

I paced the room and battled with my emotions. My overriding feeling was anger at what I had seen and I felt desperately sorry for those people. Down and outs they may be but no one deserves to be treated in such a way. I like to think of myself as self-aware and knew without any doubt that I wanted to not only get evidence of what was going on and nail those involved, but I wanted to stop it and help those people. With a sigh, I looked up and saw Ren looking into my eyes and I knew that he knew what I was feeling.

"That's not enough though is it Joss," he said quietly.

"No," I shook my head and held his gaze. "I'm sorry buddy but I have to help those people. I'd never live with myself if I walked away now."

"I understand," he smiled and nodded. "And I'm with you all the way. We're in this together remember? I'd get no more comfort from leaving them than you would."

"Thanks," I sighed.

The next three weeks were going to be a little flat for us, until Donal could secure the use of the fluid drill from his colleague. I hoped that it would allow us to see through the wall in the abandoned transport tunnel. After saying our goodbyes, Ren and I headed back to our apartment to collect our bags and headed off to Halimantera for our break away from the city. I really felt the need for a couple of days away from this job, just to relax and collect my thoughts and formulate some sort of structured plan of action. It was a four-hour flight and dusk was beginning to fall as we landed in the most beautiful rolling countryside I had seen in years.

A range of mountains loomed in the distance, rolling hills enclosed us on both sides and the campground nestled in the floor of the valley. I set my ship down and unloaded and within an hour, we were enjoying a meal. The air was fresh and the views, breathtaking and we quickly relaxed. A swiftly flowing river rushed along to our right and the narrow mouth leading to a neighbouring valley curved away in the far distance ahead. The sky darkened and filled with stars and night birds serenaded us as we worked out by the light of our campfire. Ren carved a couple of branches into crude wooden daggers and gave them to me.

"Time to arm yourself now Joss," he grinned. "You're really getting the hang of the movements now so I'm going to up the pace a little. It's time to learn to fight."

For a further hour, he taught me to use the skills I had learned in a combat situation rather than just as a form of exercise, as we had so far done and I found the movements made sense to me now that I had an opponent. He taught me how to block, attack and go for the kill shot in an effective but stylish way and I loved it. It was not only getting me fit but it allowed me to shed all the stress this job was piling on me.

"That's great Joss," he encouraged. "You'll need all these skills tomorrow when I take you hunting."

"Hunting?" I asked. "What is this hunting you keep on about?"

"You'll see," he grinned. "Now thrust, lower the knee a bit more, that's it."

I don't really know what I was expecting but it certainly wasn't anything like what I experienced when Ren took me to the Halimantera Warrior Games Station the next afternoon. A large wooden building stood a couple of miles further down the valley, surrounded by trees. Ren showed me in and registered us both and gave me a badge with a number on it. We were then led into a large separate room where a team of men helped all the participants to put on special armour.

"The armour isn't for your protection Joss," Ren said after I commented on the thinness of the material. "It's for scoring your performance."

"Huh?" I frowned. "My performance?"

"All over the armour are sensors and they register when your opponent gets a contact shot. Different areas of the body are worth different points and you lose life force in different amounts, depending upon where you get hit."

"My opponent?" My eyes were now wide with horror and he laughed.

"Relax buddy. You're going to be fighting with holographic opponents. You won't be harmed."

"Really?"

"Yeah. They're pretty realistic too, depending upon the power of the unit they're using to generate them, but they can't actually harm you. If they make contact with you, the sensors in your armour go off and your available life force is altered accordingly. Likewise if you get a shot into them, theirs goes down. Both you and your opponent score points and the one either still alive or with the most points at the end of five minutes, wins."

"That sounds awesome," I smiled. "Who will my opponent be?"

"Not who Joss, what." I was just about to ask him to explain when a man entered and called us over. "Okay now it's time to choose your opponent. We'll see what's on offer and I'll advise you okay?"

"Okay," I nodded.

"Okay let's see what we have," Ren said as he scanned the list. "Ahh here we are. This one is perfect for a first timer. My buddy here will take a Picanitch, level 1 and I'll have a Nasmurian, level 4."

"Nasmurian?" the guy said as his eyebrows went up. "Wow, you must be good, or stupid."

"Oh he's good," I answered immediately.

Ren saw my angry look and grinned. "It's okay Joss, there's a very good reason why he would assume I'm stupid."

"There is?"

"Nasmurian Warriors are probably the most fearsome fighters known," the guy grinned and Ren nodded. "And as your buddy here has asked for a level four warrior, he's either extremely skilled or extremely stupid. We've only ever had three who won against such an opponent in all the years I've been here, and all of them Damiklonians."

"How many levels are there?" I asked.

"Five is the highest skill level," he replied.

"And would I be right in saying that the thing you got me down for is little scarier than my cleaning lady?"

"A little," Ren said and laughed out loud.

We had a couple of hours to kill before our turn so we went out the back to a warm up area and sparred. Ren pushed me as hard as he dared and had me on my back a couple of times, but I made him stumble once and within a few minutes we'd drawn a crowd of onlookers, all keen to see a Damiklonian at work. I was proud to be sparring with him and, knowing others were watching inspired me to try harder. By the time we stopped for a breather, I was exhausted.

When my turn finally came, Ren clapped me on the shoulder and grinned. "Remember Joss, concentrate and watch him. Don't be fooled by his appearance and take the first opportunity for a kill shot. You've learned enough to do this easily and you might even get to despatch a level two as well. You're good enough."

I entered the arena to loud applause. A guard checked my armour and fitted the Damiklonian dagger Ren had given me with a holographic emitter so that the machine would correctly register every shot, and stepped aside for me to enter the fighting area. The circular fighting area was roughly twenty feet across. A large machine stood just outside and it was from here that my opponent would appear as a life size hologram. The guard instructed me to stand in the waiting zone and ready myself. I hefted the dagger and crouched, as I had done while sparring with Ren, and waited. An alarm sounded and this freaky little thing leapt out and ran at me. He was no more than four feet high and looked like a cross between a standard humanoid and some domestic creature reared for its meat. In his left hand was a dagger with a flat wide blade, like a chopper, and I had just seconds to react. I leapt aside gracelessly and turned to find him already on his way back; jeez, this little thing could move fast. This time I turned to one side as he flew past me and managed to avoid looking like a bumbling idiot as I readied myself for another pass. With my dagger in my right hand, I waited for him to come abreast of me and effortlessly slid it through the target in the centre of his chest. An alarm sounded and he fell to the floor and disappeared into thin air. The crowd yelled and applauded and I grinned. That was easy and I was a little insulted that I was deemed only worthy of him.

"Level two," boomed through the speakers and the crowd cheered again as I approached the waiting zone and readied myself. The alarm sounded and a much bigger version of the previous little guy appeared but did not run at me right away. He approached with caution and crouched, his identical wide chopper held out in front. We circled and I wondered what he was going to do. I was also wondering whether I should take the initiative first, so I feigned a lunge at him and watched his reaction. He brought the chopper up and across in a move that could easily take my arm off at the elbow. I lunged again but this time used one of the moves Ren had taught me and with the use of a fairly graceful twist, coupled with a carefully aimed foot, disarmed him. I followed this up with another clean kill shot to the chest and watched as he fell and vanished.

Ren went nuts when I got back to him and embraced me like a brother. "Awesome job Joss, I'm proud of you buddy."

"That was the best fun I've had in years. Did it look good?" I asked and he nodded.

"It looked fantastic. You're gonna be a credit to the Damiklonian Martial Art. Now I gotta go, it's my turn."

Ren's performance was like nothing I had ever seen before, nor ever will again. I had watched him for the past three weeks as we had worked out but I had never seen him use all his speed and skill before, and I was stunned and proud that someone this skilled was teaching me. His opponent was the most fearsome thing I had ever seen and I could not imagine ever being skilled enough to meet one of those, even in holographic form. He was easily eight feet tall, very broad across and muscular, and obviously very strong and powerful. His head and face were quite alien to me, although I hate to use that word, as it is a little insulting. Everyone is an alien to someone, but this Nasmurian was the first sentient humanoid that I would call alien. He had a slightly reptilian appearance to his face but again, like everything else about him, it was not overt. Instead of hair, he had long tendrils as thick as my finger that hung down almost to his waist; there must have been a couple of dozen of them in total. He only had three fingers and an opposing thumb on each hand, which looked weird alongside Ren's six slightly webbed fingers that clung to his large, multi-bladed Damiklonian Dagger. The Nasmurian carried a single dagger about ten inches long with a blade unlike anything I had seen. Instead of a single flat blade, it had six vertical blades joined at their tips, forming a star shape. Each of these six vertical blades sported four sharpened recurved barbs and I cringed as I thought of the damage such a weapon could do. I learned later that this weapon is a Nasmurian Filleting Dagger and it seemed a very fitting name to me.

Ren used all of his skills. He leapt, ducked, spun, kicked and turned as the huge Nasmurian kept up the most horrific onslaught and it was with just twenty seconds left on the clock that he finally got the kill shot. He dropped to his knees and heaved deep breaths, the sweat pouring off his body. The crowd erupted and I yelled along with them. He stood and accepted the applause before rejoining me and this time it was me that hugged him like a proud little brother.

"My god Ren that was awesome," I grinned. "I'm speechless buddy. You're amazing."

"Thanks," he said, his grin the equal of my own. "That was hard work Joss. Now you can see what you're aiming for huh? We'll have you in there with the Nasmurians before you know it."

"I sincerely doubt that buddy," I laughed. "That kind of skill takes years to perfect."

"And we have those years of friendship ahead in which to achieve it, don't we?" he asked.

"We sure do," I nodded, knowing without a doubt that this guy was gonna be a friend for life. I'd never had a male best buddy before and it felt good.

The following day saw me gain my level three with the Picanitch and Ren once again successfully downed a level four Nasmurian. I got a digital chip with my scores and achievement on, so I could go to any Warrior Games Station anywhere in the galaxy and get an opponent fitted to my skill level. Ren had his own chip updated and we went back to camp laughing and proud. By the time we returned to Bygora Vandos we were relaxed, happy and bonded in the way only two men can understand. We both felt ready to take up the job again and made a vow to return when we next got the time. I was hooked on the Warrior Games and hoped one day to be able to emulate Ren and fight the Nasmurian. I knew that with his teaching and my own determination and discipline, I would get there.

The next three weeks slid by slowly and all of us were frustrated at our impotence to do anything proactive to end this situation. We checked in with Donal and the boys regularly and went to see the shuttles landing and everything was the same as the first time we had watched. The shuttles were loaded with the drums, the lines of grey people shuffled and got their injections and the security guards stood, stoic with their snarling Hymilonts by their sides. It was during this three-week period that Ren started gently pressuring me to tell him more about Merellia Gilden, the girl I had loved and lost twenty years before. I resisted of course, but he was skilled in the art of getting me to talk and soon I was confiding about her for the first time in my life. It was emotional but it was like unburdening myself and I knew it was healthy to get it out from wherever it was festering inside. Eventually I told him about the day I got a call from the man who had taken her and how he had held the phone out so I could hear her crying and screaming for me. He laughed at me when I swore revenge on him after he recorded himself raping her and played it to me over the Unicom. My heart stopped when I heard him shoot her seven times, then he told me where I would find her body and cut off the call. I raced around to the abandoned warehouse within twenty minutes and found her lying on a pile of rubbish, naked and bleeding. I stayed with her body for hours before calling Tinnias and my law enforcement colleagues, and finally I confided how I had never been able to allow myself to get emotionally attached to a woman since that day. Fishing amongst the various bits and pieces in the hold on my ship, I found the wedding chain I had made for us, when she accepted my proposal and showed it to Ren. On Sigma, when two people get married, they are wrapped in a chain during the ceremony. It is symbolic of joining for life and I had kept it in a locked box ever since. He embraced me when I broke down and cried for her for the first time since that day I found her, and he listened to my guilt trip without judging me.

"When someone we love dies on Damiklon," Ren said when I was composed enough to listen, "we make a list of all the qualities we loved about the person and we honour those qualities by actively encouraging them within ourselves. It is our way to honour them and their presence in our lives and it is a way to keep them alive within us. By keeping alive those qualities we loved so much in them, we feel we are keeping them alive in our hearts. What were those qualities within Merellia that drew you to her?"

"She had an innocence that was very attractive," I replied with a smile as I remembered. "She wasn't naive though, far from it. She just had this ability to give off an innocent energy that made me feel like I wanted to wrap her up in my arms. She could look at something ordinary, like the clouds in the sky and she'd see shapes in them, animals and stuff like that and she'd make up stories about these creatures and have us both laughing. She never lost that child-like ability to see wonder in everything, even though she was street wise and knew how rough the world could be. She was very affectionate too and would hug and touch me all the time, letting me know she wanted to feel me in her life. I never felt loved that way before and it was intoxicating."

"Then those are the qualities you should encourage within yourself," Ren said. "Remember the way she was and try to be the same way and you'll be keeping the best of her alive in your heart and letting go of the pain of her passing. Don't let her memory be a painful thing Joss, that isn't honouring her in the way deserving of someone who loved so completely."

I nodded. I understood his wisdom, even though I was too emotional to acknowledge it. He stayed with me as I let out the pain and listened to me go through all the guilt one final time and when I fell asleep on the sofa, he covered me with a blanket and sat alongside me until I awoke in the early hours, puffy eyed and headache pounding. I thanked him for being there for me and we man-hugged. I went to bed feeling emotionally drained but knowing I had passed something that had been blocking me for years and I had not even realised it was there until it was gone. Ren was being the best friend anyone could wish for, and I hoped we were to be friends for a long time. Little did I realise how much time we had for our friendship. If I had, I would have made more of an effort to repay his love and wisdom.

CHAPTER TWELVE

The interminable time of waiting finally dragged by and it was time to go and watch the arrival of the bigger shuttlecraft. My shift pattern had rotated again and I was due another week off, which Ren and I had agreed to use for another visit to Halimantera after he managed to get another three-day vacation by swapping days off with a colleague. We had kept in regular touch with Donnis and Marlo who kept assuring us that their surveillance of Palko had revealed nothing of concern. This pleased us both and I reckoned that whatever his father was up to, he was keeping it a secret. I kept up my workout regime and Ren said I was progressing well. Despite my belief that he was just being kind to my ego, he allowed me to start sparring with him after our daily workout and run. He bet me a hundred that I would easily achieve level four with the Picanitch at the Warrior Games Station and I hoped he was right.

This was my last night on night shift and once again, I had to wait it out with my buddies in the Security HQ while Ren and the guys watched things live, via the Consoria. I crept into the apartment to find everyone sitting up waiting for me. They all had grave expressions on their faces and I guessed that either something had gone wrong, or I wasn't going to like what I was to see.

"You have to see the film Joss," Ren said. "Sleep afterwards. This can't wait."

"Okay buddy," I nodded, concerned at his obvious distress.

These shuttlecraft were half as big again as the normal ones and the reason why became obvious as soon as the first descended. The hatch opened and after a stream of dirty looking new workers were off loaded at gunpoint, given an injection and led away out of range of the camera, we saw hover carts laden with what could only be bodies wrapped in silver bags being loaded. It was obvious to me that they were indeed getting their workforce from the down and outs of different worlds. Every one of them looked unkempt and down trodden in the way that only living by your wits and not knowing where or when your next meal was coming from could do. The cartload of bodies were loaded by several of the grey, shuffling workers who themselves looked as if they should have been inside those bags. Once they were loaded, the workers climbed into the shuttles and the hatches closed. I guessed that these workers had reached the end of their usefulness and were serving as labourers, after which they would probably be killed and disposed of alongside those they had helped to load. When all the shuttles had taken off and Calmarin returned to normal, we sat back and I noticed Ren wiping tears from his face.

"Hey buddy," I said gently. "We'll fix this y'know."

"I know," he nodded. "It's just, those poor people. How they're suffering and then to be treated like that at the end. They're nameless and faceless; untold thousands of society's unwanted, the humanoid trash that no one cares about. But even so, do they deserve such an end?"

"No they don't," I replied. "And we will get justice for them, I promise."

"Yeah," he nodded. "We will. I'm sorry guys, it's just I hate to see people being mistreated. They don't even let them keep their names. They call them by a number, how can I get my head around that."

"Don't ever apologise for caring Ren," Palko interrupted. "Not ever, you hear me? If more people did, then none of this shit would be happening."

"We may never be able to identify all of them and we may never know where they were taken, but we will get justice for them," I said.

"I feel very ashamed that this is happening on my world," Donal said. "I intend to do all I can to make sure everyone knows about it so that it never happens here again."

The three boys nodded in agreement as Donal got up and went to the kitchen to make drinks. We sat in silence for a while, each lost in our own thoughts and all our hearts bleeding for those grey, shuffling souls without names or identities and all of us determined to bring an end to it.

"I got a call from my colleague yesterday," Donal said. "I can have the drill for a couple of days in three days' time."

"That's fantastic," Palko said. "We'll get through that wall easily and finally get some more film as evidence."

"I'm picking it up sometime during that morning, so as soon as everyone can get around to the store, we can begin."

"Well I'm off all week so I'll fit in with everyone else," I said.

"I can be there anytime," Doniss said.

"I can be there any time after mid-day," Marlo added.

"I have to go visit my grandmother with my parents in the morning," Palko said. "Father has to work in the afternoon so I can be there from early afternoon."

"I get off work at four," Ren added, "so I can be there by four thirty."

"Okay then let's make it four thirty," Donal offered and we all nodded. "Three days from now, at my store. Bring warm clothes and something to eat. It's likely to take several hours and we'll probably have to finish it the next morning. Remember we only have the drill for two days."

"That's okay," Marlo said. "Once you've shown us how to use it, you and Ren can get some sleep and the rest of us will work through the night."

"And I'll be able to continue the next day with Joss while Ren goes to work and you boys get some sleep," Donal replied. "I've got some camping gear in the store so we can bunk down and sleep in relative comfort."

"When I go back to work after my week off, I'm going to mention to the supervisor about maybe transferring to R and D security," I said as I put down my cup. "Hopefully things will speed up from now on."

"We have to be aware that you might get turned down," Ren replied. "In which case we'll need as much film as we can get as it'll be our only evidence."

"We can blast our way in through the wall and storm the place," Doniss said. "We can have our members armed and ready within a day."

"Hell no," I almost yelled at him. "You boys aren't going anywhere near there. Not with that poisonous shit in there. You've seen what it does to people."

"But you'll need troops Joss," Marlo countered. "Especially if you don't get the transfer."

"We're not storming the place," I insisted. "I'll find a way to get in somehow and no one will know I'm there. I'm sure a couple of my work buddies will be only to keen to be involved once I tell them everything we've found out. They're experienced security guys and won't need me to babysit them. Trust me please, you promised guys."

"Okay," Doniss sighed. "But we're here if all else fails okay?"

"Okay, thanks," I nodded. "Now come on, Donal needs to get to bed and Ren and I are off to Halimantera for a couple of days."

"You going to the Warrior Games?" Palko grinned and I nodded.

"Yeah, you should see him in action. He's awesome," I grinned and nodded at Ren, who blushed.

"Well let's make a date guys," Palko said. "When this situation is over successfully, we'll all go together and have a day at the games huh?"

"Agreed," I nodded. "That'll be fun."

Our trip to Halimantera proved fruitful. I got my level four Picanitch and even had a go with a level five and would have won if I had ten seconds more life force left. Ren again beat a level four Nasmurian with ease and decided to have his first try with a level five. He died within a couple of minutes but was extremely happy to have the chance to get a feel for the highest-level opponent the Warrior Games has to offer. He received a standing ovation that lasted a whole minute, despite having lost the bout just under half way through and was grinning for hours afterwards.

When Ren came back to the apartment after his first day back at work, he told me the position for the R and D security guard was now available and posted on the main bulletin board. He suggested I apply right away, despite being on leave for a week, so I decided to call in the next day to see Kobey and apply. While he took a quick shower, I packed the food I had prepared during the day, and then we set off for Donal's store. The three boys were already there and Donal was showing them the fluid drill. I was impressed when I looked at it. It had several sizes of drill tips, the smallest of which was just a millimetre across and I decided that this was the best one to use once we got close to breaking through.

"We don't want to make too big a hole," I said. "They could see it and we'd be done for. We can use one of the bigger ones to start off but once we get close, I vote we go for the smallest hole possible. The HairCam will show us everything."

"I agree," Donal said as he carefully unpacked the HairCam. This was a fine wire as thin as a hair, designed to fit through the tiniest of holes and the minute camera that ran through it would give almost as good a display as the Consoria P30. "By the way, have you eaten Ren? You've only just got off work."

"Not yet but Joss has packed something. I'll be okay till we get there."

"You're gonna make a wonderful housewife one day Joss," Palko laughed and everyone grinned.

"Okay let's go shall we?" I snickered.

We spread the bags of gear between us as Donal locked up his hover car and we set off to walk through the forest. When we reached the turn off and walked past the derelict buildings, I noticed Ren appear at my side as we walked. I looked at the buildings and Merellia flooded into my mind once again, her laughter, the twinkle in her eyes, her smell and the way she would hold and touch me whenever she could. It was a few minutes before I realised that for the first time, the memories were good ones, and not once did I find myself thinking of the sight that met my eyes when I found her. I sent a thought out into the Deligon afternoon that I hoped she was at peace, that I was grateful for her love and that I had never stopped loving her.

We picked our way down the steps and began the trek through the dark tunnels and the uncomfortable hobble along the transport rail to the room with the wall that adjoined the Calmarin Research Station underground complex. Once ensconced within the room, Donal unpacked the Sobberlander and Palko listened against the wall so that the drilling could start once the guard had passed by. Donal used the time to unpack the fluid drill and showed us how it operated. He attached a medium drill bit and then clipped on the cone shaped guide to the front before dragging an old table across to the wall and climbing up.

"It would be best if we try to get through fairly high up the wall," he said. "It'll be less obvious and there'll be less likelihood of them seeing the camera. We don't know what their wall is made of but if it's a uniform surface, any slight difference will be immediately obvious."

"Good point buddy," I nodded. I watched as he placed the large end of the cone shaped guide against the wall and flipped a switch on the handle. The machine began to emit a very quiet hum and Doniss kept a watchful eye on the tank of fluid that sat atop the generator on the floor.

"Each tankful of fluid should last a couple of hours," Donal said, "since we're using a fairly small drill bit. We've enough fluid for sixteen continuous hours of drilling, which will take us through the night and when I take Ren to work in the morning, I'll call in to the store and get more. How about we do an hour each at the drill huh? It does make your arms ache after a while."

"Sure thing buddy," I nodded. "Who's up next?"

"I'll do the next hour," Ren said. "I'd like to pull my weight before having to sleep."

"Okay, then have something to eat first huh?" I replied as I handed him the cartons of food I'd prepared. "Here's your spice."

The drilling continued throughout the night, in twelve-minute blocks to allow the guard and his snarling Hymalont to pass by without hearing anything suspicious. I woke Ren and made him a hot drink over the small fire we had made out in the transport tunnel, then handed him a sandwich for breakfast.

"Sorry it's not much but it'll keep starvation at bay until lunch time," I said. "Did you sleep okay?"

"Not bad," he said as he stretched himself and winced, "apart from a stiff neck I guess I'll survive. Did you get any sleep?"

"Yeah I got a few hours. I did the last hour of drilling before waking you so I got four hours straight."

"How's it going?"

"Donal reckons we should be through by lunch time. I'll get a recording transmitter attached so we can see everything from my camera back at the apartment and we can all watch it in comfort. It'll be set up and running by the time you get home."

"That's great. Remember to call in and see Kobey about the job in R and D."

"I won't forget. I hope I get it. It would really help us out."

"In a way I hope you don't," he replied and looked me in the eyes.

"I know buddy and I agree on a personal level but those people in there, they need help. Even if we can't bring them back to health, at least we can stop it happening to anyone else. To do that I need to get in there."

"We'll need to be off in a few minutes Ren," Donal said as he came over to where we were sitting. "Did you sleep okay?"

"Yeah, not bad thanks. I'll just take a pee and then I'm ready to go."

"I'll escort you both back through the tunnels," Palko said. "We don't want you getting lost."

Once Donal and Ren had left, I got myself a drink and ate a sandwich before getting my head down for a couple of hours. In my dream, I saw Merellia; beautiful and smiling as she held out her arms to me. She was perfect and her body showed no signs of the damage I remember from the last time I saw her. She told me she loved me and was always with me and I woke up with tears on my cheeks.

"You okay Joss," Palko asked. "You were crying out in your sleep buddy. Nightmares?"

"Huh? Yeah I'm okay thanks," I replied. "I dreamed of someone I haven't seen in a long time."

"Can't have been a comfortable meeting," he remarked, "judging by the way you were calling out and tossing around."

"She was murdered," I said and found myself not worried about telling them about her. "It was my fault she died and I found her body."

"I'm sorry," he said. "Forgive my flippancy."

"No problem," I said. "I've kept it at the back of my mind for years but since I met Ren, he umm."

"He's encouraged you to face the demons of your past," Donal said and I nodded. "That's a Damiklonian for you Joss. They're empathic and with their naturally compassionate nature, when they form a bond with someone, the other person's pain becomes their pain. You can be assured that he feels your emotions almost as clearly as you do yourself and will always encourage you to deal with the feelings directly. He won't allow you to hide or run from emotional baggage. That's one of the things about having a Damiklonian friend so you're gonna have to get used to it."

"I haven't spoken about Merellia since it happened," I replied. "Not to anyone but within days of finding out about it, he had me bringing up all this stuff that I thought I left behind years ago."

"Yeah. You'll never be able to hide anything from him or lie to him so don't even try," Donal smiled.

"I've already noticed he seems to have an uncanny ability to read me."

"He's the best friend you could wish for and you're extremely lucky that he's taken you to his heart close enough to form that empathic bond with you. Damiklonians don't often bond with other races so closely. You can rest assured that he will be your best friend for life."

"I'm real glad about that. I just wish I could be as much of a friend to him."

"You are Joss. By accepting him the way he is and letting him form that empathic bond with you tells him that you trust him completely. Trust is everything to Damiklonians and by letting him into your mind, into your deepest fears and the darkest places within your heart, you're showing him that you trust him with your feelings and that you accept his presence there. That's a huge deal for him so don't under estimate what he's getting out of your friendship."

"Thanks buddy," I smiled. "That helps me to understand."

"Another thing too," he said. "I can probably count on my two hands, the number of non Damiklonians who've been allowed to learn their martial art. They're very secretive about that so you're honoured to have him voluntarily teach you."

"Really?" I exclaimed. "He never told me that."

"He won't. To remind you of what an honour it is would be egotistical and he could never allow himself to do anything driven by ego. I envy you Joss. I've been one of his contacts since he first came to Deligon but he's never formed a bond like that with me. You're a very lucky guy."

I sat down in Kobey's office and accepted the drink he offered me.

"How can I help Joss?" he said as he sat opposite me. "It's your week off."

"Yeah but I heard there's a job going in R and D security."

"Oh," he said and gazed into my eyes. "And?"

"And I want to apply for the position if that's okay," I replied as I held his gaze.

"Of course you can apply," he said. "If it's really what you want."

"It is Boss," I smiled.

"And I can't talk you out of it?" he said suddenly.

"No," I replied. Moments of silence hung between us as I wondered what to say. "I have to know, and this will help me do that."

"Please don't," he replied.

"Why not?"

"Because you're a nice guy with a nice life and nice friends. This is a very good way of destroying all that."

"Many others lives are already destroyed Boss. I have to try. People are suffering like you couldn't imagine."

"How do you know?" he asked.

"Just believe me," I replied. "I just do. I know you like to obey the rules and I respect you because of that but this time I have to cause some upheaval around here. I'd like to think you'd help me but even if you can't, I have to try."

"It's all just rumours Joss," he countered.

"No it's not," I cut in before he could continue. "I can prove it. It's more awful than you could ever believe. I've seen a bit of what's going on, down there."

"You have?" He looked at me astonished and I nodded.

"Yeah. Believe me Boss, this could wipe out Bygora Vandos, maybe even the whole of Deligon if something isn't done."

He looked down at his hands for long moments, his lips pursing and twitching as he fought with his decision. Suddenly he banged on the table and made me jump.

"I like to run a tight ship Joss. I believe in rules and obeying structure without question. That's what I've always done and I've come to realise that only by keeping a tight structure, are things done quickly and efficiently. When people start flying off and acting from their emotions, everything gets messed up and things go wrong. I've run my whole life and career by schedules and I hate the idea of fucking up that schedule."

"I know Boss," I said, suddenly afraid that I had completely misread him and sure I was in trouble. "I respect you for all those reasons."

"Good old reliable Kobey," he said quietly and I looked at him. "Oh I have ears Joss. I know what people say about me. Solid, reliable Kobey. He'll stick to the rules no matter what. Never expect good old Kobey to use his initiative or think for himself."

"I've never heard anyone talk like that," I said truthfully.

"Then you haven't been listening." Another moment of silence while he fought an internal battle. With another bang on the desk with his fist he looked me right in the eyes. "Well I intend to show them just how much initiative I can muster. Tell me what you know. Trust me with that and you'll have my full support."

An hour later he signed the document and sighed. "There you go Joss. I've recommended you for the position of R and D security guard. Here's my Unicom number and my address. If you get the job, we'll not meet again here at the station so keep in touch with me. I'll do whatever I can to help you.

"Thanks Boss," I said as I took his address and handed him my own. "Here is mine and my Unicom number. "For what it's worth," I said as I stood to go, "I knew you'd be an ally the first time I met you."

"You did? He seemed genuinely surprised.

"Yeah," I nodded. "I saw past that firm adherence to rules right away."

"Thank you," he nodded.

Ren was aghast when I told him of my encounter with Kobey.

"You what?" he almost yelled at me.

"It was the right thing to do," I said defensively. "I just knew it was right. You'll have to trust me on this. He's okay if you look past that stiff exterior. Come on buddy you of all people can see a person's true nature."

He glared at me for a couple more seconds before his eyes softened and he sighed. He ran a hand through his hair. "You're right. I'm sorry for yelling at you. I guess I've not paid him much attention. He's not in my line of command so we don't have contact and I hear what the others say about him. Forgive me."

"Hey don't worry," I said. "There's nothing to forgive, really."

"Please Joss," he said. "I can feel it from you but I need to hear it, it's just my way I guess."

"I forgive you buddy, absolutely."

"Thanks. So he's given you an official recommendation?"

"Yeah."

"You're sure? He wasn't just saying that to get you to confide in him?"

"No. I saw him sign it right there in front of me and put it in the mail chute."

"Wow. You know it's not beyond the realms of possibility that you could actually get the job."

"I'm hoping for that," I replied. "This is the one thing we have no control over and I could sure use a bit of luck. I'm not confident we could actually do much without getting access down there."

"The film we have would go a long way but those involved would have plenty of opportunity to get away before we could use it," he said and I nodded.

"Yeah. Now Donal and the boys are coming round in two hours for dinner and to see what the camera has picked up this afternoon so do you want to work out and go for a run?"

"This is good Joss," Doniss said as he shovelled food into his mouth. "Delicious."

"Thanks buddy," I grinned.

"You are a good cook Joss," Donal said. "I mean it."

"Well being on my own for so long I guess I've had to learn how to take care of myself."

"I took the liberty of bringing along a bottle of wine for after dinner," he said. "I hope you don't mind."

"Not at all," Ren said. "What type is it?"

"Attan Blue."

"Wow, you have great taste Donal," Palko said. "Father says it's expensive. He has three bottles at home but has always refused to open one. He says he's saving them for when I get married. I hope it doesn't go off because I intend to have a few more years of fun before settling down."

"It gets better with time," Donal grinned. "I was given this when I retired from law enforcement and it was ten years old then. I've never known when to open it but now that we're actively engaged in fighting to get our world back, I reckon that's something worth celebrating. Even if we don't succeed, making the effort needs to be acknowledged."

"I completely agree," Ren smiled.

After dinner Donal opened the wine while I set up my camera so we could see what the HairCam in the tunnel was seeing. We saw white tiled walls and floor, an arched roof and a door straight ahead. The corridor went across our view and at the moment, it was empty. Ten minutes later we heard the unmistakeable sound of a breather unit that signalled an approaching guard.

hiss, thunk, foo
hiss, thunk, foo
hiss, thunk, foo

As he drew closer, we heard the click of claws on the tiled floor and then they came into view and we all took a breath in shock. The creature reached the guard's hips and was even more fearsome looking close up than it was on the Consoria camera. Its body was indeed covered in dark grey scales, very small scales that gave it a smooth and sleek outline. The head was large and wedge shaped with short, wide jaws that jutted out in front, the lower slightly further than the upper and each with a pair of long fangs that overlapped the lips. Above the eye sockets were a pair of short pointed horns and long whiskers sprouted from each side of the upper jaw. In a way, it was a handsome animal, perfectly adapted to its predatory role and I thought it rather emasculating that such a creature should be patrolling a corridor with a security guard. Every fifteen minutes the guard and his Hymalont would pass by and we chatted in between times. After an hour and a half, the door opposite suddenly opened and a man in a white coat appeared.

"That's Deniko Pasnel," Marlo said. "He's the Assistant to the guy who's retiring, the R and D Chief."

Pasnel walked towards the camera, into the niche and fished in his pocket. The guard passed by and he called out. "Guard, do you have a light?" The guard approached and fished in his own pocket and lit Pasnel's cigarette. "Thank you. It's very bad for the health you know."

"Then you should take up drinking instead," the guard replied.

"I don't like cold drinks," Pasnel responded.

"I prefer them hot myself," the guard said.

"What the fuck?" I began but then realised. "That's a code word. This could be interesting guys."

"Oh," Palko snickered. "I wondered what the fuck they were on about."

"How long until we go?" Pasnel asked.

"A couple of weeks, maybe three," the guard replied.

"No sooner?"

"Sorry. Best I can do."

"How much?" Pasnel asked.

"Seven thousand apiece."

"What? That's crazy."

"I know but that's the cost."

"Any room for negotiation?"

"None. Sorry."

"Okay then. Seven thousand. Let's do four this time."

"Right," the guard nodded. "Four it is." He stepped back out into the corridor and resumed his patrol. Pasnel stamped out his cigarette and walked off to our right and out of sight.

"What the fuck was that all about?" Marlo asked.

"That's good news for us," Donal said and Ren nodded.

"How?"

"Because it means Pasnel and one of the guards are doing some obviously secret deal. That is very useful for us to know because it's something we can use to persuade them around to our way of thinking if we need to."

"Oh you mean blackmail," Palko said and Ren winced.

"Ouch," he said, shutting his eyes tightly as if in pain. I laughed out loud.

"No buddy, persuasion around to our way of thinking," I said as Ren regained his composure."

"Right, gotcha."

"So what is your plan of action Joss?" Donal asked.

"Well I umm," I began. "I guess I get to know my way around down there and keep my eyes and ears open for starters. After that I need to find out where they're shipping the stuff and what it's being used for and I guess a sample wouldn't hurt."

"Your duties will be shorter in R and D," Ren said. "They do six hour shifts. Five days on and two off. Their pay is triple yours. If you get the job you'll be expected to live on site for the first whole week while they train you, so we'll only be able to keep in contact via Unicom."

"Okay," I nodded. "Then we'll agree that I'll call you every day, no matter what. As soon as I get to know the routine, I'll be able to set times aside to call you and we can update each other. Don't anyone call me okay?" Everyone nodded.

I was excited that the job seemed to be gaining some momentum at last. With the prospect of access to the underground complex I felt confident that I would be able to take a pro-active role at last. I was also acutely aware of the ever-present fear of becoming one of those wretched souls, grey and shuffling and I prayed that I would be spared that fate, whatever happened.

I am going to stop here, go shower, and get some sleep. I will catch you all in the morning. This is V-Log reference LB734/A data log reference point 3380133/8397

CHAPTER THIRTEEN

V-Log reference LB734/A data log reference point 3380133/8398 continuing report.

I spent the next couple of days watching the feed from the HairCam in between doing household chores and although I was beginning to get cabin fever, I did not want to miss anything. Ren and I worked out each afternoon when he got home from work and I cooked while I was off work. We were looking forward to visiting Donal for the shuttle arrival and whilst it was still a couple of days away, I was bored and contemplating redecorating the apartment just for something to do. I had called Tinnias and sent him the feed from the HairCam and the Consoria so he could watch it anytime he needed to without having to wait for me to call him and play it. He was as shocked as the rest of us were.

"This looks bad Sam," he said. "How the hell have they been getting away with this for so long?"

"That's one question that needs answering," I replied, "and maybe things need changing so it can't happen again."

"Oh they will be, I promise you that."

"Have you any news for us Sir?"

"Yes actually. We've had surveillance teams on the various members of the Abydell-Mirras family and from the initial intelligence we're getting, it seems as though they have another invisible company which we believe might have been set up to deal with the Zanbedellium."

"Oh?"

"Yeah. This company doesn't even have a name as far as we've been able to tell. It hides behind Heibat Power and Energy and Heibat Bio Research and officially doesn't exist at all. Those shuttles we've been tailing eventually arrived at an uninhabited moon of Uraloma 4. They've built some sort of storage facility there on the dark side of the moon where it isn't tracked by Uraloma security as the planet itself is uninhabited and of no interest to anyone."

"So at least we know where the stuff is going," I said.

"Yeah and we're already getting the documentation together for a seize warrant so when the time comes we can just storm the place, seize the stuff and arrest all personnel."

"That's great news Boss."

"We sent a troop ship out to you some time ago which should be arriving at the Deligon system anytime now. I'm sending the emergency Unicom channel to you now, it should be arriving at your handset now. When you need the troops, just call channel 006725 and they'll be with you in under two hours. They know to wait for a call from Space Cop 257 so use your usual handle when you call them."

"Thanks, it's good to know they're around."

"We also finally managed to track down a sample of Zanbedellium."

"You have? That's fantastic. Can you tell us anything about it yet?"

"Well yeah but it's weird Sam. It's a silvery coloured rock in its unprocessed state and, get this, completely harmless as a rock."

"What?" I exclaimed. "So what causes the effects we're seeing on those people?"

"It's only harmful after processing into a gaseous or liquid form, so those drums obviously contain a liquid. They're not gas drums so what you're looking for is not lumps of rock and if you do find that, you don't need to worry about it harming you. It's liquid processing you're looking for and it's that liquid that is harmful. Very harmful so don't touch it; even a single drop will start the effects."

"Okay that's good to know," I said. "But if they're not using it as a gas, why do the guards wear breathers?"

"Because the liquid does give off faint fumes which, over time, can affect you and give you similar effects to those of the liquid or gas forms of the stuff. You'd probably survive even after some time inhaling the fumes from the liquid but best not test that theory unless your lives depend on it."

"So am I to get a sample of this liquid or just confirm its existence?"

"Don't touch it Sam, that's an order. Just confirm its presence on site, by documentable evidence. Hack in to their computer system and retrieve data, get a witness to testify or even just film any data readout you happen to see, anything that confirms the presence of Zanbedellium liquid. We need evidence of the stuff being there but we do have some leeway on that, due to the danger levels. We need something though but remember, your lives are the top priority okay?"

"Okay. I've applied for the position of R and D Security Guard and Ren thinks there's a good chance I'll get it. I've also taken my current security supervisor into my confidence. His name is Kobey and I know he'll stand with us if need be, my colleague Hitch too and maybe a few of the other security guys I've been working with."

"Good, I'm glad you two won't be fighting alone."

"Is there a way of reversing the effects Sir? Those people down there, the workers. It's awful to see them like that."

"Unfortunately not. Once the liquid Zanbedellium is in their systems they're on borrowed time and our scientists have tested the sample we found on lab animals and none of them lived more than a week. A humanoid body might have a little more resistance but it is a death sentence I'm afraid. Our guys reckon that those injections they're giving those folks down there maybe some kind of sedative, to keep them compliant perhaps, or they may even be using them as lab specimens to test how to use the stuff. That's another thing we're hoping you'll find out but even if you can't, your main priority is to shut the place down and restrain those responsible."

"What could they possibly want with such dangerous stuff?" I asked.

"We haven't the faintest idea but our best guess so far is that they think it's a cure for something or other or maybe some kind of weapon. Can you imagine what would happen if you sprayed gallons of the stuff down on your enemies in a war situation?"

"Shit."

"Exactly. Now how are you both for money?"

"We're fine."

"Okay good. Now I want daily reports from now on. I've got a law enforcer's hunch that things will reach a climax pretty soon and I don't want to be left out of the loop when I'm so far away."

"Right, I'll call you every day Sir, no problem."

Ren was very relieved to know that we had plenty of troops at our disposal but upset at the knowledge that we couldn't make those poor wretched souls better. We worked out, went for a run, and after dinner, we spent a couple of hours checking our armoury and restocking with ammo. Just as we were about to sit down to watch a terrible vidicom movie, my Unicom beeped.

"Hi Joss, it's Marlo here."

"Marlo, hi buddy, what's up?" I looked at Ren and switched over to loudspeaker.

"I uh, I have some bad news for you."

"Bad news? What the fuck has happened?"

"And an admission too."

"Come on Marlo," Ren said. "We're in this together so out with it."

"Well umm. Well we've been tailing you both since this thing started."

Ren and I looked at each other in shock. His eyebrows shot up and I shrugged my shoulders.

"Okay," I replied, annoyed but happy that his surveillance of us would have revealed nothing out of the ordinary. "And?"

"Well, we had to be sure that you're both okay y'know? Don't be mad guys, this is serious shit and we had to be sure."

"Hey it's okay buddy," Ren said. "We'd do the same in your position. It's basic good detective work. Now what's the bad news?"

"Well, while tailing you both, we've found that as of today, you're also being tailed by others."

"What the fuck?" I said and looked at Ren who looked just as shocked as I was. "Someone else is tailing us?"

"Yeah," Marlo confirmed. "It started today and they're from Calmarin. R and D security guys working overtime checking you both out."

"Shit and fuck," I yelled and ran both hands through my hair. "Just what we don't need."

"Listen," Ren said suddenly. "You've just applied for a job in R and D so they're probably just checking you out to make sure you're who you say you are, and as we live together, they're checking me out too, especially as I also work at the station. It's obvious when you think about it."

"He has a point Joss," Marlo said. "We may find it stops once you've got the job, or not got it."

"Right," Ren nodded. "So let's wait a while before we panic okay? At least until we know if you've got the job or not. Until then you boys and Donal have to keep away from us. We can't take the risk as they're bound to know he's ex law enforcement and they might even know about your links to Bygora's gang network and we can't be seen to be engaging with that if we want to endear ourselves to Calmarin."

"That's why I called you," Marlo said. "I didn't dare let you keep our appointment at Donal's apartment for the shuttle landings without at least letting you know what's going on."

"You did the right thing buddy," I said, "and we can all be thankful that you decided to tail us. If you hadn't, we wouldn't know about them tailing us. Good work. I'm proud of you."

"Thanks Joss," Marlo replied with a sigh that told Ren and I he was very relieved that we were not annoyed.

"We'll only be able to keep in touch via Unicom from now on then," I said. "Can you make sure everyone else knows? I'll call you three boys and Donal each day, just to touch base and exchange any news okay? I can also tell you that we have some troops ready and waiting for the signal, so don't worry about us not having back up."

"You have? That's great."

"Yeah. Now I'll call again tomorrow and each day from now on okay? Even if there's nothing fresh we need to keep in touch."

"Okay, take care guys."

At first, the knowledge that we were being tailed made us feel reluctant to leave the apartment but after talking about it, Ren and I decided that the best ploy was to continue to act like two normal single men in a large city. With this in mind, we went out that evening for a few drinks and ended up in a club where I found a delicious looking redhead for hire. Ren, as always, was more than willing and decided on a black haired beauty, so we enjoyed their company for a couple of hours before getting some take-out food and heading back home. We made sure to talk about our fake shared experiences in the military, laughed about the women whose company we had enjoyed and made plans for a future visit to Hallimantera for the Warrior Games. We hoped that whoever was following us was bored shitless and the following day I decided to get my own back by visiting a local art gallery and sat in front of a large painting for two whole hours. I spent the time revisiting some of my memories of past jobs in my mind and made further plans for making some video logs of my adventures. I left the gallery confident that my follower would be losing the will to live and I smiled all the way to the store. I spent another fifty minutes slowly and carefully browsing the wares and taking my time to make up my mind what to buy to restock our kitchen. By the time I left the store, I had read the labels of every single item they had in stock despite them all being written in Deligonian which I was not able to understand. Once back at the apartment, I cleaned up, prepared dinner and then went back out into the neighbouring park and lay back on a bench and dozed for an hour and a half. By the time I went back to the apartment to make dinner, I was hoping my follower was bored because I most certainly was.

Ren laughed aloud when I told him about my day.

"You're a bad man Sam. That's awesome buddy."

We worked out and went for a run, after which I called Tinnias and updated him while Ren showered. He was annoyed that we were being tailed but agreed with Ren that it was most likely due to my application to join the R and D department. I then called Donal and he assured me that everything was fine with him and not to worry, he would call if he had any news. Marlo laughed when I called him.

"Joss you're fantastic man, I almost peed myself watching you today. The guy tailing you was bored shitless and twice called someone on his Unicorn and asked to be allowed to cut his shift short."

"That's awesome," I grinned and Ren laughed loudly.

"I do have more news though. Adlion Garmast had another secret meeting with Professor Jakelham, the guy he met the last time. The device we fixed to his hover car allowed us to hear their conversation clearly and it's good news, I think."

"Really?" I said. "Well we sure need some."

"It seems that Jakelham is a spy for Garmast."

"A spy?" Ren asked.

"Yeah. He told Garmast about what he called the cargo, which we took to mean those drums. He told him how much of the stuff was shipped since their last meeting, its value, which runs into the tens of millions by the way, and he also told him about you applying for the job of R and D security."

"He told him about me?" I asked. "I wonder why he would do that."

"That's not all," Marlo continued. "Jakelham kept referring to you as Sinclair."

"Oh shit," Ren hissed.

"Wait buddy," Marlo interrupted before I could add my own colourful curse word. "Garmast and Jakelham's conversation made it clear that not only did they both know who you are and why you're here, but that you are to be given all possible assistance when everything blows up, as Garmast put it. It would seem that you have another ally you're not yet aware of."

"Wow," I replied as I took in this news. "That's umm, good. Isn't it?" I asked as I looked at Ren, who nodded.

"It would seem so, yeah, he said.

"So once you get down there," Marlo said, "and meet up with Jakelham, you'll know where his allegiance lies."

"That's good to know," I said. "Thanks buddy, you guys are doing a top job."

I called Tinnias again and gave him the news. He was surprised and delighted and promised to do some digging into Jakelham and get back to me, which he did twenty minutes later.

"Professor Jakelham is a very highly qualified physicist," he told us. "And he's been a law enforcement spy for eight years. He's worked on five major cases in that time, all relating to bad practice in a scientific environment and Garmast has been using him at Calmarin since the day the company expanded its operation on Deligon. When the research station expanded, which we can assume is when they discovered the Zanbedellium and realised the money they could make out of it, Garmast planted him into a top Research Science company that Calmarin often head hunted their top men from. His real name is Sifflen Belding and he's from Laxmair 3 originally."

"That's a relief Boss," I replied.

"I thought it might help you sleep better. It's been interesting to find out just how seriously Garmast has been working this case these past few years."

"Thanks. We'll call again tomorrow."

Ren suggested that as the time was drawing near when we would both inevitably be called to fight, possibly for our lives, it would not hurt to work out more vigorously. I agreed this was a good idea so we spent three hours each night sparring and he concentrated on drilling me on disarming my opponent and bringing him down in as quick and effective a way as possible. I was nowhere near as proficient as he, but when the time came for me to report back to work, I was confident that I now had very useful combat skills, should my gun be useless or absent. I did not know what to expect so I just reported in as usual and chatted with the guys as we got ready to head out to our allotted patch. Ren had given me one of his Damiklonian daggers, which now snuggled against my back under my work uniform and I felt some measure of comfort at its presence, cold against my skin.

Hitch and I were patrolling the southern sector when we heard a hover cart approach. We turned to see Kobey pull up and jump out.

"Hi Boss," Hitch and I said in unison.

"Morning guys," he replied with a nod. "Joss, I have to call you off duty for an hour. Can you manage alone Hitch?"

"Sure thing."

I followed Kobey and sat in the passenger seat as he gunned the engine and headed back towards the buildings in the distance.

"Is there a problem Boss?" I asked.

"You have an interview with R and D," he replied quietly. "For the security position."

"Oh. Great."

"I know what your reasons are Joss, and they're noble and I'll be there to back you up when it comes to it but I still wish you weren't doing this."

"Thanks for caring," I replied and gave a weak smile. He didn't smile back.

A man I'd not met before was waiting for us in Kobey's office.

"Joss," Kobey said, "this is Janost Spurrell, head of R and D security."

"Pleased to meet you Joss," he said with an insincere smile that had me immediately on my guard. "I'm here to interview you about the position you applied for."

"Okay Sir," I replied and gave my best fake smile.

We talked for an hour about my military background, my time in security, my family background and even my friendship with Ren. He looked over my Calmarin work record and finally checked the recommendation Kobey had signed for me.

"You have an excellent military record Joss."

"Yes Sir, thank you."

"I see you did just ten years."

"Yes Sir," I nodded.

"Was there a problem? You didn't want to continue?"

"Oh there wasn't any problem. On Sigma, you only ever do ten years unless you want to make a lifetime career of it. It's standard practice back home."

"Ahh I see," he nodded. "I notice that one or two of your subsequent security positions were with companies that deal in potentially sensitive information."

"Yes Sir," I nodded.

"And that didn't bother you? The secrecy of it I mean?"

"No Sir. My job was security. That was my reason for being there and that's what I did. And if I may say so myself, I was damn good at it. I don't poke my nose where it's not supposed to be. I want a decent pay check so I can enjoy my life."

"That's good to know because the research we're doing here is of a sensitive nature and you may very well see things and hear things that we would expect you to keep to yourself. Will that be a problem for you? If so, say so now and you can get back to work."

"That's not a problem at all Sir," I said. "I'm used to keeping my eyes and ears closed and I don't gossip. I just want a good job with decent pay so I can have a good life. I've done my time saving the universe and I did it to the best of my ability and now I just want to enjoy the time I have."

"What about your Damiklonian friend, Balien Renimir?"

"What about him?"

"Is he the curious type?"

"Good lord no. He works here too so he knows I won't be able to tell him anything. We talked about it when I first considered applying and he's okay with it."

"He has an excellent record here. That's good. You will be expected to live on site for the first week, while we train you."

"Yes Sir, Ren told me."

"Are you okay with animals?"

"Animals Sir? Oh you must mean the dogs the other guys talk about. Yes I'm fine."

"Indeed. You will be issued with a security trained guard animal. They're rather frightening looking things but very obedient."

"That's fine Sir."

"One more thing Joss. If you decide, at the end of your first week's training period, that you made a mistake applying for the position, you realise you won't be able to return to your old position. You're employment effectively relies on your decision whether to continue with your application."

"I understand that Sir, and yes, I wish to continue."

"Okay then," he said with a smile that was as equally fake as his first had been, "I will now formally offer you the position." He extended his hand, which I shook.

"Thank you very much."

"You're welcome. Now go home and pack two changes of underwear and all your washing necessities. All other clothing will be provided. I'll meet you back here in Kobey's office in, say two hours?"

"Okay, two hours. I'll be here and thank you again."

I raced back to the apartment, called Tinnias and told him his updates would be coming from Ren for the next week. He was pleased I had secured the position and reminded me about the troops waiting in covert orbit around Deligon. I then called Donal and the boys, and reminded them not to call me at all until further notice. They assured me that was okay and I assured them that I would check in daily when I could and asked them to make sure Ren was okay while I was gone. They promised to keep an eye on him for me and I hung up. After setting up my vidicom camera to collect the feed from my tiny surveillance button camera, I left a detailed note for Ren on the kitchen counter and packed my stuff. On impulse I decided to take the dagger he had given me, just in case, and headed back out to catch the hover bus back to the research station. Kobey offered me a drink and I accepted.

"I hope you've brought your Unicom with you Joss. I want to know about it if and when you need back up okay?"

"I have it, and thanks. I might very well have to take you up on that offer."

"Do so. Now the guy who interviewed you, Janost Spurrell. He makes my skin crawl. I don't know why and I might be doing him a disservice but my feeling is that he is not to be trusted. Be careful of him."

"I picked that up from him too," I replied. "There's something very off about him."

"There's a man called Jakelham who seems nice," Kobey continued and I smiled. "At least he always smiles and says good morning when I see him in the corridor."

"He's a good guy," I replied with a grin and Kobey gaped at me.

"He is?"

"Yeah, he is," I nodded. "I can promise you that. You have sharp instincts Boss."

Kobey looked into my eyes for long moments without speaking. It was as if he was trying to read me. "You're more than you say you are, aren't you Joss? You know what you're doing, don't you? And you've done it before."

"Like I said," I replied. "You have excellent instincts."

"Promise me one thing?" he asked. I looked into his eyes and noticed they were full of emotion. "Promise me you'll bring this to an end, whatever this is. All I know is, it's terribly wrong but I'm powerless to stop it. If you can stop it, if you have that power, please end this."

"I promise," I nodded.

He gave another quick nod and made a call informing Janost Spurrell that I was back and ready to be taken into R and D to begin my training. While we waited for him to arrive to escort me, he came around from behind his desk and extended his hand.

"Be safe Joss and a swift end to this."

"Thank you for your support," I replied as I shook his hand.

I followed Janost Spurrell along corridors and out into the open air just as I had followed Kobey on my first day of employment. This time though, instead of walking past the mysterious door with the weird looking locking mechanism, we walked right up to it and Spurrell took out a key card, which he slid into a slot. Three beeps and then a loud click and we were in another corridor. Unlike the previous one, this corridor was all highly polished surfaces, glass and bright light. Hundreds of reflections of myself walked beside us as I followed Spurrell, and all of them, as nervous as I was. There was a single door at the end of this short corridor and we entered a long narrow room sectioned into cubicles, each containing a chair, a small table, a shower and toilet.

"The R and D facility is a clean environment Joss," Spurrell explained as I looked about the sparse room. "So everyone who comes in must shower before going any further." He indicated to the first cubicle on my left. "You can use this one here. That box on the table contains your uniform shirt, pants and a pair of boots. Change your underwear for a fresh set and put all of your own clothes back into the box. They will be laundered and returned to you by the end of the day and you can use them when off duty. I'll come back in twenty minutes and show you to your living quarters and then you can have some lunch. You'll find our facilities of the highest quality and you will enjoy your meals here."

"Thank you Sir," I replied as I opened the box and took out a brown shirt and matching pants and a pair of sturdy but high quality boots. I placed my bag on the table and retrieved a fresh set of underwear and my wash things as Spurrell turned and left me alone. Fifteen minutes later I was re-dressed with my Damiklonian knife safely snuggled against my back, Unicom in my pocket and tiny button cam attached to the front of my shirt. When I heard the door open quietly I bent down and put on my boots.

"Perfect timing Joss," Spurrell said as he appeared almost silently within my cubicle.

"Yes Sir," I smiled as I stood. "I'm ready."

"Great. Leave the box of clothes on the table but bring your other bag with you. You'll be in cubicle seventeen for this week. The accommodations are basic but you'll have your privacy and the beds are comfortable. Follow me."

I picked up my bag and followed him down the long room and through another door at the end into another bright and shiny corridor. Down a set of steps and a security desk greeted us.

"This will be one of your duties Joss," Spurrell explained. All the guys take a shift on the desk once a week. It's boring but everyone does it. Senker, do you have Joss's pass and badge?"

"Yes Sir, they're right here," the guy on the desk said as he handed Spurrell a key card and badge. If you could sign for them Mr Gilden?" He asked as he handed me a digital console. I signed and took possession of my key card and gave an internal sigh of relief that I finally had entry through that mysterious door.

"Here's your badge Joss," Spurrell continued as he handed me a small cloth patch. "Sew it onto the jacket you'll be issued with later on, just like

Senker's." I looked at the guy behind the desk. On the right hand side of his jacket, above the breast pocket, was the bright yellow Heibat logo, the capital H with the lightning bolt.

"Right, no problem Sir," I nodded.

"Good. Now follow me and I'll show you to your quarters.

CHAPTER FOURTEEN

The room was very small and, as Spurrell said, basic, but at least I was not sharing with anyone so calling Ren and the others should not be a problem. Like everywhere else I had seen so far, the room was white tiled and brightly lit. A single bed stood against the far wall, by the side of which was a small bedside locker on which was a clock, a pitcher of water and a glass. The smallest closet I had ever seen stood to one side of another door, which I found led to a tiny white tiled bathroom containing just shower, basin and toilet. There was nothing decorative, nothing mentally stimulating and looked more like a prison cell than staff accommodation. I found myself extremely grateful I only had to endure a week here for I knew I would go stir crazy before too long.

"This is your room Joss," Spurrell said as he handed me a key card. Cubicle seventeen. It's basic but you're only here for a week and we find that basic accommodations help to focus the mind on the task at hand."

"It's perfectly adequate Sir," I nodded. "My needs are minimal."

"Good. Now I'll show you to the mess room and you can have an hour for lunch, then I'll take you to meet your security animal."

The food was surprisingly good and I ate well. In different circumstances, I would think I had landed on my feet with a job like this, and thought back to the nutri vend on board my ship. Having been eating real food for several weeks, I knew it was going to be very hard for me when things got back to my usual routine. Spurrell returned at the end of the hour to escort me along another white tiled corridor and stopped outside a door.

"Now Joss. In this room are fourteen security animals. They're called Hymalonts and they're pretty freaky looking but don't be scared okay? You have to find the one that wants to work with you."

"What?" I frowned and Spurrell grinned.

"We can't just give you any one. They choose their owner and once they've made their choice, they won't work for any other handler."

"So how will I know which one?"

"Oh you'll know. Don't worry. Just be yourself and let them get on with it. We'll be watching from the adjoining room through the one-way glass. They get nervous if they see others watching when meeting a new handler and could get aggressive, so we've found it best to be a little sneaky. Once you've paired up, you'll spend every moment of this week together."

"Every moment?"

"Every moment. It helps them to seal their bond with you so that once you go back to normal shift patterns and go home each day, they don't get nervous and worried with you gone. Now, in you go." He reached out and opened the door a crack and encouraged me to enter with a hand in the small of my back.

I almost shit my pants when I entered the room and heard the door click firmly shut behind me. My hand went instinctively to the blade, hidden beneath my shirt, but I just managed to stop myself in time. Fourteen pairs of eyes looked up at me; fourteen shiny-scaled bodies stopped what they were doing and stood still as statues. I was convinced my cover was blown and that this was my punishment. The adrenaline coursed through my body as I realised I was going to die in horrible agony and I almost started to cry. What happened next saved me from screaming out. One of the animals then gave a huge, jaw-cracking yawn, flopped down on to the floor, rolled onto his side, and fell asleep. Another two snorted and turned away to play some kind of wrestling game together and another sat down and started licking his balls. Three came towards me, sniffing. Two lost interest before they got within three feet of me and the remaining one sniffed my legs, snorted in what I can only describe as disgust and walked off. One by one, they sniffed me. One stuck her nose into my crotch and another licked my hand, the others gave a tentative sniff and walked away. Eventually there was just one still stood looking at me and we locked eyes.

"Hey there girl," I said nervously. "I'm Joss." We remained there, eyes locked for almost thirty seconds before she came towards me, stood up on her hind legs and licked my face all over. Her tongue was rough but warm and the more I tried to avoid it, the more expertly she washed my face with it. "Hey, stop," I snickered as I put my arms around her body and hugged her. Despite being covered with scales, she was warm, and I could feel her solid musculature beneath the skin. Those huge fangs in my face were disconcerting to look at but after a few minutes getting to know her, I did not really notice them. She rolled onto her back and demanded a belly rub and then we play wrestled and although she took my hands and arms into her jaws on several occasions, she never bit down. I guessed she had decided I was the one.

"Well done Joss," Spurrell's voice came over the intercom. Now if you'd both like to exit through the door behind you, I'll meet you there." I got up and turned towards the door and was about to motion for her to follow when I noticed her at my heels, already following. "We were beginning to think she would never choose a team mate," Spurrell said. "She will automatically follow you everywhere you go now until we uplink you both."

"Uplink us?" I asked.

"Yes. A masterstroke of humanoid and animal communication. You'll be fitted with a special headset that will transmit your brainwaves to a receiver that she has already had implanted into her brain. That way you'll effectively be able to communicate your needs to her via your thoughts."

"Really? You're kidding."

"No kidding Joss. Now, until you get your headset and learn how to use it, she is conditioned to automatically go into a working aggressive mode whenever you put on her collar and leash. For this reason, never leash her unless you want her to work."

"Okay."

"The first thing you must do is name her. It'll be the first thing you tell her when you use the headset, so if you haven't got a suitable name in mind, get thinking because you'll be needing it first thing in the morning."

"Essy," I said with a grin. "She'll be called Essy."

"Okay," Spurrell nodded. "Good name. Now. let's get you kitted out with the rest of your gear. Follow me."

Well, Essy did indeed follow me everywhere and would answer only to me. I spent that first afternoon learning to give her basic voice and hand signal commands and boy, she was a fast learner. By the time we went in for dinner, she was obeying me without question and I never had to admonish her once. After dinner there was exercise class for an hour and she and I ran on a treadmill, then she played with some of the other Hymalonts who were still without handlers, while I worked out and practiced the Damiklonian martial art. It was mid-evening by the time I had showered and had returned to my room, Essy at my heels, and relax. Spurrell told me to be up at six am, for breakfast at half past, and I was tired so I did not intend to stay up late. Before heading to the recreation room to watch a vidicom movie, I decided to make some calls. I called Donal first and he confirmed that the HairCam was still in place and transmitting. He also told me that everyone would be at his apartment tonight to watch the shuttles land. I thanked him and told him I would call each day. Next, I called Marlo, who confirmed that Ren was still being tailed, so we both agreed that it would be best if he stayed away from Donal's apartment. He promised to update me the next day, and confirmed that their surveillance of Palko still revealed nothing of concern. Then I called Ren.

"Hey Ren, how ya doing buddy?"

"Joss, I got your note. You okay?"

"Yeah I'm fine. Just finding my way around down here at the moment."

"Have you found out anything interesting?"

"Well no, not yet. I've not seen anything we saw on the film yet. I guess that must be on a still lower level. I've only come down one level from the surface so far."

"How's your day been, and what's that rumbling noise?"

"That's Essy," I grinned.

"Essy? What's Essy?"

"She's my Hymalont and she's lying here on my bed and enjoying a belly rub. That rumbling is the noise she makes when she's happy."

"You're shitting me Joss. You're giving one of those things a belly rub?" I heard him laugh out loud.

"No shit Ren," I snickered. "She's very friendly, to me anyway. Apparently once they bond with you, they'll only work for that one person and no one else. Tomorrow I get some gizmo that means I can control her by my thoughts."

"Now you are shitting me."

"I'm not shitting you. Actually it might come in useful when the shit hits the fan here. Knowing she'll only obey me, and being able to give her commands by my thoughts means she'll be useful as extra defence should we need it."

"That's a good point Joss. I called Tinnias by the way. He's glad you got the job and told me to call him at least every day with updates or just to let him know we're still alive if there's no news."

"Great. Marlo told me that you still have your follower by the way, so we both think it wise that you stay away from Donal's apartment tonight."

"Shit. Okay, thanks for letting me know. I was planning on going as I'd assumed the surveillance would stop now that you have the position."

"I'm gonna be calling each evening so as soon as he informs me you've lost your tail, I'll let you know. Now I'm going to watch a movie, or rather we're going to watch a movie. Take care buddy, I'll call tomorrow."

"Be careful Joss."

I spent the following day getting the headset that would enable me to control Essy by my thoughts and learning how to use it. It was weird, very weird, but by the end of the day, I was getting the hang of it. There is a knack to using it, and once you learn to focus your thought in a particular way, it is just practice. At first, I just could not get it, but once I did, I realised that if I tried too hard, it ruined it, so I learned to relax my mind when I wanted to control her. It was cool and on the third day, Spurrell was impressed enough with my command of Essy that he let me leash her for the first time, and the change in her was scary. Whereas normally she had been friendly and docile, once I leashed her she was immediately alert and growled at everyone foolhardy enough to come into her line of sight. I sent her a thought to be quiet but alert and she quietened immediately. The rest of the day was spent in security exercises where I was tested on my ability to control her in an emergency. The first couple of times she successfully ripped all the holographic targets to pieces and I felt embarrassed at my total lack of control. After taking some time to refresh my skills with the thought headset, we tried again and I managed to save the lives of most of the innocent holograms. After lunch, we were back at it and by the end of the day, I knew I was getting the hang of it. Each evening I called everyone and we were all getting very frustrated at the lack of momentum. I had thought, no, hoped, that once I got into R and D, I could have the situation sorted out quickly but this was proving to be a slow moving job. I still hadn't seen any of the lower levels and guessed that it might be some time before I was trusted enough to see what was really going on.

On the fourth day, everything moved a step forward. Spurrell told me that I was to take on my first duty and that I would be partnered with an experienced security guard who would show me the ropes. He called me into his office and offered me a seat. With Essy curled up on the floor, he began to open up to me about what I was to see. I had to stop myself from kissing him and thanking him for finally breaking my boredom.

"We're pleased with how you're progressing Joss."

"Thank you Sir."

"We've decided to let you do a full duty this evening. You'll be partnered with another guard who will explain things and show you what to do. Basically you'll just be patrolling, much like you've been doing on the surface with Pendle and the other security team. Things are quite different down here though and there are things you'll see that you'll not have seen before. As you know, we're a research establishment and as such, we experiment. That's how we find out what we need to know in order to move things forward for everyone. I know we had the conversation about discretion when I interviewed you, but I need to remind you of it again and give you a chance to decide finally whether the job is for you or not."

"Sir," I replied. "I did ten years in the military and have worked in security ever since, in all kinds of situations. I've seen things that have greatly disturbed me on a personal level but I've always carried out my duties to the best of my ability and if you check my work history you'll see I don't have a single mark against me for not carrying out my allocated duties."

"Why did you go into the military Joss?" he asked.

"Why? Well umm, to help people learn to live together in harmony I guess. For me, the military wasn't about being tough, it was about peace making and peace keeping and through all the killings and the things I witnessed and even took part in, the knowledge that this was leading to peace kept me going."

"Then you'll understand perfectly where we are coming from here at Calmarin," he replied. "In order for us to further our knowledge of how to bring medical cures and help to people who are in pain and suffering, we need to experiment and do tests. Those experiments are sometimes uncomfortable for people but knowing their bravery will bring help to millions of others makes it all worthwhile."

"I understand perfectly Sir," I lied.

"Okay, then follow me and I'll give you a tour of the lower level."

Along corridors and down another set of steps, Essy and I followed Spurrell and found ourselves in a corridor with an arched roof just like the one I had seen via the HairCam. I wondered if this was the actual tunnel that connected with the transport tunnels and kept my eyes open for the niche in the wall opposite an office door. Sure enough, there it was and I looked at the wall and grinned, Essy looked up at the wall too and I remembered that we were linked by thought. He showed me along corridors until we eventually found our way into what I immediately recognised as the shuttle loading room I had seen via the Consoria P30 camera that was still stuck in the grass and transmitting. The place was huge and I looked to see the long tunnel disappearing into the rock above me, down which I had seen the shuttles descending.

"Remember when you tripped over on your first day here and hurt your ankle?" Spurrell asked and I nodded. "That area of ground you noticed so expertly hides the entrance to that tunnel above us."

"Oh?" I replied, trying to sound amazed. "Wow."

"The substance we're manufacturing here is taken via shuttle, up through that tunnel and away to where it is stored. It saves us having to haul everything up those flights of stairs."

"Right, yeah that makes sense," I nodded and hoped I was doing a good enough acting job.

"Now we need to get issued with breather units before I take you into the next part. The fumes are dangerous."

"Okay," I replied, resisting the urge to question why, if this medical advancement was designed to help people, would the fumes be dangerous. We entered a small room and were issued with breather units. Spurrell asked me if I'd used one before and I assured him I'd used them plenty of times in the military. I asked him about Essy and whether the fumes would hurt her and he shook his head.

"Hymalonts are immune to the effects," he said. "That's the main reason we use them, that and their useful habit of being easy to manipulate into thought control." I was delighted to know she would not be harmed and realised that I was getting emotionally attached to her. It then occurred to me that when this job was finished, I might find it hard to leave her behind to be dealt with by whatever authority took over when this Calmarin business was out in the open. There were a couple of freelance law enforcers I knew of who had pets with them, so I knew she would not interfere with my work. In fact, she could be helpful in dangerous situations. What I did not know, was anyone who had a pet Hymalont, and she was a big fearsome looking creature. How would she act when I had company, as I sometimes do on jobs? Occasionally I have guests accompany me when I am on a job, and having something like Essy around might make it awkward. I decided it would be best to test her people skills when I got the opportunity. When she was unleashed, she just ignored everyone except me so that was not a problem, but I needed to know if I would be able to trust her completely.

The breather unit was heavy and uncomfortable, but there was no way I wanted to risk becoming one of those poor wretched shuffling husks, so I bore it without complaint. Another heavy door with a key card lock barred our way and Spurrell indicated for me to use my key card to unlock it. I did so and we entered a long narrow room with what looked like cells on either side, each occupied by one of the grey shuffling people.

"What's wrong with them?" I asked, trying to keep the emotion from my voice.

"They are suffering from a terrible affliction, from which we are trying to cure them."

"I thought you were just sorting out the problem with the trees," I said.

"Oh we are Joss, but in the course of our investigation into that, we found that what's poisoning the trees, has a medicinal benefit that might be able to cure a deadly disease called Palmax Syndrome."

"What is that?" I asked.

"It's a disease indigenous to people from the three inhabited planets in the Palmax System. It's a terrible plague to them and if we can help to cure it as well as stop the trees dying, we'll do two good things instead of just one."

"Oh I see," I replied, not knowing what else to say. I had never heard of the Palmax System and I have been around, but it is not beyond the realms of possibility that it could be genuine. I decided to ask Ren to mention it to Tinnias next time I called him.

"The disease they're suffering from can be passed in many ways, one of which is by airborne particles that they breathe out. That's one of the reasons to always wear the breather unit whenever you're near them."

"Okay," I nodded. "So you know what it is that's poisoning the trees then?"

"Yes, but we don't yet know how to cure them or stop it happening to more trees, although we have been able to slow down it's progression a little. Ahh, here we are. Just through here."

We entered another large room that contained several huge tanks. I saw metal steps snaking their way up the sides of the tanks at regular intervals and a visible cloud of fumes hung over the whole room.

"What the heck is that cloud?" I asked,

"Come, I'll show you." Spurrell indicated for me to follow him up the nearest set of steps. At the top I looked out over the vast acre of tank and the still fluid covering a layer of silver sediment. "This is what we're calling Heibat Zanbedox and it's what we hope will cure Palmax Syndrome. This cloud is the fumes from the liquid and if you were to take off your breather while standing here, you would undoubtedly die horribly."

"How can it cure people if it's so dangerous?" I asked.

"The secret is in the dosage, and that's the part we're still wrestling with but we'll get there."

"So where do you get this stuff?"

"That's what I'm going to show you now, this way."

We left the room with the tank and entered a small compartment. Spurrell indicated for me to stand on a plate in the corner. Overhead was what looked like a showerhead but when I pressed the button he indicated, a strong jet of air rained down over me, after which he indicated that it was safe to remove my breather unit.

"The fumes leave a fine residue that can build up over time and become toxic to the touch. This jet of air gets rid of the residue and prevents build up. Place your breather unit over there and it will be thoroughly cleaned before being put out for use again."

After the two of us, and Essy, went through the air shower, we went through another three locked doors until I found myself in a tunnel that looked like it had been hewn out of the bedrock. After walking for what seemed to me like a half mile, the noise of an engine reached me. Turning a corner, I found myself at a dead end at which a machine with a large drill head worked, the chunks of silver rock falling onto a conveyor that went up and over our heads, through a hole to an upper level, and away out of sight.

"This is the rock from which we get the substance," Spurrell said.

"Isn't this dangerous?" I said.

"Not at all," he replied and reached down and grabbed a rock as big as his fist. "In its natural state it's harmless, see? It's only by grinding it to powder and mixing it with a particular fluid that it becomes both dangerous and miraculous."

"So if it's not dangerous, how come it poisoned the trees?"

"Because we found that by a complete coincidence of nature, this seam of rock came into contact with a small pool of this liquid, which is also a naturally occurring substance. Normally, the geological conditions necessary to produce this rock are totally different to those needed to produce the liquid and the two cannot be formed in the same environment. There must've been an earthquake at some time in the past that created a pathway between these two neighbours. As we all know, liquid flows when it has the chance and when these two combined, the result was a slow poisoning of the trees in the ground directly above. We drained off the liquid, and we're mining the remainder of the rock so that we can combine them in a controlled environment and use the resulting product to help cure Palmax Syndrome."

"Oh, I get it," I nodded. "So umm, if you've drained the liquid off, it can't be poisoning the trees anymore, can it?"

"Not directly no, but you see when the liquid and rock powder combined, the resulting mixture will have leeched into the soil for untold numbers of years. Rather than remove the trees and soil, find somewhere safe to dump it and then replace it, we thought it would be better and cheaper to try to find something we can add to the soil to counteract the effects."

"Right, gotcha," I said. So far, everything he'd told me was entirely plausible and if true, noble. Why then did I not believe a single word he said? On the way back through the tunnels and corridors, I thought of another question and wanted to see how he got around this one.

"Boss? Sorry to keep asking questions but it's interesting. How come you need us guys? Surely the security guys outside are enough aren't they? Why the special security?"

"Because our patients, those poor Palmax Syndrome sufferers you saw, get very violent. It's a side effect of the syndrome you see Joss. It affects the brain in such a way that they become dangerous and can pass on the syndrome by biting, scratching, spitting and clawing. Until we find a cure, we need you guys to protect us and the outside world from the disease they carry."

"Right, yeah I understand."

I made my calls that evening and updated everyone and they were amazed at the amount of information I had been given. Ren was astounded when I told him everything I had seen and been told and promised to call Tinnias and pass it all on to him. He then made a comment that I've so often wished I took more notice of. He was showing me the depth of his wisdom and I, of course, failed to take heed.

"Be careful Joss. There's something not right about all this."

"What do you mean buddy?"

"I can't explain, it's just a feeling. It's just, oh I don't know but it seems real weird to me at how quick they've opened up to you about what they're doing, even if they haven't told you the whole truth."

"Yeah he didn't go into detail about the shuttles or the regular influx of new people who don't look at all sick when they arrive."

"It's just too perfect," he said.

"How so?"

"Well think about it. You've only been in the job four days and already he's told you all this stuff. How the fuck does he know you're not going to blab to everyone once they let you out at the end of your week huh? Doesn't that seem like the most outrageous risk to you?"

"I get your point," I replied. "But so far what he's told me is just how nobly they're trying to find a cure for everything. The only wrong doing he's admitted to is not telling anyone outside exactly what they're doing. On the face of it, they're trying to do a great service to everyone on both Deligon and all three planets in this alleged Palmax System. The whole lot could be a total fabrication."

"You have a valid point too Joss, but I've got this feeling y'know? Please don't take anything for granted huh? Promise me."

"I promise buddy, and you take care too okay? I'll call you tomorrow."

Essy nudged me and wriggled her head under my arm and began making that rumbling noise she makes when she's happy.

"Okay girl, let's go get some dinner huh?"

I was on duty promptly and met my colleague, a guy named Brelik. He turned out to be a nice guy and chatted non-stop to me the whole time. His Hymalont was named Lokka, a big dark and foreboding looking male who took quite a shine to Essy and they got along like a house on fire. Essy completely ignored Brelik and Lokka totally ignored me. We patrolled the corridors and twice watched as lines of grey silent people shuffled past.

"Where are they going?" I asked.

"To get their injections."

"Oh right, the medicine Spurrell told me about, for the Palmax Syndrome?"

Brelik looked at me for just a moment too long before snickering. "So that's what he's calling it now is it? When I joined a year ago it was Canlium Poisoning and a couple of my buddies were told something else again."

"Really?" I exclaimed, feigning surprise. "You saying he's covering something up?"

"Hey buddy, I ain't saying nothing because my wife values my balls almost as much as I do and if you value yours, you'll stop wondering what's really going on and just do the job."

"So there's sufficient need to worry about losing them then?" I replied and he nodded. "I guess whatever they are doing is pretty serious then, wouldn't you think?"

"Hell yeah," he nodded. We carried on down the white tiled corridor in silence.

hiss, thunk, foo

hiss, thunk, foo

hiss, thunk, foo

Merita King

CHAPTER FIFTEEN

The remainder of my week's incarceration at Calmarin passed in a similar fashion to the first four days. I spent my days training with my Hymalont, Essy, and soon gained a good level of control over her and found the thought transference headset easy to use. It just takes concentration and once I learned the knack of focussing, it was easy. After the evening meal, I took a shift with one of the other guards and we patrolled the corridors. On the evening when the shuttles were due, Spurrell called me to duty to help oversee security during the loading of drums. I watched as the cart loads of drums were loaded and taken away and noticed that security was heavy. There were fourteen guards with Hymalonts in the loading bay alone, not counting the ones on the surface, and I knew I would never be able to do this alone. I would have to call in the troops that were waiting in covert orbit to help me. Tinnias had said it would take them a couple of hours to arrive on site, so this could not be a spur of the moment thing. It would need careful planning and I was grateful that things seemed to work to a tight and predictable schedule at the station.

Once the shuttles had gone, an alarm sounded and I looked at my co-worker and frowned.

"It's time for the new batch to go into the mix Joss," he said. "Follow me. We have to make sure none of em run off or anything."

"What do you mean?" I asked.

"The people," he explained. "They're a new batch so they might be a little argumentative."

"Huh?"

"Don't you know anything?"

"Sorry buddy, I'm new remember?"

"Yeah, sorry. The stuff they make takes a week to brew and it needs to be stirred three times a day. The people go into the tank with paddles and stir the mixture for an hour. Once they ship it out, the people go in and clean out the tank and a new batch goes in. The people need to be supervised so they don't try to run away or anything."

"The people?" I said. "You mean the ones with the sickness?"

"Oh so that's what they told you huh?" he laughed. "Listen Joss. There's no sickness and there's certainly no cure. The people are used to make the stuff they ship out, the liquid in the drums and we're here to ensure they do as they're told. That's all."

"So why do they look so sick?"

"Because working in the tank makes em like that," he replied. I then remembered wondering what Deniko Pasnel meant when we'd all heard him talking to the guard about immersion. I now knew the answer and my heart fell.

"What about the injections they give them?" I asked. "What are they for?"

"To keep them obedient. It's some kind of stuff to make them quiet I guess. Come on, get your breather on or you're toast."

We donned our breather units and entered the tank room. A long line of people were filing out from a door to our right and heading for the tanks. They filed past a guard who handed each a broom as they headed towards the stairs that led up the side of each tank. Once on the rim, they stepped over and descended another set of steps into the belly of the tanks and out of our sight. Hoses ran from the ceiling and I could hear liquid being sprayed and brushes scrubbing. Suddenly, one of the people yelled something and ran from the line and headed towards the door.

"Okay big boy," my partner said to his Hymalont, "time for dinner."

"I got this," I said quickly. "It's good practice for me and Essy huh?"

"Well all right then," he grinned and nodded at me. "She's all yours."

I mentally sent Essy after the woman and made sure she knew that she was to prevent her escape but not harm her. She leapt at her and grabbed her arm and sent her sprawling to the floor, where she stood over her growling menacingly. The terrified woman covered her face with her arms and screamed in fright as a man in a white lab coat approached her with an injector. Once the woman was subdued and compliant, I called Essy back and grinned at my co-worker in triumph, to find him frowning at me.

"What the fuck are you doing Joss?" he hissed.

"What?" I asked, confused. "I stopped her getting away and now she's back on the job. What's the problem?"

"You think these bad boys here are just for decoration?" he said as he rattled his Hymalont's leash.

"Of course not," I glared back. "They're for security, which is exactly what I was doing, upholding security and preventing her escape. I didn't have to kill her to do that."

"There's hundreds more where she came from," he countered. "If you don't want to get a reputation as weak around here, don't hold back next time okay?"

"I couldn't give a Flatmid Eldor's asshole about reputation," I replied. "I do my job and if there's no reason to kill, then I won't. These are the animals around here," I shook Essy's leash to emphasise my point. "Or maybe they're not the only ones." I held his gaze for a few seconds to push my point home, before turning away and resuming my watch.

I found that my standing within the workforce changed significantly after that episode. There were two distinct sides; those who enjoyed using their Hymalonts to kill whenever they got the chance, and those who tried to avoid it at all costs. I knew I had joined the right side, but I was also aware that it was not the strongest. New people now said hello to me in the mess hall, and some who previously used to, no longer did. I had made a public statement about myself and I would have to live with the consequences.

My last shift before my week's incarceration ended was my first solo duty. I found myself patrolling the corridor that adjoined the transport tunnel so when I passed by the niche in the wall where the tunnel had been blocked in, I turned and waved so the guys would know it was me. Three hours into my shift, the door opposite the niche opened and I saw Deniko Pasnel, the man I had seen talking in code to one of the security guards via the HairCam, and made a quick decision.

"Excuse me, do you have a light?" I called. He stopped mid stride before turning slowly and looking me in the eyes. I turned and headed into the niche and leaned against the wall as nonchalantly as I could. For a couple of agonising seconds I wondered whether he had taken the bait, but then he appeared and looked at me, before joining me in the niche.

"Do you have a light?" I repeated as he looked at me. "They're very bad for the health you know."

"Then maybe you should take up drinking he said, the suspicion evident in his voice.

"I don't like cold drinks," I replied immediately.

"I prefer them hot myself," he replied and stood next to me.

"Mr Pasnel I presume?" I said and he nodded. "Tell me about your little arrangement with the guard."

"What little arrangement?" he replied, his attempt at faking surprise wasn't bad but wasn't nearly good enough to fool me.

"I have it on film," I said, "so either you tell me about it or I hand it to Spurrell and you can explain it to him." Pasnel visibly paled so I guessed

173

that suggestion was not one he would choose to implement if given the choice.

"Who the fuck are you and what do you want?"

"I'm the guy who has the upper hand," I said, "so explain."

"You're that new security guard, the one transferred from surface security aren't you?" he said. Joss Gilden."

"Pleased to meet you," I hissed. "Now, explain."

"Maybe I should call Spurrell and tell him you've tried to blackmail me into telling you things," he challenged and I grinned.

"Fine, you do that," I said as I pushed myself away from the wall and headed back out into the corridor. "Don't say I didn't warn ya."

"Okay okay," he hissed and waved me back inside the niche. "Look I really don't want any trouble. I'm just trying to do the right thing, and look out for myself too."

"So am I," I replied, "but I need all the information you have to help me do that. Y'know buddy, it's not beyond the realms of possibility that you and I could be on the same side here." He sighed deeply and ran a hand through his hair.

"I don't like what's happening here. It's got too big. There's a disaster waiting to happen and I don't want to be a part of it. The people, so many people. I never wanted that, but no matter how I tried to persuade them, they wouldn't listen. Here and there, I try to get a few out but it's just a drop in the ocean. Every time the price goes up and the number I can get out goes down."

"So your conversation the other day was about getting some of the people out of here?" I asked and he nodded.

"Yeah. They want seven thousand each this time and I have problems raising that kind of money. I've managed it this time but I'm afraid I won't be able to raise any more. How will I help them then?"

"Who else is in on your scheme?" I asked.

"Professor Jakelham and a couple of the security guards. They have contacts on the outside who they get donations from." Pieces were beginning to fit together inside my head.

"Adlion Garmast," I said and he nodded.

"Yeah. How did you know that?"

"Oh I'm clever like that buddy," I replied. "Tell me, how do you get them out?"

"There's a secret entrance that leads from the back of store room seven. The shelving is attached to a false wall that leads to part of the old transport system tunnels. It comes out in an alleyway between the city hall and museum next door. It just looks like a metal door into the rear of the museum but it's actually the old entrance to one of the underground transport platforms. We have to get them out during the first three days of their arrival here or they're too far gone to be able to have any kind of quality of life outside."

"Why is that?" I asked.

"Because there's no cure, even after one shift in the tank and the effects are cumulative. After three or four day's exposure in the tank, their brain is too poisoned for them to be able to function normally."

"I know they go in the tank every day?" I nodded. "I thought it was just for an hour at a time though."

"Yes, but they do three one hour shifts every day, and there's the cleaning too, it all adds up."

"Why don't they give them waterproof suits to wear or something?"

"Because the liquid isn't water," he sighed. "It's able to seep through even waterproof materials and it quickly destroys the material anyway. They would need a new suit every time they go in the tanks and the powers that be, don't want to spend that kind of money. People are cheaper to replace. I hate seeing them become affected. I feel so helpless."

"So did you get the last lot out okay?"

"Yes."

"Good. Can you tell me what they're doing all this for?"

"Power Joss. Massive amounts of power. Each drum of the liquid they're shipping out of here has the potential to provide power for a city the size of Bygora Vandos for three or four months. They're hoping to sell it to the highest bidder and disappear before any of the buyers discover how dangerous it is."

"What's the story on those seven people who died?" I asked. "Symeal Gloak and that woman who certainly did not die by falling whilst climbing. There were seven in all whose deaths were obviously covered up. What's the real story?"

"I liked Mr Gloak," he sighed. "He was an honourable man. All of the seven were technicians here and all made it obvious they didn't approve of what is going on. Each of them threatened to tell the authorities about it and no amount of bribery would change their minds. Spurrell had them chained naked into a bath of the liquid and they died within four days. Their bodies were shipped out and left so they would look like accidental deaths."

"Shit," I sighed.

"Yeah," Pasnel nodded. "Indeed."

"Can you help me get hard evidence of what you've just told me? I need access to computer records or something, documentation so that I can help stop this."

"Yes I can," he nodded. "But not for a couple of days. I do a weekly back up of all the week's research which normally takes an hour or so. It's in room 37a, at the end of corridor four. I always do the backup late in the evening when all the researchers have gone for the day so the record is kept as up to date as possible. Meet me in there at midnight, three nights from tonight and you can have all the evidence you need."

"Thanks buddy," I nodded.

"Can you really stop all this Joss? Do you really have that power?"

"Yes I can," I replied as I headed back into the corridor, "and I will."

I called Ren as soon as my shift was over and after apologising profusely for waking him, I told him everything I had been told. He promised to call Tinnias right away and update him and said he would upload the film of my conversation with Pasnel for him to see. Tinnias had told him there was no Palmax system and therefore, no syndrome either.

"It looks as if everything will go down three nights from tonight. When I get out of here I'll call the troops and arrange it with them. Can you get the boys to blow the tunnel wall so we can lead some of the people out?"

"Sure, I'll call them first thing in the morning and arrange that with them. Do you want me to let Garmast know?"

"See what Tinnias says first," I replied. "If he's okay with it then do it. I'll be back tomorrow so we'll talk about everything then. I've got a couple of days off and then I'm on night shift."

"Okay, see you tomorrow Joss."

I was glad to be back in our apartment and took a long shower before making myself a rather large and indulgent lunch. Then I called Tinnias and asked him how things had been while I was out of sight.

"Ren's been calling me daily Sam," he said, "so I've been kept up to date with everything that you've been reporting. I can't tell you how relieved I am about Garmast; the thought that he might be a double agent was too terrifying to contemplate."

"I know Boss, I felt the same."

"So it looks like we have a go for the night after tomorrow huh?"

"Yeah. If the troops can start a diversion, Ren and I can take advantage of the chaos to download as much information as we can find from Pasnel's computer console. We also have all the film footage. That should be enough shouldn't it?"

"Yeah, we'll have those bastards Sam. I've been discussing things with Garmast and told him that there will be something of a hiatus at the Research Station the night after tomorrow and that he's to ignore all calls that aren't from either yourself or Ren. He's promised to have his officers ready and waiting for your call. You will have to call him when the troops have things under control as he has official jurisdiction in Bygora Vandos. He's doing us a big favour by holding back and letting us do the initial work so don't offend him by keeping him out of it okay? Let him make the official arrests."

"Okay no problem. Boss? What will happen to the Hymalonts?"

"Come on Sam, don't get all mushy on me now."

"Sorry. I guess I've got a little attached to the thing. She's got such a sweet nature."

"You can't go carting a Hymalont around with you on jobs. An animal like that is too much of a responsibility and a great danger."

"Yeah I guess you're right. Promise me she'll be treated with compassion though huh? Even if she's to be destroyed."

"I give you my word. Call me if there are any more developments okay? In any case call me during the afternoon, the day after tomorrow so we can finalise your plans."

"I will."

I then called Marlo who confirmed that Ren and I still had our followers, which annoyed me but I guess it was to be expected. I asked him if the three of them could prepare to blow the wall in the tunnel to give me an escape route and he was delighted to be involved.

"Sure Joss, that's no problem at all. The guys and I will go and set it up tomorrow and it will be ready for you to give the word. All four of us will be there on the day so don't hesitate to call when you need us okay?"

"Thanks buddy, I really appreciate the help. There's going to be a lot of troops descending on the place so keep well out of the line of fire. I don't want any of you guys getting hurt."

"Okay. I'll call you tomorrow and confirm everything's ready."

Ren and I worked out for hours that evening. We both felt the need to be physically ready and the routine helped us relax and focus. Our conversation was all about tactics and all possible scenarios that could occur. Then we checked and re-checked our armoury; we did not want to forget anything. The plan was for me to go into work as normal while Ren would meet the boys at the tunnel. I would then call in the troops and use the time until they arrived to meet with Pasnel as arranged and download as much information as I could. Once the troops arrived and all hell broke loose, I would call Ren and the boys to blow the tunnel wall. Ren would then join me and cover my back, after which we would both beat a hasty retreat through the tunnel. I decided to call Kobey and tell him to prepare for the troops and maybe even help to ensure they got onto the site with as little trouble as possible.

"Hi Kobey, it's Joss here. Joss Gilden."

"Hi Joss, how's it going in R and D?"

"Do you umm, remember our conversation the last time we met? You said you'd like to be involved in a umm, party?"

"Hell yeah, I love a party. Just tell me where and when and I'll round up some friends. We'll make sure everything goes with a swing."

"That's wonderful. The day after tomorrow, a large crowd of friends will be arriving to join in the fun around midnight or so. Maybe you could show them where the real fun is to be had huh?"

"I'd be glad to Joss. Hell, this is just what I need to make me feel young again. Thanks for inviting me buddy."

"It wouldn't be a party without you Kobey. See you the day after tomorrow. Take care."

The following day was Ren's day off so we decided to spend a couple of hours in the morning working out. Once we had showered, we went out for lunch and found a nice quiet restaurant just around the corner from our apartment. We both expected this to be our last chance to enjoy Bygora Vandos before our little party at the Research Station so we blew the budget and had a feast. When neither of us could face another morsel, we staggered out of the restaurant and headed for a nearby bar. Three hours later we limped back to the apartment laughing our heads off at the way the gorgeous blondes had helped us recover from our over indulgence.

"I thought you weren't into blondes Joss?" Ren said as he pressed the button on the elevator up to floor seven.

"Yeah well," I blushed. "I guess I changed my mind."

He turned and looked at me for several seconds and then smiled. "Merellia was a blonde wasn't she?"

"Yeah," I nodded.

"That's good buddy. It shows you're getting past the pain and finding your balance with it. I'm proud of you man."

"Thanks. It does feel kind of, different now, when I think about her."

"How different?"

"It feels good now, her memory I mean. It used to feel bad but now it doesn't." I shrugged but Ren nodded in complete understanding. I will never be able to understand that guy's wisdom.

"That's wonderful. Once you've dealt with the pain, it can't hurt you anymore. The more you tried to bury it and ignore it, the stronger it got and the worse it got. Only by expressing it can it go away and just leave the truth behind."

"The truth?" I asked.

"That she was a beautiful woman you loved who made you happy."

I nodded. I understood.

We spent a couple of hours relaxing over a dreadful vidicom movie and then went for a run and worked out for a couple of hours, after which we went over our plan again and checked our armoury for the fourth time. Marlo called and confirmed the tunnel wall was rigged and promised that Donal and all three boys would be on site by ten the next evening. They would be waiting for our call and would blow the wall. I then called the troops on the number Tinnias had given me and relayed the information to them. They said they would arrive at midnight and would look for Kobey and a bunch of men in security uniforms who would be waiting to assist them. Now that everything was in place, I called Tinnias and told him everything was set to go at midnight the next evening.

"Okay guys, we have a go. Everything is set. Are you sure it's the right time? It's not too late to delay if you need to. Remember time is flexible on this one."

"There would be no benefit to further delay," I replied. "We have enough vidicom footage, I have a small sample of the raw Zanbedellium from when Spurrell gave me the tour and there's Pasnel who would probably be willing to testify and knows just about all there is to know. We will need to ensure he gets away safely by the way."

"They'll extract him safely, don't worry. Now once you've got your download, you get out of there to the tunnel. Ren, you promise me you'll both get the fuck out of there without any heroics."

"I promise Sir," Ren replied

We both awoke early after having decided to get an early night. We wanted to be rested and I had slept surprisingly well considering the pressure of the imminent showdown. After weeks of boring my ass off waiting for things to come together, the knowledge that I was just a day away from snapping my cuffs on someone made me excited. We breakfasted lightly and discussed how we both hoped the mission would go.

"If everything goes like clockwork, we could be having a celebration meal with Donal and the boys tomorrow," Ren laughed and I grinned. Suddenly a wild idea flashed into my mind and I looked at him.

"Hey buddy. After this job is over, why don't we team up? We work well together and we get along fine and it'll be fun."

"I was wondering the same," he replied, "but I never suggested it because you always say you prefer to work alone."

"I'm used to working alone, sure, but I don't prefer it." I noticed him frown at me and I blushed. "You know this work Ren, we can't have proper friendships or emotional commitments and it's always been easier to keep a little detachment from people. I don't like the idea of letting people down by not being a reliable friend y'know? I've never had the chance to have a best buddy before, especially one that knows the job and one I don't have to lie to about what I'm doing. I never realised it felt this good having a buddy that's all. We'd make a great team. But you're right, it's probably a silly idea," I said, trying to cover my embarrassment and disappointment with a snigger.

"I agree," Ren replied quickly, "and I'd love to."

"You would?" I exclaimed.

"Yeah. I've only been doing the job for five years but I know what you mean about the solitude. Not being able to confide in someone is hard for me sometimes. Where I come from, we're social people. We don't do solitude. We could pool our resources and buy a bigger ship with a couple of runabouts and pool our contacts too. We'd be a force to be reckoned with across the whole galaxy."

"That's awesome buddy," I grinned and reached across the table. He shook my hand and our deal was sealed. I was happy at that moment, happier than I had been in many years and it had taken the friendship of another man to help me achieve it. At that moment I was determined our friendship was going to continue and was so relieved when he agreed.

I was clearing up after lunch when Marlo called to wish me luck. He promised to help Ren shake off his follower long enough for them all to get away safely to Donal's store, where they were meeting before heading to the tunnel complex. My shift was due to start at ten so we arranged that I would leave at nine, as would be normal and Ren would leave at quarter past, after having got a call from one of the boys assuring him that his follower was taking a nap.

I was immediately alert when I got a call from Spurrell at four thirty telling me they needed me to come in early as there had been what he would only refer to as 'an accident' and all security staff were being called in. All my senses switched to high alert and I knew at once something had gone wrong and rang Donal straight away. He assured me he would call the boys and get Ren as soon as he got in. It was then that I realised Ren should be home any minute now and contemplated waiting for him. I hung around for ten minutes but my gut was getting more and more knotted up, so I left a note and raced from the apartment. After doing this job for so long my law enforcer's hunch is not often wrong and I just knew something was up. All the way to the station, I could not shake a nagging worry about Ren, although nothing had occurred to put me on alert other than him being a few minutes late home from work. As the hover cab purred through the city, I tried to talk common sense to myself. His hover bus could be late or he could have stopped into a store on his way home; there were any number of reasons but none of them calmed my inner turmoil. I sat in the hover cab and worried for my friend.

Once at the station, I raced into work and found Spurrell waiting for me by the main security door into the R and D department. He was talking to another guy in a white lab coat and smiled as he saw me approach.

"Thanks for coming in early Joss," he said and although his mouth smiled, his eyes didn't and I knew at once he was faking it.

"No problem Boss, what's up?"

"You get yourself showered and kitted up as normal and I'll explain everything in my office. Thirty minutes?"

"Sure, okay."

Thirty minutes later I was kitted up and had received a huge welcome from Essy, involving lots of face licking and belly rubs and both of us were standing outside Spurrell's office. I raised my hand to knock but a thought raced through my mind and I looked at Essy.

"I need you to obey me without question tonight baby," I sent her the thought and she looked up at me, her eyes focussed in that way I had come to recognise as understanding. "I will ask you to do some things that are a little different from our normal work but I need you to trust me and obey." We locked eyes and I knew she understood and I breathed a sigh of relief as I knocked on Spurrell's door.

"Come in Joss," he said as he stepped aside. "Thanks once again for coming in at such short notice."

"No problem," I replied. "What's the panic? You said there was an accident?"

"Yes, one of our latest umm, patients went a bit crazy and injured a couple of our security guys. It started a bit of a riot and we had to lock the place down to contain it."

"Oh I see. Are the guys okay?"

"Yeah, they'll live. They're in the infirmary now. It took several guys to hold the patient down so we could get some sedative into him. He's calm now."

"Where would you like me to begin my patrol Sir?"

"If you go and relax for a while and maybe begin at eight? Is that okay with you?"

"Of course Boss."

"Thanks. You'll be starting with the patient's cubicles tonight so report there for duty at eight okay?"

"Yes Sir," I nodded and turned to leave, Essy at my heels as always. I raced back to the staff accommodation and went into the same room I had used the week before. First, I called Marlo and asked if Ren had got home okay. His reply chilled me to the bone.

"He never arrived home Joss. We're worried sick."

"Oh shit no," I said as I remembered my conversation with Spurrell just minutes before. "I think they have him prisoner here. Oh fuck I have to get him out of here."

"What can we do?"

"Get to the tunnels as quick as you can and wait for my call. I'm going to call in the troops now, which will mean we have two hours until the shit hits the fan."

"Okay, I'll round everyone up and we'll be there within the hour. Be safe buddy."

I then called the troops, gave them the details, and heard the siren going off in the background as I spoke with their commander.

"We'll be with you in two hours Joss. Just hold on. We'll have you both out of there, I promise."

Another call to Kobey sent him into a panic, which did not surprise me knowing his obsession with schedules. He rose to the occasion though and said he would do what he could with the guards he had on duty and promised the troops would not encounter any problems when they arrived. The next two hours dragged by, the slowest two hours of my entire life and

I spent every minute worrying for Ren. Eventually I couldn't stand it any longer and reported for duty fifteen minutes early. Spurrell was in the patient cubicle when I arrived and smiled when he saw me enter.

"Hello there Joss, nice to see you eager for work tonight. Come and meet the source of all our problems."

I sent a thought to Essy as I walked to the end of the narrow corridor lined with patient cubicles. "Be ready girl, watch my back." She slowed her pace a tiny bit and fell into line behind me. I reached the cubicle at the end of the corridor and slowly turned to look through the glass partition wall. He was hunched on the floor, one knee drawn up, his head resting in his hand. Bloodied scraps of cloth dotted around the small cubicle explained why he was shirtless, the bruises already forming over his chest and shoulders telling me of a severe beating.

I leapt forward and banged on the glass. "Ren, buddy. What the fuck? Why is he being held here? He's my friend, he works here. I don't understand. What the fuck is going on?" I yelled at Spurrell, who took a step back from my angry onslaught. I heard growls from behind me and turned to see Essy holding off an approaching lab guy who wielded a huge injector. Instinct drove my hand to my tranquiliser pistol, hidden beneath my jacket and shot Spurrell at point blank range. He was unconscious within twenty seconds and I turned back to see how Essy was doing. The lab guy was retreating towards the door at the far end. He didn't make it; the sedative dart ensuring he was out cold before he was halfway there. I turned back to Ren, who was almost unconscious in his prison.

"I'll be back for you buddy, I promise." I called Essy and together, we raced out into the corridor.

Merita King

CHAPTER SIXTEEN

Thoughts were racing around my head, all jumbled and in my panic, I wasn't able to make sense of any one of them. What the fuck had gone wrong and why? Had someone given us up and if so, who? Why was Ren in a cell? He hadn't done anything except read a few personnel files. I was determined whoever did this to my friend was going to pay dearly. The first thing I did was ring the boys and tell them what had happened. They were already on route through the forest and promised they would blow the tunnel as soon as they arrived. As I ran along corridors, I heard the siren go off and saw lights flashing up in the corners and I guessed the troops had arrived on the surface and hoped they were finding their way down here. I pulled down my breather and tried to look like just another security guard racing to help sort out whatever the problem was and as my work colleagues rushed passed me in all directions, none of them stopped me so I guessed the attempt on my life was not yet general knowledge. Sighing with relief, I was grateful for that; at least I would not have to bother with fending off security guards and angry Hymalonts.

My first task was to find room 37a and download as much information as I could, so I raced along to corridor four. Men in lab coats were running in all directions, the panic in their faces obvious.

"What do we do? Where do we go?" one of them asked me. I was a bit taken aback before I realised he expected me, as a security guard, to know what to do.

"Head up to the surface and out through the main door. Someone is there to do a head count. Go on, go," I commanded and he obeyed without question, followed by all the others who had heard our exchange. This would help ensure the main door was open for the troops, as I knew Kobey did not have a key card for it and I had not been able to secure one for him. Room 37a was tucked away at the far end of the corridor, so I yanked open the door and entered, to find two guys in lab coats standing at the console. One of them was Pasnel. Panting from running and panic, I removed my breather and looked at him.

"Oh it's you," he sighed with obvious relief. "Shut the damn door would you?"

"Who are you?" I demanded of the other guy.

"This is Jakelham," Pasnel replied, "and he's helping me upload this week's report so you can download everything, so be nice. It's far earlier than we normally do this, but I guessed you'd find your way here. We both want to make sure you get as much information as possible."

"Oh, okay," I nodded at the guy, who nodded back. I jammed a chair against the doorknob and set Essy to guard the entrance. "Don't let anyone in girl." Jakelham and Pasnel operated the console while I paced and tried to remain calm.

"What the fuck happened?" I demanded. "My best friend is being held prisoner in the patient cubicles and someone tried to off me with a syringe. What the fuck's going on?"

"The Chief got a call about you," Jakelham said.

"The Chief?" I asked.

"Roben Abydell Mirras."

"Calmarin's head honcho?"

"Yeah. He got a call just over a week ago, telling him all about you. You were already working here by then so he ordered that you be brought in and dealt with and when you applied for the job down here, it seemed the easy way to deal with you."

"But why is Ren here?"

"There were two reasons. Firstly, he's your buddy and with you two living together, your disappearance would make him suspicious and he might start an investigation that Mirras wouldn't approve of. Secondly, the caller who told us about you, also mentioned that Ren is a law enforcer too. When Mirras realised we'd had a law enforcer working here and peering into the personnel records for the past few months, it was felt prudent to deal with him too."

"It was felt prudent?" I almost yelled.

"Quiet, for fuck's sake Joss," Pasnel hissed.

"Sorry, but I'm having a little difficulty adjusting to the, the, grand scale and organisation of all this. Lives are just collateral damage are they?"

"To these people, yes," Jakelham nodded. "You've no idea of the amount of money they're hoping to make out of this. The power it will give them is way beyond anyone's comprehension. That kind of thing is powerful inducement to bend your normal morals a little."

"Or a lot," Pasnel added and Jakelham nodded again.

"So why are you two working against them?" I asked.

"Well first because it's totally, utterly wrong and secondly because we were planted here eighteen months ago to work our way into the heart of the place and see what was going on. We pass information back and get a few people out when we can and those we really answer to have been slowly building their case against Calmarin."

"And just who is it you work for?"

"We're ghosts," Jakelham replied.

My jaw dropped in shock. All law enforcers have heard about ghosts but I had never actually met one and many people thought they were just invented by conspiracy theorists. Ghosts are ultra-secret agents who work for an officially non-existent arm of the Inter Galactic Law Enforcement Agency. They are planted into situations and work their way into the community, become a part of the community and gather intelligence from the inside and slowly, carefully, work up a case against them. It takes time doing a ghost's job and sometimes, as in Jakelham and Pasnel's case, it can take years. There are rumours that many of the jobs I, and other law enforcers like me get, come from years of research and information gathering by diligent ghosts and although I have never quite known whether it's true or not, the secrecy and mystique surrounding them intrigued me.

"Wow," I replied. "I've heard about you guys. I've never quite known what is true and what's just rumour though. You guys do an awesome job. Thank you."

"Thanks Joss," Pasnel replied. "We seldom get gratitude for our efforts."

"So who was the call from?" I asked. "The call that sold Ren and I out?"

"Manno Lashling," Jakelham said and grinned at my raised eyebrows.

"So that's how he fits in all of this."

"Yeah, he's one of the Mirras lookout guys. He's got contacts everywhere and one of them knew about you and Ren."

"I wonder who?"

"Who hates you?"

"Could be anyone of a thousand people from hundreds of planets. Where the fuck do I begin to search through such a long list of names?"

"You'll probably never know."

"But this mission was kept real secret," I replied. "It must be someone in law enforcement."

"An inside man?" Pasnel asked and I nodded. "There's always an inside man isn't there? Damn, how predictable."

"Is there really no cure for those people?"

"None," Jakelham replied quietly. "We've been working on finding an antidote but we've failed so far. That stuff is the most evil and poisonous substance I've ever heard of."

"What will happen to them?"

"The new intake can be cared for and live reasonable lives with most of their minds intact," Pasnel said. "The others who've been here longer will be dead within another week or so. Right, that's the upload done, now here, you do your download so we can all get out of here."

I stepped forward and retrieved my data recorder and a docking adaptor from my back pocket. After attaching the adaptor to my recorder, I docked it with the console and tapped the screen to begin the download. Behind me, Essy growled as she glared at the door. The door handle rattled and all three of us jumped. I sent a thought to Essy to be quiet but remain on guard as the door handle rattled again. After a third attempt, we heard boot steps running away up the outer corridor and we all sighed.

"We have to get out of here," Pasnel said and Jakelham nodded.

"I'm organising a way out," I told them as I tapped the keys on my Unicom and called Marlo, who informed me that they would be ready to blow the wall in ten minutes. I told them to wait for my call, which would be pretty soon. "You're welcome to join me if you want but I need your help first."

"How can we help?" Jakelham asked.

"I need to rescue Ren from the patient cubicles. He's been given some kind of tranquiliser and is almost out cold. Is there something to wake him up a bit? He's a big guy and I'll get him out quicker if I don't have to drag his body."

"Yes, there is something I can give him," Pasnel nodded. "It's kept in the medical supply cupboard at the end of the patient cubicle section."

"Thanks. All we have to do is get Ren out and back down to the corridor with the niche in the wall, where you and I had our conversation." They both nodded.

We heard the sounds of gunfire from above and we looked up.

"What the fuck is going on?" Pasnel said.

"That'll be the troops," I replied. "Relax, they're here to sweep the place." A beep from the console told me the download was finished and I yanked my recorder from the docking plug and shoved it into my pocket. I put an ear to the door but all was quiet outside.

"Ready guys?" I asked and they both nodded reluctantly. "Keep behind me and Essy and stay close okay?" Gingerly, I pulled open the door and stepped into the empty corridor. It was eerily silent so I beckoned the two men to follow and jogged up to where the corridors intersect. I sent Essy a thought to be on her guard as I pulled down my breather and headed into the crowd of scared workers all running for the main exit. The patient cubicles were down a corridor to our right and the three of us headed down there, Pasnel shutting the door behind us. Sickened with worry, I raced along to the end cubicle to see Ren still crouched on the floor but not so out of it as he had looked the last time I had seen him. His body was obviously dealing with the sedative very quickly and I was pleased.

"Let me get by," Pasnel said as he headed for the medical supply cupboard. He shot a look at Ren and his face darkened. "Oh, he's Damiklonian. Shit."

"What do you mean shit?" I demanded.

"It must've taken a massive dose to get him this quiet and it'll take another massive one to wake him up. It could harm him."

"Just give him some," I said. "Even a small dose might help wake him a little bit won't it?"

"Okay," he said as he fumbled with an injector and a phial of blue liquid. "I'll give him the same dose as we give to the Gildenarians. That should help a bit without doing damage. Okay step aside." He pressed a code into the cubicle locking mechanism and the glass partition slid aside. I raced over and grabbed Ren, who reacted defensively and tried to fight me off.

"Hey, it's okay buddy it's me Joss. Relax Ren, it's me. I'm here to get you out, just trust me okay?" I felt him relax a little and I held him as Pasnel delivered the injection. Then I noticed the antidote tube was missing from Ren's arm and guessed he had put up one hell of a fight. Spurrell had told me two of his guards were in the infirmary and the missing tube of antidote told me Ren must have bitten them. I hoped they were suffering.

"That's it buddy, come on now, we gotta run so help me out here okay or do I have to drag your sorry ass?"

The sound of more gunfire, this time on the same level as ours, came to us from right outside the door. I didn't want to get taken for one of Calmarin's security guards so I threw off my breather unit. With great care, I opened the door to see several of the troops laying down fire on the advancing guards and their Hymalonts and I slammed it shut quickly. My thoughts turned to Essy and I was suddenly worried for her. There was no other way out, so I opened the door again and signalled to the nearest of the troops, who immediately turned his gun to face me. I held up my hands.

"Whoa stop, it's me, Space Cop 257. Sam Sinclair. I'm on a rescue mission here, don't shoot, we're the good guys." The soldier lowered his gun and nodded, before signalling with a movement of his gun for us to move out and away. We stepped out and I just had time to register the look of shock on his face before I remembered Essy was with us. "No", I yelled and stepped in front of her. "She's mine and she won't harm you." He lowered his gun and nodded, keeping a sharp eye on her as we stole away down the corridor. With my free hand I fished for my Unicom and called the boys. "Now guys, blow the wall now and wait for us. There's four of us and my Hymalont so don't shoot us okay?"

We heard a distant rumble and I sighed with relief.

"What the heck was that?" Pasnel hissed.

"Our way out of here," I replied as I tried to shift Ren's weight off my arm which was quickly getting numb. "Can one of you take Ren's other arm, he's getting real heavy." Jakelham hoisted Ren's right arm over his shoulder and took some of his weight off me.

"Come on Ren, wake up buddy, we need you to walk now huh? Sleepy time over, come on, wake up," I hissed into his ear. I heard a groan in response and felt his legs moving against mine. "That's it buddy, help us out here huh."

Three security guards appeared from an office to our left and we froze. They stared at us and we stared back. One of their Hymalonts started to growl and I knew we were going to have to fight our way out. Suddenly all three of the Hymalonts fell to the ground with a squeal, followed shortly by all three security guards. I hadn't shot them so who had?

"Well don't just stand there, for fuck's sake move," the voice commanded. From around the bend in the corridor appeared the three boys and Donal, all packing heat. I was both annoyed and relieved to see them. We raced after them and headed down the corridor towards the next intersection. Suddenly Marlo fell with a scream, his knee spouting blood. I spun around and opened fire and downed the two guards who'd shot him whilst Donal and Doniss dealt with the Hymalonts. Palko helped Marlo up and together we hobbled along to the intersection. This intersection was deserted and we rushed across the open space into the corridor we knew would take us to the wall. I sighed with relief when I saw the debris lying in the corridor and we all headed towards the hole in the wall and the relative safety of the transport tunnels.

"Where do you think you're going Joss Gilden, or should I say Sam Sinclair?" We froze on the spot and my heart sank as I recognised that voice. "Not trying to desert your post I hope?" We turned and I looked into Spurrell's face. "Whatever it was you darted me with, it was quite a kick. Shame it wasn't longer lasting though. You see I'm from Haxion 2 and our bodies get rid of all injected substances real quick, but you weren't to know that were you?"

"Screw you asshole," I replied. "I don't care what you're doing here or how you're doing it," I lied, "I just want to get my friends out safely, it's not their problem."

"You think you can come in here and ruin everything we've worked for? Do you realise how much time and money this operation has cost? Have you any idea how mad this has made a lot of people? People with influence and money are gonna be out for blood Sam."

"Look buddy," I said. "I couldn't give a fuck about that. Now since there's five guns here to your one, it looks like we have the upper hand so just turn around and go away before we shoot you."

"Well someone is going to. It was my job to ensure security and you fucked that all up and that means my head is for the block. I'm pretty sure your five guns will do me quicker and easier than anyone connected with Calmarin will."

"I'm not interested in giving you an easy way out buddy," I replied. "If you want to make a bargain, go and give yourself up to the troops and they'll take care of you in return for information to help them put those responsible behind bars. You'll get a comfortable bed and three meals a day."

"And be tortured in prison? Are you stupid? You've really no idea how far these guys' reach is have you? No that's not the life for me Sam."

"Fine, then kill yourself," I hissed angrily.

I was about to say something else, when a shot rang out and Spurrell fell to the floor. From around the bend in the corridor, four troops appeared. We turned and headed for the hole in the wall and I was relieved to be away from the chaos at last. Just as Pasnel and I were helping Ren through the hole, another shot rang out and Ren gasped. I became aware of wetness down the front of my legs and looked down at myself, but could not figure out where the blood had come from. I had not been shot, at least I did not feel shot and I was confused. Ren coughed and spat blood and I turned to look at him as realisation dawned.

Time slowed almost to nothing, my hearing disappeared and although I was vaguely aware of several more shots, they didn't register in my brain. I dragged Ren through the hole and felt the wetness of his blood against my shirt as he collapsed in my arms. He was heavy, and I screamed his name as his legs gave way and I dropped to my knees as I clutched his body close.

"Stay with me buddy, please stay with me," I begged as I cradled him in my arms and tried to stem the flow of blood from the wound in his chest. "Please stay with me, please."

"Joss," he whispered as he looked into my eyes. His far too big and strange blue grey eyes growing visibly dim as he strained to stay with me. With a huge effort of will, his trembling fingers fished beneath his shirt collar and he pulled up the necklace he always wore; a long, white curving fang carved out of some kind of hard stone. He was never without it. "Take this Joss," he gasped between coughing blood and fighting for air. "Take this and I will always be with you. All of Damiklon will be your friend."

"Ren, stay, please," I begged as my tears splashed onto his cheek. "You're my best friend, don't leave me."

"I will always be with you. Remember me in the good way; don't lock me away inside."

"I promise," I nodded, my voice just a whisper as my emotions fought with me for control. Ren nodded slowly and tried to smile, his eyes never leaving mine. With a deep sigh, his head fell against my chest. He died in my arms, and I was beside myself with anger and grief. Placing his head gently onto the floor of the dirty little room, I closed his big eyes for the last time and removed his necklace. "Thank you my friend," I cried as I put it around my neck and hid it safely beneath my shirt. Anger flooded through me; the blood surging through my veins so hard I could feel the throb in my neck and I stood, raised my gun and stepped over the remains of the wall and back into the corridor. Without caring to check whether the corridor was safe or not, I strode over to where Spurrell's body lay.

"Joss, don't," a voice behind me said but I ignored it. The kid had no idea of the shit life can bring you, but he will learn in his own time, I could not hold that against him. Wiping away the tears from my eyes, I put down my gun and took hold of Spurrell's body. A full five minutes later, Donal and the boys physically dragged me away from the mess. My two broken fingers and bruised knuckles giving testament to how fully I had allowed my grief to express itself. Ren made me promise him I would not try to bury my grief this time and I meant to keep that promise. Spurrell's unrecognisable face and smashed skull was evidence to that.

"Come on Joss," Donal soothed. You've made sure that asshole has paid the price. Now spend some time with Ren huh?" They helped me over the wall and I looked down at Ren's body. Essy was there, laying down beside him, her head on his chest and I realised that I was still wearing the headset that allowed me to control her by thought. She had picked up my grief and was expressing it herself. Donal and the boys left us alone for, hell I do not know how long and I said all the things I guess I should have said to Ren when he was alive. I thanked him for being my best friend and I promised him I would keep up with the martial art practice. With a smile, I reminded him about some of the fun things we had done together and I thanked him for showing me how to have a good time. A hand on my shoulder made me start and I looked up to find a group of soldiers waiting on the other side of the wall.

"It's all over buddy," Donal said. "Garmast has made more arrests tonight than in the last five years put together. The troop commander has taken control and is waiting for us up top."

"I'm not leaving Ren here," I said.

"We're here to take him up top," one of the soldiers said quietly. "We'll take him to the Bygora Law Enforcement Headquarters and make him comfortable." He stepped over the wall with a stretcher and crouched down beside us. "We'll take care of him, don't worry." I nodded weakly and allowed Donal to steer me over the wall.

We made our way along silent corridors, our boot steps and the click of Essy's claws on the tiled floor, eerie in the deserted research station. The night air was fresh as we stepped out of the main exit and into the darkness. Twenty or so troop shuttles filled the immediate area and crowds of men shuffled about. A hand touched my shoulder and I turned to find Kobey looking at me, Pendle, Hitch and a couple of the other security guys behind him.

"Well done Joss," he said. "You did it. I'm proud of you. I'm so sorry about your friend. If there's anything I can do, just ask okay? Don't be shy."

"Thanks," I nodded. "Thanks for your help, all of you." I noticed Adlion Garmast walking towards me and looked up at him. "Did you get them all?"

"I got a lot of em, yeah," he nodded. "All thanks to you and Ren. Your bravery made this possible and all of Deligon will be in your debt. I'm so sorry Ren was lost. He's a first class law enforcer and will be missed by the force. We're taking him back to my headquarters, where he will be looked after until he goes home and you can come and spend as much time with him as you wish. I called Tinnias, he's waiting to talk to you. Come with me," he indicated the nearest of the troop shuttles and I followed him inside. "Take all the time you need," Garmast said as he turned and left me alone.

"Boss?" I said.

"I'm so sorry Sam. What the fuck can I say to make it better?"

"Nothing I guess."

"I'm proud of both of you."

"Thanks. We were gonna team up y'know? We were gonna pool our contacts and resources and team up."

"You'd have made a formidable team."

"Yeah, we would," I smiled at the thought. "Garmast said he got a lot of the people he needed to collar. I downloaded a load of stuff from their console too. By the way, two of the guys here are ghosts. Pasnel and Jakelham."

"Umm, yeah I know," Tinnias replied.

"You know?"

"Yeah. Hey I'm the boss for a reason y'know. It means I get to know about stuff. One of the few perks of extra responsibility."

"Yeah, I know. I was just surprised when they told me. I've never met any before."

"Well don't be surprised if you never do again. They're not called ghosts for nothing."

"I'm keeping Essy Boss," I said, changing the subject suddenly. "Nothing you can say will talk me out of it and if you won't allow it, I'm resigning."

"Okay Sam, don't worry. If you're happy to take responsibility for any of her potential misdemeanours, we won't have a problem."

"She'll be no trouble, I promise."

"Okay."

"Thanks. They don't live that long actually, about five years maximum but she's imprinted on me now and could never be taught to obey anyone else. If I left her now I would be condemning her to death and she's only got about three and a half years left. I couldn't lose another friend, not so soon."

"I understand Sam and it's not a problem."

"Thanks. Now umm, do you want me to give all my data and film to Garmast or should I send it over to you?"

"Give a copy to Garmast and send me a copy. That way we're both in the loop."

"Okay."

Well, that's just about the end of the story of Bygora Vandos. I gave all my film and data to Garmast and sent copies to Tinnias. Those members of staff Garmast had managed to arrest were only too happy to spill their guts about what had been going on, and several more arrests were made in the following weeks. Tinnias had ordered troops to raid the moon where the drums had been shipped and stored, and the stuff was taken and sent by unmanned rocket into a suicide nosedive into an uninhabited system's dying sun. Those surviving Hymalonts who had imprinted on the now imprisoned guards were unfortunately put to sleep. The vast amount of data gleaned from the Station's records showed us that the tree disease that started this whole affair was indeed a result of a seam of raw Zanbedellium rock mixing with a naturally occurring pool of some oily liquid. The authorities sent in teams to mine the rest of the seam of Zanbedellium rock and use it as landfill elsewhere. Once there was no more Zanbedellium rock for the oily liquid to mix with, there would be no more danger to the trees. The diseased trees were felled and the topsoil was removed and dumped onto a lifeless planetoid where the combined effects of the very low temperatures and vacuum of space would soon render it inert and harmless.

Supreme Commander Manno Lashling was stripped of his military honours and court martialled. During questioning he bargained for a lower prison term in exchange for the inside man who had ratted me out. I was shocked rigid when Tinnias gave me the news.

"What?" I almost yelled. "Mr Gilden? Are you sure it was him?"

"Yeah," Tinnias replied. "He's some big noise in information security on the galactic web and he's been hacking into our system for years and selling information to the highest bidder. When he saw that you were off to Deligon, he sold the information to Calmarin, where it was picked up by Manno Lashling and passed from him, down to the people at the station. We picked him up and he didn't even deny it. In fact he seemed proud of it. He said it was your fault he lost his daughter and he is glad he was able to help make sure you lost someone you love."

I hung around Bygora Vandos for a couple of weeks. I had official stuff to do anyway but I wanted to take the time to properly say goodbye to Donal and the Boys. Donal asked to become one of my contacts and I told him I would be proud to have him on board. We all went out for a meal to celebrate the success of the mission and to celebrate Ren's role in our lives. We ate too much and drank too much, Ren would have been proud. All of us remembered him and the many ways he touched all our lives and I was determined to remember him in the way he taught me. The qualities I loved about him most were his compassion and wisdom, his honesty and dedication. I promised him in the silence of my mind that I would endeavour to cultivate those qualities I loved in him, within myself, and in doing so, honour him and keep him alive in my heart.

I met with two representatives of the Lavastra Valkerian, the Damiklonian spiritual leaders who came to collect Ren's body and take him home. We had a long talk about my friend and they were nice people. I showed them the necklace he gave me as he died and they confirmed what Ren had said; that while I wore it, all of Damiklon would be my friend whenever I need them. They told me he would have a hero's funeral and that his personal journals told them of his love for me as his friend and how proud he was that I seemed to be happy to let him form a deep empathic bond with me. They said that showed without doubt that he regarded me as the closest of friends and that my name would be included in his Sovenda Lonraal, the list of closest loved ones who still mourn that would form part of his funeral ceremony.

Essy remained with me and fitted into my job without a problem. She was happy just being with me and the unpredictability of my job seemed to suit her. There were many times when she was very useful in situations where my life was in danger. She gave her life saving me from a bullet, eight months after she first bonded with me. I buried her on a beautiful hillside on Kalien 7 and mourned her by the light of its twin moons. She helped me while I mourned for Ren and brought fun and companionship to my life in those short months and I missed her terribly for ages after she had gone.

As I said at the beginning, the cost of this job was high for me personally. It cost me my first and only best friend and the pain was almost too much to bear. A lot of good was done as well and although Calmarin Research Station took many lives in a horrible way, many countless others were saved by bringing the place down. This job was one of those defining moments in my life and I knew it changed me in many ways. It tired me too, and I took a leave of absence for a couple of months, to mourn my friend and let my mind get rid of the pain. Essy's company helped; her sense of fun had me back on track within a few weeks and I was able to get back to work with my mind fully on the job, as Ren would have wished. I still miss my friend; I will always miss him but I feel a part of him is always nearby.

Losing Ren was another reason I decided to think more seriously about putting my video logs up onto the galactic web and sharing them with people. I wanted people to know how special he was, and how unique his people are. He gave his life helping me and that is something that needs to be acknowledged. It is such a big universe out there, that it is almost impossible to get your voice heard and your accomplishments acknowledged, but I was determined that Ren's sacrifice was not going to get lost in the void of space.

Now I had better sign off as another job has just come in. Some nut job has escaped from a psyche facility and Tinnias wants me to go to a planet called Lilea 4 and see if I can recruit the guy's brother to help me catch him. And, get this, the brother is that guy who killed those Transmortals a few years ago, how about that huh? I never thought I would be getting to meet him. Tinnias reckons his presence will help flush the nut job out as they have some bad history between them. It has been a while since I have had a passenger accompany me on a job. I just hope this guy is not an asshole.

This is V-log reference LB734/A, data log reference point 3380133/8399. Sam Sinclair signing off.

THE END

COMING SOON

Delectus Morbidium
Twenty Tales of Horror

By Merita King

An anthology of short horror stories, designed to disturb, frighten and shock you to the core.

Just what does the cleaning woman discover when she presents herself for work at the home of the recently widowed elderly woman?

Brandy is excited when her new boyfriend asks her to come and meet his parents for the first time, but little does she know what lies in store for her up at the rambling house on the other side of the wood.

Santosh has been a fan of singer Louise Black for years, but a chance meeting with her quickly destroys his infatuation. Little does he know, when he vents his anger on his website, the effect those words will have on him later.

~ and more ~